A WISH SO DARK

SLAVES OF SANDSPIRE

Z.R. ABADDI

CHAPTER
ONE

Whoever said that the Glass District was the worst place in the Sundara desert was an ignorant fool because, had they visited the marble mines of Sandspire even once, they would know the truth.

There are worse hells than a little glass-sharded sand.

The torch in Reema's hand crackled, staving off the darkness as she led the way through the tunnels. White marble walls pressed in on them from all sides. It constricted the air and reflected the hollow silence back onto them. The pressure built in their ears as they went deeper into the earth.

Her gang of slaves followed closely behind, tools resting against their shoulders, each wearing the same simple, coarse tunic—sturdy linen that reached their knees. Their hardened gazes were fixed on the dancing shadows. Like Reema, each one of them had spent most of their lives in the mines. They knew the dangers that lurked, from the ever-present threat of the earth collapsing to the gnawing madness that threatened to consume them whenever the torchlight began to fade. But as dangerous as those threats were, there was one greater still.

Other miners.

The miners of Sandspire were like cockroaches, scurrying through the earth. No matter how many died, they just kept coming back, forming new gangs that grew bold enough to encroach on Reema's territory. She couldn't allow that. Not at all.

She'd fought hard for this section of the mines, clawed it from the dying hands of countless men and women in the dark, left their bloodstains all along the white marble walls so that there could be no mistaking it: the southern mines belonged to *her*.

When Reema reached the end of the tunnel, she ran her hand over the stone, her fingers drifting over the ridges, searching for any fine cracks that would waste days of work. She'd had to learn over the years what marble was good for harvesting and what wasn't. And that knowledge was painfully gained.

Content with the tunnel, she marked the sides with black chalk and gave her gang the look to get started. None of them spoke as they moved, setting up reinforcements along the walls, draping a blanket from the ceiling to catch the sound, and establishing a guard at the back. It was important to stay quiet, because this deep in the tunnels, sound carried. And when that happened, others came looking.

Once they'd finished their work, Reema took the pickaxe from Asif and stood before the great, white marble. Her lip curled as she stared at it: this piece of the earth that would defy her, that dictated whether the guards that worked for the slave master on the surface would give them food and water.

Her rage burned, flames sparking from the ever-burning coals at the pit of her belly. She ran a hand over the stone again, remembering that this sundamned *rock* was why the surface dwellers made slaves of men and women.

It was why her sister was dead.

But just as she knew the white marble was the source of her misery, she also knew it held her peace. She lifted her pickaxe, and with a sharp breath, she swung.

White marble dust filled the air. She paused, fitting a piece of cloth over her mouth while Javid checked the marble to make sure the cut was clean. She glanced back at Asif, motioning toward the blanket. He gave her a thumbs up. Any sound that did make it past the blanket was muted enough to pose no danger.

Javid gave her a nod before joining Hadi to guard the tunnel. The cut was good.

She set her feet and swung again.

Over and over, she imposed her will on the earth, demanding that it give up a piece of itself, just as she had given up a piece of herself the day the light had left her sister's eyes.

With every swing, she imagined a different face from among the guards who had long become familiar to her. She imagined burying the pickaxe into their chests, hot blood spurting out to drench her in sweet justice. She imagined hearing their screams as she tore their bodies apart.

As she worked longer, breathing became more difficult, the air thickening with marble dust. But still, she swung, her muscles glistening with sweat, her mid-length dark hair sticking to her forehead. She thought of the nameless Bloodlined slave master who smirked at her before the guards threw her and her sister's body down the hole into the mines.

His face lingered in her mind longer than the others. His glowing blue eyes had never seemed so dark, and she knew that despite the Angel's blood running through his veins, there wasn't an ounce of goodness in him.

A hand tapped her shoulder, pulling her back from the inferno of her rage. She blinked the slave master's face away and wiped the dust from her face. She passed the pickaxe to her second, Asif. He ran his hand over his bald head and through his long beard as he took her place.

Then he continued harvesting the marble, his soft grunts of exertion a reminder that he was like her. The whole gang was; they'd all suffered at the hands of the slave master.

She stepped away, working to catch her breath. Gangs came and went in the mines, living and dying as territories were claimed and lost. But her ruthless band of five had survived through the years, bonded by the depth of their rage that endured even these shadowy depths of the earth.

Reema pushed past the hung blanket and pulled

away the cloth from her mouth. Particles of marble dust still floated in the air, but it was easier to breathe now.

Javid leaned against the wall, his gaze locked onto his shiv. He'd made it years ago, crafted it from sharpened marble. He might be a muscled brute with no sense of his own strength, making him useless for mining marble, but she wouldn't want to have any other man by her side in a fight. He was born to kill.

She glanced at Hadi, taking in his wiry frame and beady eyes. He was nearly as short as she was, but he had the best eyes out of all of them, and he had proved his value by saving them more than once by spotting miners trying to get the better of them. She stood next to him as they stared into the deep dark, each listening to the muffled sounds of Asif attacking the stone.

"It's too loud," Hadi whispered.

She glanced back at the blanket. He was right. The blanket wasn't doing its job well enough. It was probably time to replace it. The issue with the cloth fabric was that over time, the stone chips flying from the marble and the dust coating its surface wore it down enough that tiny holes appeared. Omar had checked it before they descended into the tunnel, but holes this tiny were hard to see.

She leaned in toward Hadi, "We'll need to pick one up off the next miner we see, then."

He nodded, "Let's hope it's on our terms."

She agreed. This was not a good place to get caught, not this deep down in the earth. Most miners never ventured this deep into the earth because of the risk of the earth collapsing in on them; the earth was sensitive down here, and she knew that it wouldn't respond well if another gang appeared and a fight broke out. Men screaming from a mortal wound? That'd be enough to do all of them in.

This was her territory. Other gangs should know better than to enter it, but she'd been down in the mines long enough to know that desperate men and women had little common sense.

A few more minutes painfully passed, but despite the sound escaping the blanket, nothing appeared out of the dark. Reema patted Hadi's shoulder and went back to check on Asif's work.

He paused, resting his hand on the pickaxe and catching his breath. She blew away the dust and wiped it away, checking the holes that he'd struck into the marble. Good cuts, all of them.

"Omar, Ra'ad. You're up."

The twin brothers were masters of their work, and in all Reema's years in the mines, she hadn't seen anybody better at guiding the cracks. They slid a thin pair of wooden feathers into the holes, before fitting a wedge between them. With a hammer, they tapped the wedge into place. The tiniest hairline fracture appeared between the cuts that she and Asif had made. The earth groaned around them and each one of them stopped, fearful eyes flickering up to the ceiling.

Then it came to a stop, and they all breathed a sigh of relief.

Omar and Ra'ad continued their hammering, soft at first, ensuring that the fractures lined up, before striking it with reverberating thuds. Once they had done their work, Reema struck a few more cuts into the marble, helping drive the work. The earth groaned again, and this time, it shook all around them, dust falling off the ceiling down onto them.

When it stopped, they exchanged glances.

"Maybe we should stop for today," Omar said.

Reema stared at the rock, a vile hatred for it rising up in her. They must have seen the look in her eyes, because Asif rested a hand on her shoulder. He was always the one they relied on to calm her.

"It's not a bad idea. The earth is being difficult today."

She shook off his hand, "When is it not difficult? This is the job, boys. We're close, I can feel it."

Omar and Ra'ad exchanged another glance with each other, communicating telepathically in that way that only twins can.

Reema snarled, "Do I need to do it myself?"

They immediately started back in on the marble. They knew that angering her any further would lead to bad things. Each one of the crew had proven themselves in a fight, but they knew that there was a reason Reema was the gang leader. None of them were as terrifying as she was when her anger came on.

The earth groaned again, deeper this time. But they stood their place and continued to work. It was only when the final, resounding crack snapped through the air that they stopped. The earth calmed.

This time, she didn't have to tell them what to do. The brothers worked to get the rollers into place as Asif levered a bar underneath the stone. Together, she and

Asif lifted the marble block just enough to get it onto the edge of the roller.

"Get the blanket down, and let's move this out of the way."

One of the brothers tore down the cave reinforcements and the blanket, drawing Javid's attention. He began to stretch his arms and back, aware that he was in for a long stretch of work. When it came to hauling the marble blocks back to base camp, he was as good as three men.

Reema passed him a pair of wooden hooks worn smooth from years of use, and he fitted them to the sides. With a heavy groan, he pulled the marble block onto the rest of the rollers. They slowly moved it further from the wall, inch by inch, replacing each roller with the next.

Once it was far enough away, it was her turn to shine. Every person in her gang brought value in some way that no other person could. And that didn't exclude her. She had strength and endurance enough to carry her weight in cutting the marble, and she was small enough to squeeze between the tight space of the wall and the marble block once it was pulled away.

Taking hold of a long leather strap, she squeezed herself into the tight space, her hot breath bouncing back off the stone against her face. It would be impossible to explain to the surface dwellers, but the earth *breathed*. That was only something you could understand when you were trapped as she was between the earth and a marble block. It pressed against her on all sides, scraping against her skin. At times she had to pause, let the earth loosen up enough for her to squeeze through. And she had to be quick about it, otherwise the earth pressed too tight for *her* to even get a breath. But she had a lifetime of practice now, and she knew the earth more intimately than even the men in her gang.

She made it onto the other side of the block. Once she tightened the strap into place, she signaled for them to pull with a rap of her knuckles. She heard the faintest sound of Javid's muffled groan as he pulled. The marble block began to move faster then, and with the brothers keeping the rollers in place, she knew they could make it quick time back to base.

With this block, they had their quota for the month. The guards would send them another month's worth of food and water down, and that was another month they'd get to live—so long as they guarded it from the other miners, of course.

But Reema didn't care as much about that in the moment, and neither did the other members of her gang. They had chosen to risk venturing this deep into the earth for a reason, and it wasn't to harvest the marble blocks. There were safer places to do that.

Despite the danger of the torchlight going out, they passed it to her. The heat was sweltering in the tight space, but she endured it as she studied the marble, searching for some sign of the myth they had hunted all these years.

Her heart began to fall into the empty pit of her stomach as she saw white upon white. She closed her eyes and rested it against the cool marble, fighting back a growl of frustration. She started to turn away, but just then, she saw it.

A single speck of black.

Her breath caught in her throat. She knelt before it, hoping it wasn't a simple vein of color running through the stone, like the last time she thought she had found a sign of what she searched for. That mistake had cost them months of their lives.

She ran her hand over the speck of black. It didn't trail anywhere else, though. And studying the rest of the wall, she didn't see any other sign of black.

"Reema?" Asif's whisper reached her.

She'd been quiet too long.

She looked back through the space she'd squeezed through and saw his dark brown eyes.

"Pass me the chisel."

His eyes widened. "You think we found it?"

She stuck her hand through the gap. "The hammer and chisel, Asif. Be quick with it."

He nodded, and a moment later, she had the tools in hand. She rested the torch on the ground and worked the chisel against the marble. A shard broke away.

She lifted the shard and studied the black speck more closely in the light. It wasn't a vein. Adrenaline pumped through her as a surge of excitement passed through her. She knelt down and studied the marble again.

The black speck had gotten bigger. Only a bit, but it was enough.

When she squeezed back through the gap, her gang stood before her, their eyes wide with anticipation and hope.

She lifted the shard.

"We found it."

They loosed a loud cheer that echoed down the tunnels, and not a single one of the gang cared. Years of bloodshed, sweat, and tears had led to this moment.

Reema grinned. "Let's get this block back to base. Keep a sharp eye out for any of the poor bastards who come our way."

They hauled the marble slab back to base with an energy they hadn't felt in years. And the whole way, Reema could not take her eyes off the black speck.

A decade ago, she'd stumbled on a dying stranger in the mines, a mad old man who kept to himself. On the cusp of death, he told her a myth of black marble, and the being that lived within it. He spoke of the Djinn, who had power enough to free them from the mines; power enough for her gang to have their revenge on the slave master.

In her hands, she held the first proof of the mad man's myth. If the black marble existed, then perhaps the Djinn did too. And if he did ... well, she might just have justice for her sister after all.

CHAPTER
TWO

Every month, when they mined a marble block, they delivered it to the guards at the Hole. The cave was aptly named, as it was the only place the surface could be accessed via a platform that could raise marble blocks up. It was also the only place that sunlight reached the mines.

Reema knew that some of the other miners looked forward to seeing the Hole, as it reminded them of where they came from. For Reema and her gang, they hated going there. The sunlit cave made it harder to adjust back to the mines' darkness, and the guards took great pleasure in reminding them they were nothing more than slaves. Still, they had to appear to get water and food to survive. Trying to poach it from other gangs rarely worked out long term—she had seen more than one gang die out because of that approach.

Reema, Javid, and Asif were the first to arrive this time. Omar and Ra'ad stayed back at the base to guard it, in case other miners got the clever idea to invade their territory while they were up here.

While Javid and Asif caught their breaths from pulling the marble block, Reema stared at the tunnels the other gangs would appear from.

At the moment, there were only five gangs that mattered in the mines of Sandspire, each ruling their own section. There were others, of course, led by aspiring miners who roamed between territories, constantly fighting to carve out a piece for themselves. Reema didn't know their bosses by name, but she never ignored the danger they posed. After all, she was one of them once, and look what she'd done: she'd taken over a whole section for herself.

Most of the five kept to themselves, content to defend and mine their own sections. But between the continual harvest of marble blocks and collapsing tunnels, the territories were constantly evolving. It wasn't uncommon to see one of the five go up against another, and for the power dynamics to shift.

The darkness in the northern tunnels began to soften. Voices reached Reema, and soon, so did torch light. Renfri stepped out of the shadows, wearing her ever-present smirk. She was followed by four men drenched in sweat as they pulled the marble block behind them.

Reema studied Renfri. She was the only other woman who led her own gang, and damn the deep, she *was* beautiful. Her gang was full of men she seduced and controlled, and the graveyard was full of those she grew tired of. Nobody lasted very long in her gang, not that they seemed bothered.

"Reema," Renfri said. "You're still alive. That's good to see."

"Is it?" Reema asked.

Renfri's smirk inched wider. "It is. Can't let men rule all of the mines, now can we?"

Her gaze passed from Reema to Javid behind her, lingering there appreciatively. "Don't suppose you're willing to part with your big man there?"

"Javid?" Reema called out.

"I'm good, thanks," he answered.

"What a shame," Renfri said. She addressed Javid. "Perhaps one of these days we'll encounter each other in the dark, and you'll ... reconsider."

Javid blinked. He knew as well as Reema just how many bodies Renfri had left behind. She took great pleasure in ruining men, especially large men.

"Don't take the bait. The sex isn't that good. Trust me."

Renfri's smile soured as they turned to see Zayd, the third gang lord, emerging from another tunnel, pulling a marble block himself with a pair of attached straps looped around his shoulders.

He was the only other man Reema had seen rival Javid's size, and as much as she believed in Javid, she knew that Zayd would put him flat on his ass. There was something unnatural about how quick he could move.

Zayd winked as his gang brought forth another marble block. Reema and Renfri both scowled at him. Though there had never been a formal agreement among the gang lords, there was a common understanding that none of them would try to exceed the quota. Doing so risked the slave master realizing they were capable of more and upping the quota, which wouldn't be good for any of them.

The way Renfri stared at him, Reema had no doubt she would seek out her own special brand of revenge— both for the comment he made and for being foolish enough to bring a second marble block.

The third gang lord made his entrance, quietly standing aside as his men and women worked as a team to roll their marble block forward. Salman was well known to be the most cunning of them all, and though the individual members of his gang were weaker than those of Reema's, Renfri's, or Zayd's gangs, he never seemed to have any trouble defending his territory.

He locked eyes with Reema, and she nodded back in acknowledgment. Though they never spoke, at some point she reached a quiet understanding with him. As long as she left him alone, he'd leave her alone too.

And last came the most vicious of them all, the man who made them all seem like angels in the dark: Mehdi.

He strode forward from the last remaining tunnel, a toothy white grin showing through a face caked in blood. Shirtless men pushed a marble block forward. Their backs were striped with scars, and the moment one fell down, it became apparent why.

Mehdi's second, a vicious man who took as much delight in delivering pain as he did, whipped the man across the back. The sharp snap echoed through the sunlit cave. Once, the sound might have made Reema flinch, but now she'd grown numb to it. She'd seen far worse things.

Mehdi's gaze swept through the cave, lingering on Reema for a moment longer than on the other gang lords. Meeting his gaze with a cold one of her own, she knew he must be thinking about when he'd tried to encroach on her territory, only to scamper back to his section of the mines with a fresh scar stretching from his brow to the corner of his mouth. She drew back the veil on her rage, allowing it to show through for but a moment. And that was all it took to make Mehdi look away.

As terrifying as each of the gang lords seemed, they knew her as something worse.

With each of the five main gangs present, Reema knew she shouldn't expect any more sudden appearances. Before she had an established territory, it never made sense for her to show up to these things. She was more concerned with taking from the other gangs than making an appearance with the guards. But now she had no option.

A shadow disturbed the light filtering down through the Hole.

"Hello, all of my beautiful little monsters."

She shifted her gaze upward. The captain of the guard, Hamza, stood there, his hands on his hips and a smug smile plastered on his ugly, pockmarked face. He lifted a pipe to his mouth and loosed a cloud of ember-dust smoke. His smile inched wider.

More guards appeared on either side of him, doing their best to appear intimidating. But Reema could see by the way each of them gripped their sheathed swords with white-knuckled grips that *they* were the ones intimidated. These guards were bottom of the barrel, relegated to a simple babysitting role that served zero strategic importance. Their jobs began and ended with standing around and waiting to collect the once-a-month quota of marble from the slaves.

Not that it bothered Hamza. The slave master was rare to show his face, which left him content to play the part of king so long as he delivered on the marble blocks.

"Did you miss me?" Hamza asked.

Each of the gang lords bristled in silence. The urge to strangle the captain was the one thing they all shared; that and the fact that, at the end of the day, they were just slaves who had to do as their master bade. One wrong act, one wrong word, they were out of food and water for the whole month. Without that, they'd be forced to attack other territories.

"My, my, you are quiet today. Nothing to say? Not even you, Renfri? Are you sure?" The quiet threat played under his words.

Renfri's eyes narrowed, but she answered, "Not today. My throat's a little parched, captain."

Hamza smiled and held his hand out. One of the other guards passed him a heavy skin of water.

"It's a good thing I've got your water here, then," he said.

He uncapped the lid to the water skin and lifted it to his mouth, watching her as the water spilled down his beard and wet the sand surrounding the Hole. He swallowed the water with an audible gulp.

"Ah, how *refreshing*."

He tossed the near empty water skin down the Hole. It landed with a soft thud, the sound echoing through the cave.

"Come get your water, Renfri." He leaned forward on one knee, his eyes gleaming with humor.

Renfri's knuckles popped, and her lips pursed. But she obeyed.

"That's a good slave." He straightened and clapped his hands. "Well, I have important things to do, important places to be. Shall we get on with this?"

Reema seriously doubted that, but she and the rest of the gang lords nodded.

"Good. Mehdi, let's start with you first."

Several guards worked to lower a wooden platform. It descended through the air, until it hit the cave floor with a soft tap. The others unsheathed their swords in case the gang lords tried anything, but none of them would. Despite the fact that they were slaves and their lives were worthless, they were still too stubborn to die.

Mehdi signaled to his men to push the marble block onto the platform.

Once the block was in place, the guards up top heaved the platform upwards, using a pulley system that made lifting easier. But even with that, the veins in their necks still strained against their skin as the platform creaked slowly upward.

Reema could remember when they had slaves do that job for them, and when they realized that with *more* slaves in the mines instead of sitting around on the surface, they would get even more marble.

They hadn't anticipated that they'd be killed off so quickly.

The block reached the top, and after a moment of inspection by the captain, the guards moved it away. Reema could hear their curses even when they were out of view.

"Did you have to make it so bloody, Mehdi?"

Mehdi stared blankly at the captain. Then he smiled.

The captain cackled and drew another puff of his emberdust. His pupils began to dilate. "I like you, Mehdi. Always have. Now piss off."

Mehdi waited silently.

The captain's laughter came to a halt. He lifted a brow. "Do you need something?"

"You're a smart man, captain. You know I do."

"Beg me, then."

Mehdi's smile faltered. His gaze flicked to Reema and to the others. He stiffened as he bowed his head.

"Please, can we have the food and water?"

"That sounds like you're asking. Not begging."

Mehdi bared his teeth, but got down on one knee. He folded his hands and looked up with dead eyes at the guards above. "I beg you. The food and water."

Hamza laughed again, pointing his pipe at one of the other guards. "You hear that?"

The other guard grinned down at them through the Hole.

"Very well, give the slave what he wants. He did beg."

A sack of lentils and dates landed with a heavy thud next to Mehdi, along with several water skins.

Mehdi wasted no time. He signaled to his second,

who quickly organized the other slaves into action. They grabbed the sacks and waterskins before disappearing back into the tunnels.

"You see that?" Hamza asked the remaining gang lords. "Mehdi knows his place. Who's next?"

None of them answered, until with a growing scowl, Renfri stepped forward. "Do you need me to beg too?"

"Beg? No, I don't think so. Why don't you do something ... else?"

Renfri stared at him. Then, without breaking eye contact, she stripped her top off. Hamza's grin widened, his gaze unabashed. The other guards laughed as they goggled at her.

"It's a shame you're down there, and I'm up here," Hamza said, running his smoke-tipped fingers through his greasy hair.

"We can always change that," Renfri said.

Hamza shook his head. "You can admire a slave, but you don't sleep with it."

He motioned for the other guards to toss down the supplies. They landed with a thud, and without asking, Renfri's gang retrieved them. They disappeared back into the tunnels. With her top still in her hands, Renfri stared up at the captain and drained the last of the near-empty water skin before tossing it aside. Then she left without another word.

Something drew the captain's attention away from the Hole, and for a moment, he stepped away. Salman quickly had his gang position the marble block onto the platform. The guards at the Hole looked to see where the captain had gone.

"Do you really want to stand around all day?" Salman asked, his voice calm and measured.

The guards frowned at each other before shrugging and raising the platform. Once they had it, they dropped the lentils down along with the water skins.

Salman was gone before Hamza returned. Something he wasn't too happy about.

"Damn! Couldn't you wait?" Hamza spat at the guards, shaking his head. "Fine. Who's left?"

Zayd stepped forward with a big smile.

"Oh, yes, you. What shall I do with you?" Hamza asked.

"Nothing."

Hamza raised a brow. "And why would I do that?"

"Because unlike these other lazy bastards, I brought you *two* blocks of marble." Zayd waved for the members of his gang to pull the blocks forward. Hamza's eyes lit up.

"Good work," Hamza said, as the guards raised the platform and two sacks of lentils dropped through the hole. "The master will be pleased. Let's see you do this again, yeah?"

Zayd beamed at the sight of the two sacks and lifted them with one hand. He saluted the captain, "I'll see you next month, captain."

He disappeared down his tunnel, his whistle echoing back. Reema shook her head as Asif and Javid pushed the marble block onto the platform. She stood quietly, staring up at the captain as he inspected the marble. It was flawless. Not once had she ever delivered anything less, and they both knew that. But still, they had to play this game.

Water skins fell through the hole, landing at her feet. She waited for the lentils to follow, but the look on the captain's face told her none were coming.

"Is there a problem, slave?"

If she was smart, she would turn back. But sundamned hells, she was *tired* of the cruelty. Behind her, Asif and Javid tensed. They knew what she was like.

"There is, actually. Where the hell are my lentils?"

"Faizan?" Hamza asked.

The guard to his side responded, "Yes, captain?"

"Do we have any more lentil bags?"

"No, Captain, we gave the last of her share to the other slave—the big one."

Reema clenched her teeth. Even with their rationing, they had very little lentils left; not enough to survive her gang for another month.

She slipped her hand into her pocket, gripping the black specked marble shard. They'd have to waste time hunting other miners for food, instead of digging deeper into the earth.

She spat to the side and started to turn back.

"Hold on. Where do you think you're going, slave?"

"Back!" Reema shouted over her shoulder.

"But you didn't see what else we have for you."

Reema paused. Her nostrils flared as she breathed. She closed her eyes, trying to calm herself. Revenge and justice was close, so close. If she screwed up now by walking away when Hamza wasn't done with her, then she endangered everything they'd worked toward.

Asif dipped his head when she locked eyes with him, encouraging her to turn back. If there was even a tiny chance that Hamza had food for them, she needed to play his game.

Reema returned and stared up at the captain.

"What do you have for me?"

The captain straightened, shifted himself, and said, "Hang on, I've got to take a piss. Stay right there."

He pulled his dick from his trousers and the other guards began to howl in laughter, their voices echoing through the cave below. Reema stared up at him, unflinching, as his warm piss splashed down onto her sandals, mixing with the white marble dust over her feet. The only thing she did was squeeze that marble shard tighter, and tuck this memory away into the back of her mind as fuel for when she struck into the earth's marble.

When it was all said and done, he tucked his dick away and grinned. "You're a nasty one, you know. I cannot believe you stood there, taking it all like you did. You must've liked it, huh?"

"What do you have for me?" Reema asked, her voice dangerously low and quiet.

Hamza's smile died away. He'd hoped to rile her up. "You do bore me. Go ahead, boys, throw it down."

The guards parted and shoved a man through the gap between them. Before Reema could get a good look at him, they kicked him over the edge of the Hole.

Most people screamed or shouted whenever they were tossed down into the mines. Reema had been no exception, though she didn't know to this day whether it was out of fear or rage and despair as her sister's body landed next to her.

But this man didn't scream, or shout, or even grunt as he landed against the cold stone floor. The only sound was a soft thud when what appeared to be a book landed nearby.

Reema studied him as he picked himself up. He wore a dirtied, bloodied blue coat that seemed hand-stitched, and his once neatly trimmed beard now grew unruly beneath cracked lips. However, the most striking feature was the steel band forged around his skull, molded so tightly against his eyes that she suspected not even a sliver of light could penetrate.

Someone had blinded this poor man.

And that made him useless to her.

She watched as he pathetically searched for the book, sweeping his hand across the stone floor. He wasn't even close. The book lay in the opposite direction.

"You look disappointed."

"What am I supposed to do with *that*?" Reema asked, shifting her gaze from the blinded man to the captain. "A blind man's worthless down here. You know that."

"Are you saying you'd rather have a sack of lentils than another pair of hands?"

"Yɛꜱ."

The sweeping hands paused.

The captain clutched his chest. "Ah, that's heartless. It's a shame that the newest member of your gang isn't deaf too."

A distant voice called for the captain again, and he glanced over his shoulder with a deep sigh. "Well, that's me. Time to get these marble blocks where they belong. Maybe I'll have lentils for you next month, if you can manage two blocks like Zayd."

With that, the captain and the guards retreated from the hole. Asif and Javid stood next to Reema, the three of them watching the blind man continue to search for the book. Asif passed Reema a cloth to wipe the piss from her.

"Damn," Asif said.

Reema handed the cloth back to Asif once she was done. Her voice was low but firm. "Let's go."

The three of them began to walk away, their steps echoing off the cold, damp walls. Reema's mind, however, lingered on the helpless figure they left behind. She glanced over her shoulder, and something in his desperate, blind search tugged at her heart.

She stopped.

"Leave him," Asif said. "There's no point. He'll be dead by the end of the week."

Irritation flared within her. She stalked to the book and with a swift kick, sent the book sliding across the stone floor toward the blind man. The man picked up the book almost reverently.

"Keep up if you can," she snapped.

He tucked the book inside his jacket and pushed himself to his feet. Reema shook her head. Even from the way he stood, she could tell he was a refined man, accustomed only to money and comfort. Asif was right. He would be dead by the end of the week, because refined men never lasted in these mines.

She led the way, the torchlight scattering the shadows. She heard the man follow, his hand softly scraping against the stone walls. It surprised her, the way he managed to keep pace, never quite falling behind. She thought he'd be lost, swallowed by the mines, but he stayed just there, at the edge of darkness.

Reema glanced back again, curiosity mingled with a grudging respect. He moved with a strange confidence, each step deliberate, guided more by instinct than sight. It was as if the darkness made no difference to him. She supposed it didn't. Not any more, with that steel band around his eyes.

"You shouldn't have bothered with him," Asif muttered, breaking the silence.

Reema didn't have an answer for him. He was right. The blind man was more likely to get them killed than anything else.

She scowled, more at herself than at Asif. "Don't worry about him. We've got enough problems to think about."

Like the fact that they were running out of food, which meant only one thing: to live, blood would have to be spilled. If the blind man didn't get lost in the dark, he'd find his own death then.

CHAPTER
THREE

Reema sat by the fire with her gang members, shadows flickering across the cave walls. Normally, the cave would be full of conversation. But today, it was eerily silent, not just because they were eating the last of their lentils.

At the edge of the cave, sitting all by himself, was the blind man.

Asif, noticing her gaze, leaned in and whispered, "You shouldn't have bothered with him."

"But I did," she snapped, shoveling a small handful of lentils into her mouth. "So save me the pain of hearing you moan and bitch about it, okay?"

"It's just a surprise."

"What is?"

"That you bothered with him at all. Unexpectedly soft of you."

Omar and Ra'ad nodded quietly nearby, surprise evident in their eyes. Reema looked at Javid and Hadi. They shrugged.

"You've got a reputation," Hadi said.

Reema knew exactly what kind of reputation she had. It was one that had other gangs referring to her as the Ifrit; a nickname she'd earned in blood and fury. When it came down to it, she was the most violent of any of the gang lords.

She noticed a hint of worry in her gang's eyes. Had their fearless leader gone soft?

She snarled, setting aside her lentils. She couldn't risk them thinking she had gone soft. Not because they'd turn on her; they were practically a family now, bonded not by blood but by their shared rage. But if they doubted her, they might replace her with Asif, and she wasn't about to let that happen.

"Let's lay things out," she said, her voice cutting through the silence. "We're short on food, thanks to that bastard Zayd, and we all know what that means. We need to invade another gang's territory. What better way to get the advantage than to dangle bait in front of them? And what better bait is there than a blind bastard stumbling through their tunnels?"

Her words hung in the air. The gang members exchanged looks, understanding dawning in their eyes. Using the blind man to gain the advantage? That sounded like the Reema they knew.

Asif grinned. "It's not a bad idea."

Reema allowed herself a small, grim smile. "Of course it's not. I came up with it. So the only question is what territory do we want to go after? Because whatever happens, we'll have to finish the job. That means a gang lord's death."

"Salman's the closest," Asif said immediately. There was something he held against Salman, but Reema didn't know what.

She shook her head. "No, not him."

"Renfri?" Omar suggested.

"She is the easiest target," Ra'ad said.

"Not her either," Reema said. "I'd rather keep her in play. She's not a threat I'm worried about."

That left Mehdi and Zayd on the table. She chewed the lentils, thinking on it more.

"Zayd did land us in this mess in the first place," she commented.

"And if he keeps going with extra marble blocks, then that could be a real issue," Asif said.

She nodded. She looked to Javid. "How do you feel about finally going up against the big man?"

"In a straight fight?"

"No, we'll cheat, of course."

"Then I'd feel pretty good."

Reema looked around the fire, "So are we agreed, then? Zayd pays the price?"

Grim faces all around nodded.

"Good. Asif, start on a plan. I'll be back."

"Where are you going?" Asif asked.

Reema glanced toward the blind man. "A man deserves to have a last meal, no?"

"Not when we don't have much food left. Eat the food yourself, preserve your strength."

"Just focus on the plan, Asif."

She left a grumbling Asif to strategise with the others and approached the blind man. The way he sat, so quiet and still, he seemed like a statue. But she had to acknowledge that he was reasonably good looking. He had a strong, bearded jaw and disheveled hair that worked for him. And though his blue coat was now coated with marble dust, it must have been dashing on him once. Her gaze lingered on the soft curve of his lips. It was liberating, knowing she could watch him as much as she wanted without him even knowing.

She got the nagging feeling that there was something familiar about him. With a frown, she tried to put her finger on it, but failed.

"It's a good plan, using me as bait."

Reema flinched at the sound of his voice. It was deep and, surprisingly, calm. She crouched in front of him, studying him closer. She hadn't intended for him to overhear their conversation at the fire, but voices do carry in these caves. It didn't bother her much though. There wasn't really anything he could do to avoid being bait. He was helpless, and miners prey on the helpless. He had to know that.

"You're not going to beg me to keep you safe?" Reema asked.

He turned toward her, as if he could see straight through the steel band into her eyes. The way his silence hung in the air, she wondered for a moment if he could.

"No. I will not beg."

Reema studied him, noting the undercurrent of rage in his words. There was something different about this man, but she couldn't put her finger on it. In a voice quiet enough that the others couldn't hear, she asked, "What's your name?"

"Are you sure you want to know the name of the man you're sending to his death?"

He had a point. Why was she asking his name? The bowl of lentils scraped against the stone as she slid it toward him.

"Your last meal," she said with a gesture, forgetting for a moment that he was blind. "We'll take you deep into their gang lord's territory and make some noise. By the time they come, we'll be gone."

She cleared her throat, noticing he hadn't even bothered searching for the bowl.

"When they find you, they'll kill you. But it'll be quick. They're not the type down here to make too much fun out of it."

Still, he didn't reach for the lentils. She frowned and shoved the bowl into his arms. He glanced down at the bowl.

"Any questions?" she asked.

A second passed, then he answered, looking back in her direction.

"Just one."

She sighed. She had really hoped there wouldn't be any.

"What happens if I survive?" he asked.

"You won't."

"If I do?"

"You *won't*."

He continued to stare blindly at her.

"Damn the deep, *fine*. If you survive, I'll grant you one magical wish, sprinkled with my very own special marble dust. How about that?"

He stayed quiet.

Reema shook her head and turned away.

"Alaric."

She paused and looked back at him. "What?"

"My name is Alaric."

In that moment, his name and his face branded themselves into her mind. Staring at him now, she couldn't help but feel that, despite this man being helpless, he was the furthest thing from weak. Like her sister.

"Strong name," she said.

He lifted his chin.

She returned to the fire.

CHAPTER
FOUR

Night and day didn't exist in the mines. But men were men, and women were women, and they all had to sleep at some point. Reema and her gang waited long enough to figure that Zayd's crew had likely enjoyed themselves on a fat serving of lentils and gone to sleep before starting out into the labyrinth of the mines. It was a pure guess, but after so many years in the mines, it was a reasonable one.

And as much as Reema hated leaving her territory unmanned, she had no choice. They were invading another territory. Saving her own was pointless if she were dead, and that was something each member of her gang seemed to agree on.

The layout of the mines used to make sense. Everything used to revolve around the central pit, from the northern quarry and the deep southern mines to the western veins and the expansive eastern caverns. But some long time ago, a gang lord who ruled the central pit grew tired of having to defend against each of the territories, and secretly dispatched men to invade each and every territory. Before the others found out, his men had mined paths connecting each territory to the ones on either side.

Whoever that bastard gang lord had been, he'd ruined whatever hope the miners had of mapping this place out. Now, the only way to know how to get around, and where you were, was by chalking the walls and hoping that nobody else got behind you to wipe them clean.

Reema led the way through the tunnels with the torch in hand, running her free hand along the walls, keeping track of the old marks she'd made years ago. She'd gotten clever at some point and realized she could mark grooves in the walls with her pickaxe instead of black chalk, and they would seem like another part of the earth. She'd made these the years that she had spent roaming from territory to territory, trying to carve out space for herself.

But even with these grooves in place, she had to be careful. These tunnels changed constantly, with collapses in some and new ones being mined daily. There was the risk that someone's pickaxe scraped across the walls too. That had happened before—she'd gotten lost for several terrifying hours before finding her way back to base.

As they ascended from the depths of the southern mines, the air grew warmer and less oppressive. The weight of the silence remained, though, seeping into their very bones. The silence of the mines was unlike anything that could be experienced on the surface. It was thicker, denser, as though the earth itself had swallowed all sound and kept it prisoner in its stony belly.

Hadi walked next to her, so that he could keep an eye on the darkness ahead. Behind them, Asif gripped Alaric's arm, holding him upright so that he didn't stumble and fall. Alaric had his hands bound and his mouth muffled with stuffed cloth to keep him from causing any sort of racket until they were ready.

The last thing they needed was for him to start announcing to the mines that they were making a move.

Omar and Ra'ad followed him, their faces more serious than usual, pickaxes held at the ready. Javid was at the rear, ducking his head just enough to keep from hitting the ceiling. They'd learned long ago that other gangs were less likely to assault them from behind, knowing the hulking giant was the first man they'd have to face.

"Not much further now," Reema whispered softly in Hadi's ear. "Ready the others."

He nodded and passed the message back to the others.

The rest of her gang wrapped cloth around their sandals to keep their footsteps silent as they entered the northern quarry. The deeper they went, the faster Reema's heart beat. The silence was so deep that she could hear the sound of her own blood rushing through her veins.

When Reema felt they had gone deep enough into the territory, she brought her gang to a halt. She didn't have to pass instructions. The others knew what to do.

While the others went around the corner to wait, Asif

unbound Alaric and whispered, "Make some noise, blind man, or I'll come back here and make you scream. Understand?"

Alaric didn't respond.

Asif grabbed hold of his throat and growled, "Do you understand?"

Reema winced as his voice echoed down the tunnels. Even though this was the plan—to draw attention here—it still felt unnatural to make any hint of a noise in another gang lord's territory.

Alaric gave him a curt nod.

Satisfied, Asif released him and followed Reema to join the others. They waited for Alaric to make a sound, to draw Zayd and his men. But when no sound came, she glanced back around the corner and saw him standing there, doing nothing except staring blindly ahead of him.

"This bastard," Asif cursed. His voice echoed down the tunnel again. "I'll make this easy on us."

Reema pushed him back with an arm, signaling for him to fall silent. She watched Alaric. He did not strike her as a man to play games with them.

She passed the torch to Asif. He knew the northern quarry better than her, and he'd be better suited to lead from here. After all, he used to stay here back before Zayd came into rule.

Then the strangest thing happened.

She watched as Alaric reached inside his coat and withdrew the same damned book he'd scrambled after back at the Hole. He held it in his hands, his thumbs brushing over the cover.

When he spoke, his voice carried through the tunnels

with the strength and calmness that had surprised her earlier.

"His heart broke."

Reema frowned, her brow furrowing. Behind her, the other miners looked at each other in confusion. They all had the same thought: What was he doing?

"As he stared into her dying eyes, watching that light fade into the eternal darkness, his heart broke."

"Is he a poet?" Omar asked.

"That's not poetry, idiot. That's prose," Ra'ad said with a shove.

"Shut up, you fools," Asif growled. "Who cares what it is? He's doing his sundamned job. Let's get going."

The others began to shuffle off, but Reema was rooted to the spot, unable to tear her gaze away from him.

"This was the woman who was supposed to be his everlasting love, whose soul had been made in measure for his. And now she was gone."

The sound of clattering in the distance echoed back through the tunnel: men scrambling for their pickaxes. Zayd's voice boomed toward them, demanding his men go to meet the invaders while he defended the camp. A moment later, footsteps pounded against stone toward them.

Alaric lifted his blinded gaze to face Reema, as if he could sense she was still watching him.

"Rage consumed him with a fire that would rival even that of the seventh hell. He wanted revenge, wanted to destroy the man who had robbed this earth of its most precious light. But he knew it would change nothing."

Reema's heart slowed to a stop. Everything faded away—the sound of death marching toward them through the tunnels, the quick scramble of her own men, even the stark white marble walls. All she could see was her sister's body falling through the Hole, turning in the air, her eyes robbed of that very same light.

A tear slipped from the corner of her eye. She touched a finger to it in surprise. She hadn't shed a tear since that day, since she had vowed vengeance. She lifted her gaze to the blind one that met hers.

"She was gone."

Alaric's words speared her heart, made her vulnerable and weak.

"Reema!" Asif's voice cut through it, the anger in his voice drawing her attention to him. "What're you doing? Let's *go*."

Reema clenched her teeth and steeled her heart. Then she turned away from Alaric and began to follow Asif through the tunnels that would lead them to the other side of the northern quarry, where they could attack Zayd at a weakened base. They would have a chance to steal all the food and water he had, and ensure themselves at least another month or two to live. That was maybe long enough for them to mine deeper through the black marble and find what they'd spent years searching for.

But with every step she took, Alaric's words sounded louder in her head until she couldn't form a thought. She glanced over her shoulder. She had lied to him. Zayd's men were absolutely the sort of miners who would take their time with him.

And Alaric was helpless. Just like her sister had been.

Reema seethed, digging her fingers into her palms, her knuckles cracking. She came to a stop.

Asif stopped when he realized that she wasn't following him anymore.

"What is it?" he asked, like there had to be something wrong. He couldn't fathom that she, the one everybody called the Ifrit, would want to go back and save some useless blind man. Damn the deep, she couldn't fathom it herself.

"Go ahead."

"Don't tell me you're going back for him," he said in disbelief.

"I am."

Asif looked toward the direction of Alaric's voice and shook his head. "He's not her, Reema. Saving him won't save her. She's gone."

"I know *that*. I know she's gone."

"Then what in the sundamned hells are you doing?"

The other miners in her gang stopped at the edge of the light, looking back with questioning eyes.

"Don't question me, Asif. Do as I fucking say," she snapped.

His jaw flexed, and his gaze narrowed. He didn't like it when she spoke to him like that in front of the others, but it didn't matter. She was the gang lord here.

"Go and get the job done. I'll meet you there," she ordered.

He looked back over his shoulder, saw the others waiting, then with a sigh and shake of his head, he said, "You don't have a torch."

"I'll take theirs."

He scoffed. Not because the idea was foolish, but because he knew she would. With a resigned sigh, he nodded and stuck out his hand. "Be careful. You know what you mean to us."

She clasped it, meeting his gaze. She softened her voice. "Take care of the others."

They'd lost men in their gang before, but every time it'd happened had been felt. They were bound by their rage, but at this point, they'd become like a family.

"I will. Good luck."

Then he was gone, along with the rest of the miners.

Reema turned back, keeping her hand on the left wall. The instant that Asif and the rest of her gang disappeared into another tunnel, darkness swallowed her whole. The silence would have impressed itself on her too, if not for Alaric's voice, still echoing off the walls around her. She followed the tunnel back to him.

She stood at the entrance to the small cavern he stood in, listening to him recite the lines of the story from memory. It had been a long time since she had felt the dying need to know something. The mines had culled that feeling from her. Down here, curiosity got people killed more often than not.

She swallowed and hoped that this wouldn't be one of those times. But listening to the shouting voices and the stamping feet racing toward them, she didn't exactly feel confident about that.

A presence pressed on her, as if she could feel his gaze resting on her even through the dark. But that was impossible. Strange things could happen in the deep of the mines, but no man could see through steel, and that was a fact.

The darkness softened, the first vestiges of light starting to make its way through the small cavern from the side tunnel. She strained her eyes, and sure enough, he was staring at her. Like he sensed her there.

Then the men burst in—five of them, each as stick thin as the other. Zayd had a reputation for eating most of the food passed down by the captain, but even so, she was starting to understand why Zayd risked giving up a second block. His men needed to eat too or they'd soon starve to death, and she knew he wasn't about to give up his own portions. The flickering torchlight cast their shadows across the space. She shrank back against the edge of the entrance to the tunnel, hoping the shadows kept her hidden.

She bit a curse. Even as thin as they were, five miners was a lot to deal with by herself.

Alaric fell silent.

"What in the deep?" A man with pockmarked cheeks stared at the band of steel forged around Alaric's skull. "He's blind."

"It's a trap!" another miner cried.

Reema shrank back from the entrance, hiding herself from view as the leader waved his torch back and forth.

"It's just him, don't worry," the leader growled. Hard lines etched his face, but Reema's eyes caught on the scar slashed across his throat.

Scar-Throat stalked forward, driving his foot into Alaric's chest.

Alaric stumbled and fell onto his back, banging the

back of his head against the hard stone floor with a soft grunt.

"Who in the sundamned hells are you?" Scar-Throat asked.

Alaric didn't answer. He held his hands out, showing that he was unarmed except for the book in his hands. He remained stoic until the man ripped the book from his hands.

Then Reema saw the rage.

It was different from hers. Where her rage was hot and vicious, his was cold and quiet. And somehow, that made it even more terrifying.

He leaned up, his voice low and dangerous.

"Give that back."

The men were quiet, exchanging glances of surprise.

Then Scar-Throat laughed. "Angel be damned, did you hear *that*? He's got a temper."

He kneeled next to Alaric and slapped him with an open palm. The sharp sound echoed across the cavern.

"You'll speak when I want you to speak. You understand?"

Reema seethed, drawing her shiv out from the back of her trousers. But it wasn't time to attack yet. They were still facing her direction. They'd see her before she could get even one of them down.

Then she heard Alaric beg.

"Don't hurt me, please."

Reema frowned, caught off guard by the sudden shift in his voice. She watched him crawl backward, angling himself to one side.

Her mouth parted in shock.

He was positioning himself up against the back wall, continuing his begging as the miners laughed and surrounded him. Their backs were to her now.

"Didn't nobody tell you to steer clear of the northern quarry?" Another miner asked, this one with a crooked nose and a permanent sneer.

"He's blind," the pockmarked miner said. "How's he supposed to know what's where? Or where's what?"

"You've got a point."

"I don't care if he's blind," Scar-Throat said. "He's someplace he shouldn't be, and for that, he needs to be taught a lesson."

He crouched over Alaric and drew a shiv. It was the same as Reema's, sharpened marble. With a dark grin, he heated the edge with the torch.

She started to creep forward, her thighs burning as she kept low. She had to move slowly, otherwise she risked drawing the other miners' attention. They ripped open Alaric's coat and shirt, and with savage glee, held him tight as Scar-Throat pressed the shiv against Alaric's chest.

Reema winced as she listened to the burning hiss of flesh. She expected to hear his scream shake the cavern walls, but heard nothing more than a strained groan.

The hiss stopped, and when it did, Alaric's pants filled the air. One of the miners whistled.

"He didn't even say a word."

Scar-Throat's face twisted. Branding Alaric hadn't given him the result he wanted. He waved the torch in front of Alaric's face, ready to try something else.

"Let's see you scream now."

The cavern filled with a scream then, but not Alaric's. Reema unlocked the cage confining her rage, letting its flames consume her. Her vision turned red as she buried her shiv in the back of a miner's neck.

Hot blood spurted over her, and before the body hit the ground, she had already slashed open another miner's neck.

The men stumbled back with a shout, but Reema attacked with reckless abandon.

She thrust the shiv into the third man's gut, his sneer splitting wide into an ear-splitting scream. Instead of drawing back, she leaned into it and met it with a banshee scream of her own. She dropped his body to the ground.

"It's the Ifrit!" The pockmarked miner screamed.

He tackled her, cursing as she dragged the shiv's edge across his forearm. But he managed to get his hands on her wrists, and he pinned her down. Reema leaned forward and bit the man's ear, tearing it off with a vicious growl.

He screamed, clutching his bleeding, gushing ear, and fell back. "She bit my ear off!"

She spat the ear flesh to the side, only to be caught by a flying fist. Lights spun into existence, swimming across the darkness. A warm shiv's edge pressed itself to her throat.

"Stop screaming. I've got the crazy bitch," Scar-Throat growled.

The pockmarked miner straightened, holding his bleeding ear with bared teeth.

Reema struggled, but the shiv pressed tighter. A bead

of warm blood trickled down her throat. Her mind turned as she tried to figure out how she was going to get out of this. She was so close. With three down, there was just the two left.

Then a deep, loud roar echoed across the cavern, and a heavy weight slammed into both her and Scar-Throat. The shiv nicked the side of her throat, but not deep enough to do any real damage.

Reema looked up to see Alaric scrambling with him, swinging his fist blindly. The fallen torch gleamed off the sharpened marble in Scar-Throat's hand.

She stood up to help Alaric, only to get tackled back to the ground by the earless, pockmarked miner. She strained against him, turning her head to see Scar-Throat with his shiv in hand.

"Watch out! He's got a—"

A hand clamped over her mouth.

But it was enough. Alaric patted his hand against the Scar-Throat's arm, and just as the shiv was thrust toward him, he moved his hand in the way. The blade stabbed through his palm, drawing a deep growl from Alaric. He drove a fist down, but he was nowhere near the Scar-Throat's head, and he smashed his fist against stone.

Reema bit the finger over her mouth, ignoring the iron tang of blood gushing into her mouth. The pock-marked miner holding her screamed again, falling away and clutching his hand with gasping sobs.

"You b-bitch. I'll kill you. I'll—"

She buried her shiv into his chest and silenced him forever.

She turned and saw Alaric fighting for his life, pinned under the weight of the scarred leader. Blood was everywhere, seeping from the open wound in his hand to the numerous cuts he'd sustained in trying to fight him.

When Scar-Throat realized what she'd done, he backed away. Alaric kicked and punched blindly, but Scar-Throat wasn't there. She could see the panic in his face, even with his eyes bound by steel.

"It's okay," she said, her raspy voice calming Alaric. "I've got him now."

The leader's gaze flicked toward the fallen gang members and then back to her. Her reflection shone in his dark eyes: a small woman with dark hair clinging to her face, drenched in blood—the very image of an Ifrit, spawned from the seventh level of hell.

He didn't bother begging. He would know the nightmarish tales of the Ifrit, of the woman who offered no mercy. He swallowed, got into a stance, and waved his shiv through the air.

"Come on," he said, fighting back a stammer. "Let's finish—"

She flicked her wrist. The shiv flew through the air without a sound. A pained, wheezing gasp escaped him as he stumbled back and glanced down at his chest. Then he collapsed with a gaping mouth and lifeless eyes.

Reema yanked her shiv free from his body, wiped it dry on his tunic, and tucked it away. She retrieved the fallen torch and spotted the book in the corner of the cavern. It must have slid there during the scramble.

She picked it up and studied the cover.

The cover was a beautiful shade of burgundy, with

gold lettering styling the front. She opened it, and saw symbols running across the page. She ran her fingers over them, threads of memory pulling at her in an attempt to read them. But frustratingly, they were lost.

She was gone.

It had never bothered her before that she had forgotten to read. Her parents had taught her as a small child, but it wasn't exactly a valued skill in the mines. It had been easy to forget their lessons. But now, with those words branded into her mind, she found herself frustrated. There was *meaning* hidden behind these symbols; meaning that she desperately craved to know.

She slammed the book shut and went to stand over Alaric. He lay quietly, holding his injured hand to his chest and staring blindly up at the ceiling. If this were anyone else from her gang, they would have made a comment or joke by now about being still alive. But Alaric remained quiet, more upset than even when he'd been thrown down the Hole.

"Who was she?" she asked.

"What?"

She crouched over him and pushed the book into his hands. "You were saying something about a broken heart, and a woman who was gone. Who was she?"

He didn't answer, not at first. Instead, the silence stretched, so quiet now without the dying screams. She should be used to it by now, but for some reason, it still surprised her.

Then he spoke. "Her name was Tasneem."

He rolled over and awkwardly got to his feet before stumbling back a step. She grabbed his shoulder to keep him from falling over. She started to ask more, craving to know what this Tasneem's story was, but she stopped herself. This wasn't the time.

He shrugged her hand away, and she frowned.

"How many were there?" he asked.

"Five."

He shook his head and clutched his bleeding fist. "I thought there were four."

"Doesn't matter now. They're all dead," Reema said, with a last glance toward the man she'd gutted. He wasn't quite dead yet, but he'd passed out, and judging by the paleness of his skin and the blood gushing from the wound, he wouldn't live long enough to wake anyway.

"I would've been too, if it weren't for you," he said.

He was covered in cuts, but the worst of his wounds was the stab wound through his palm. It needed to be bound. Otherwise, he'd end up slowing her down.

Without thinking, Reema ripped a strip of cloth from the bottom of her tunic and reached for Alaric's hand. The instant her fingers touched his palm, they both jumped at the spark.

"Hells," she said with a chuckle. She grabbed hold of his hand again, wrapping the cloth tightly around the wound. His hands were soft. Warm, too. For some reason, her heart beat faster now than when she was fighting the other miners. "I'd be dead too if you hadn't gotten that bastard off me."

"That's true," he said, the corner of his mouth lifting into a soft smirk. An unfamiliar heat flushed through her.

Damn the deep, what was *wrong* with her? "You owe me."

Reema frowned. "*I* owe *you*? Did you hit your head against the rock too hard or something? We saved each other's lives. We're even."

His smirk widened. "I wasn't talking about that."

"What do you mean?"

"I'm alive."

"So?"

"Did you forget already? If I lived, you'd give me one magical wish, sprinkled with your very own marble dust."

It came back to her, and Reema snarled. She smacked her hand against his injured palm, wiping that stupid smirk away.

"I lied. Now, let's get going," she said. "My men will be waiting for us at Zayd's camp."

She started down the tunnel the miners had come from, only to realize after a few steps that Alaric hadn't moved. Instead, his head dipped, his skin flushed with embarrassment and frustration.

"I need help," he said.

She didn't say a word as she grabbed his arm and guided him in the right direction. Leaving the bloodied cavern behind, he was quieter than ever.

CHAPTER
FIVE

By the time they reached Zayd's camp, Asif and the other men in her gang had already done him in. They sat around a crackling fire, eating from his serving of lentils, while the gang lord's body lay to the side with a deep gash splitting his neck from where one of them had struck him with their pickaxe.

Even though it looked like they'd caught Zayd with only one other member of his gang, he had put up a fight. Asif had an ugly cut across his face. Javid had a visibly broken nose. Hadi, Omar, and Ra'ad each had a myriad of gruesome bruises.

They all stared at Reema, frustration, confusion, and a sense of betrayal in their gazes. She was their gang lord. She should have been here with them, earning her own share of blood taken from this territory. Instead, she was nowhere to be seen, saving the useless blind man.

Asif spat to the side and dropped his bowl of lentils, the sound of the bowl clattering against the stone echoing across the cavern.

Reema ignored the look he gave her and went to the body. Zayd stared into the distance, his eyes beginning to glass over.

"He say anything before he died?" Reema asked.

Asif didn't answer, letting the silence stretch between them.

The other gang members looked from him to her and shook their heads. It was rare for them to argue; for as long as most of them had been in her gang, he had always been at her side.

"He cursed us to the seven hells," Omar said, breaking the silence.

"Said he'd come back from the dead to haunt us," Ra'ad added.

"Take our balls from us," Omar continued.

"The usual," Ra'ad concluded.

They resumed eating their lentils.

Reema nodded. "What about their sacks of food and water?"

Hadi patted the sacks at his side. "Untouched."

"Good, good," Reema said. "Finish your meals, then we'll head back. Last thing we need is another gang taking our territory."

She realized then that Alaric stood a few feet back, still at the edge of the light, quiet and holding his bound hand to his chest.

"And give a bowl of lentils to Alaric. He deserves it."

Asif growled, "Deserves it? I'd say that from the sounds of it, you were the better distraction than him. The only reason we got the jump on Zayd was because he heard *you* fighting."

Reema fixed him with a look. "He deserves it because he's one of us now."

"One of *us*?" His gaze narrowed as he stood, towering over her. "Did you forget what we're trying to accomplish?"

"You think I *forgot*?" she hissed, her voice thick with rage.

He seemed to realize what he said and started to backtrack. "I wasn't talking about your sister."

"The only thing that seems to be forgotten is *who* leads this gang. Remind me, Asif. Who's the gang lord?"

He stared at her, his fists flexing at his sides.

"You," he ground out.

"Who brought you into the fold, kept us together and alive?"

"You."

She looked to the others. "Who promised you vengeance?"

Each one of them knew the depths of her rage, knew how unreasonable she could be when she got like this. But this was what was needed for them to ever have a chance at getting back at the captain and the slave master.

They answered in a quiet voice. "You."

Her lip curled as she stared each of them into submission. When they dipped their heads, she turned her attention back to Asif. He slowly sat back down.

"Hadi," she said. "Give my man a bowl."

"Yes, boss," he said without hesitation.

Alaric cocked his head but said nothing as Hadi led him to a seat and pushed a warm bowl of lentils into his hands. She realized that it must have been some time since Alaric had eaten, judging by the way he dove into it with his one good hand.

Reema sat next to Asif, and a private look passed between them. She might be pissed at Asif, but he was still her second. He drew a deep breath and sighed, as if expelling all the tension. He quietly fetched her a bowl of lentils from the fire.

They finished their meals in silence and packed up the rest, heading back into the tunnels. They were silent as they walked through the tunnels toward their territory. To her surprise, Asif had taken the position next to Alaric, gripping his shoulder and guiding him. She wasn't sure if he was simply interested in keeping Alaric quiet to avoid drawing attention to themselves, or if he was just trying to stay in her good graces.

She couldn't deny the reason for his anger, though. They had just found the first sign of black marble, the first sign of hope in getting revenge against the cruel bastards up top, and she was putting it all in danger by bringing a blind man into the gang. They would only ever be as strong as their weakest link, and him? He couldn't keep watch, couldn't help defend them, couldn't even help mine the marble. He was worse than useless; he was a liability. To keep him safe, they'd have to dedicate at least one of their focus to him at all times, and with what they were trying to accomplish, that would be impossible.

Reema knew it would only be a matter of time before Alaric met his end.

There was nothing she could do to stop it.

She ground her teeth, dug her nails into her palm. She and the others in the gang shared one thing: their rage. It bonded them, drew them together, made them stronger.

She and Alaric? The one thing they shared was their helplessness: him to suffer the cruel fate that befell every weak man and woman unlucky enough to be thrown into these mines, and her to watch as yet another person she couldn't save died.

Suddenly, she wished she had listened to Asif and never gone back to save him at all. At least then, she wouldn't have to feel so weak herself.

Her thoughts cleared as the torchlight revealed a mound of fallen marble rocks ahead of them. Reema's frown deepened the closer they got.

"Did we take a wrong turn?" Hadi asked.

Reema didn't answer, focused on running her hand along the walls to make sure she hadn't led them down the wrong tunnel. Sure enough, she found the groove she'd carved into it. This *was* the way back to her territory.

A bad feeling settled in the pit of her stomach. She climbed atop the first few rocks, maintaining her balance as she shifted a few out of the way. She stopped when she saw the larger blocks behind them.

"What is it?" Hadi asked, his voice tight within the tunnel.

"The path's collapsed," Reema said.

The members of her gang cursed.

"Let's get it mined away. The sooner we get it done, the sooner we're out of these damned tunnels," Asif said.

She didn't answer him. Something was wrong. Though the tunnels could be unpredictable, this small section of the mines should have been stable. She climbed further up the mound until she could touch the ceiling, running her hands along it.

"What are you looking for?" Asif asked.

Then she found it—a simple groove, stretching from one side of the tunnel to the other. This wasn't done by the earth. It was a guided collapse.

Shit.

"Go back," Reema said, her voice flooded with panic.

Her gang members exchanged glances. It was unlike her to panic.

"Go back!" she shouted, but it was too late.

A deep rumble echoed through the earth, the walls shaking on all sides of them. They shouted and pushed back toward her as the ceiling collapsed behind them, flooding the air with a wave of white marble dust.

They all choked on the air, struggling to get a clean breath. It took a full minute for the dust to settle.

The torch flickered in the dark, the shadows dancing around them as if mocking them. Reema pushed through the others, only to find another set of rubble behind them. She climbed the rocks, shoving them aside with budding fury, but whoever orchestrated this collapse had done a thorough job.

They were trapped.

CHAPTER
SIX

Javid finally had a chance to put his full strength to use. Reema sat back, drenched in sweat, her muscles trembling, as she listened to the giant smash the rubble with his pickaxe. Every time he struck, a small cloud of marble dust filled the air, drawing a cough from at least one of them.

It was tedious work. Because there wasn't much room between them and the marble rubble on either side, every time Javid made headway, they had to strategically pass the broken pieces of marble down the line and place them on the other side.

They spent most of the first hour debating which way to mine. Should they mine straight through to their side of the territory and potentially into whatever traps lay that way, or should they go back, which was the safer route?

Much to the gang's surprise, Reema advocated for safety. She knew their limits. They were tired, worn, and battered from their attack on the northern quarry.

Pushing them to retake their territory from whoever had taken it wouldn't turn out well.

She watched as the twin brothers picked up the broken blocks of marble from the rubble Javid was working on and passed them to Hadi, who then gave them to Asif, who pushed Alaric out of the way to toss the rocks to the other side.

Reema took a final breath, then stood and took her place back in the line, motioning for Asif to take a few minutes to rest.

The monotony of passing marble pieces from Hadi to Alaric freed up her mind and gave her space to wander. Usually, in moments like these, she thought about her sister, stoking the burning coals in her heart.

But today, her mind turned to something different: the book Alaric carried in his coat pocket. Its bulge was visible even now, in the dimly lit tunnel.

The words he'd spoken had weight to them, enough that she couldn't help but wonder about the story behind them. She wanted to know more about this Tasneem and the man who'd fallen for her. She wanted to know about his tragedy, if only to know that someone's pain was greater than hers.

Javid loosed a victorious shout that reverberated within the tight space, and after what seemed like an eternity, a wave of fresh air passed into the tunnel. Each gang member craned their neck to see the space Javid had forced open at the top of the mound.

"Finally," Reema said. "Keep at it, Javid. Clear that shit out of the way."

The taste of fresh air gave them the renewed energy

they needed, and before long, they had a hole big enough at the top of the rubble for each of them to crawl through. One by one, they freed themselves from the collapsed tunnel.

"What's the plan, boss?" Omar panted, his hands on his hips as his shoulders sagged with exhaustion.

"We'll find a place to lay low for a bit, until we figure out what bastards did this to us."

They gave her skeptical looks, and she understood why. The very idea of a place to lie low was laughable in the mines. But there was *one* place, a place that was the only reason she ever managed to survive the years she'd spent roaming between the territories. She'd closed the entrance to it many years ago, promising never to return.

The lingering pain in her heart twisted.

"Follow me," she said.

She led the way through the tunnels, the torch doing nothing to keep the darkness from seeping into her bones. Sometimes, the mines had a way of making a person lonely, even when they were with others. Reema felt that loneliness now more than ever, with the silence pressing in on her.

Her heart was heavy as memories threatened to climb up from where she'd buried them. They turned down a tunnel and reached a dead end.

The group looked around in confusion.

Reema handed Omar the torch and took the pickaxe from his hand. Then she turned to the side and swung at waist level, the pickaxe slamming into the marble wall. A hollow sound echoed through the tunnel.

With a few more swings, she revealed an entrance known only to her. She knelt down low enough that she wouldn't hit her head on the entrance. She hesitated for a moment, her hand resting on the cold marble wall.

Memories flooded back—the good, the bad, and the desperate times that had driven her to this secluded spot. It was a sanctuary that had turned into a tomb of memories she had tried to leave behind.

She took the torch back from Omar.

"This is it," she murmured, more to herself than to the others. With a deep breath, she ducked her head and crawled through the entrance.

The cave was half the size of their base but infinitely more beautiful. The walls were ensconced with rose quartz that reflected the lights off the torch all across the floor. She could still see where she had left things behind; the clothing she'd worn from the surface, the makeshift bed that she'd return to after terrorizing other miners as she roamed the tunnels.

A sense of dread settled over her when she heard the trickle of water. She could hear the whispers of her past echoing all around her, the walls closing in on her. All at once, she struggled to breathe beneath the weight of the earth.

She swallowed and turned to see a small tunnel leading off to a second, smaller cave. A voice at the back of her mind called for her to go that way, to see the grave she left behind. But she didn't have to go to know what she would find. The image had haunted her in the same nightmare she'd had every night for years: a small grave made from assembled marble blocks and decorated with rose quartz chips, resting next to a small pool of water.

The other members of her gang gaped in silent awe as they crawled into the cave after her.

"We'll be safe here," she said, her voice hollow in the enclosed space.

Hushed whispers passed behind her, and Reema tore her gaze away from the grave's direction.

"Why didn't she ever tell us about this place?" Ra'ad muttered.

His brother, Omar, shushed him, his eyes flicking toward Reema.

"I'll say this once," Reema said, her gaze sweeping across each of the men, drawing their attention back to her. "In case you haven't figured it out, this is a special place to me, and there's a reason I've kept it a secret. I only have one rule. Do not go down that tunnel. If I find out that you have, I promise you, I'll end you where you stand. Do you understand?"

The others nodded, except for Alaric. He might've been blind, but he seemed contemplative as he faced the direction of the tunnel.

"Make camp, and rest up. We have no idea what we're up against, but you know what's at stake. We have to take our territory back, whatever happens."

While the others took to assembling the camp, Asif approached Reema.

"This is where she's buried, isn't it?" he asked, glancing toward the direction of the tunnel.

She didn't say anything. Her silence was answer enough.

"I'll make sure nobody disturbs her peace." He clapped her on the shoulder and went to join the others.

He had to be every bit as tired as the rest of them. It felt like an age since they'd last slept. And sure enough, the second they'd finished setting up the fire, they lay down to sleep. Soon, the echoes of their snores filled the cave.

Needing some space for herself, Reema sat apart from the group, her gaze lost in the shadows. She wrapped her arms around her knees, doing everything she could to still her mind from the onslaught of memories of her sister.

She tried not to think about how she'd carried her sister's body for days, even as it decayed, trying to find a place to bury her. It was only by sheer luck that she found this place; she'd dropped her pickaxe and heard it hit a hollow section of marble.

This cave, as beautiful as it was, made every breath a struggle against the suffocating despair.

She was gone.

Damn the deep, she missed her sister so much.

Hesitant, stumbling footsteps drew her attention. Alaric was trying to find his way through the dark, his hands outstretched and his mouth parted in the worry that he'd trip and fall.

She watched him for a moment, debating if she should let him continue searching blindly for her. But it was too pathetic to watch, how helpless he was.

"I'm here," she said.

He breathed a sigh of relief, and carefully made his way to her. She guided him so he knew where to sit.

She readied herself for questions, knowing he must have sought her out for a reason, but to her surprise, he remained quiet as he settled next to her.

Something about his presence affected the dark. It wasn't as oppressive. In fact, next to him, it even seemed ... comforting.

She glanced at him out of the corner of her eye, ignoring the way her heart quickened just at the sight of him. Her gaze trailed up to the steel forged around his skull. There wasn't so much as an inch of space between it and his face, nor did it seem like there was any visible welded line. Whoever had made this had the skills of a master.

Not for the first time, she wondered what he had done to deserve such punishment.

It was a silly question, she knew. The surface dwellers did not need a reason to be as cruel as they were. It was baked into them, maybe by the sun or the way that traits pass from father to son, and it took Reema being made a slave to realize that.

The longer she stared at him, the more she wondered about him, and the more she wanted to hear his voice.

"Are you afraid of the dark?" Reema asked before she could stop herself.

A moment of silence passed before he answered.

"I wasn't." A heavy sigh escaped his lips. His voice was just quiet enough to not wake the others. "I used to love the dark. I'd go outside all the time and stare up at the stars."

"I don't even remember what the stars look like, to be honest," Reema said.

The corner of his mouth quirked, "They're beautiful, so magical that I wonder if the Angel descended from them instead of the heavens."

His smile fell away.

"Don't think I'll be seeing them again. Or much of anything else."

Reema's heart ached for him. If only there was some way to help him, but how do you help a blind man in the mines?

He was already dead. He just didn't know it.

The thought dragged a memory from the back of her mind: her sister kneeling on the sand nearby, and the moment that she had watched the last spark of hope disappear from her sister's eyes before she was murdered.

She swallowed, suddenly wishing that she could have given her sister hope in those final moments.

She looked at Alaric again. He might be helpless, but maybe she could help him where she hadn't been able to help her sister. Maybe she could give him some hope before he died.

With a heavy sigh, she reached to her side and scraped up a pinch's worth of marble dust. She sprinkled it over him.

He flinched at the sudden feeling. He frowned as he dusted himself off and rubbed the marble dust between his fingers.

"Your magical wish, sprinkled with my very own special marble dust," Reema said.

His brows furrowed above the steel band, before he

realized what she was saying. His cheeks crinkled as he smiled.

His smile reminded her of her sister, the way that it seemed like the sun had come out from behind the clouds. Reema found herself reflecting his smile before she scowled and checked herself.

"Don't get too excited. You're not picking the wish, I'll be doing that for you."

"Oh, come now, what fun is that?"

"It's not supposed to be fun," she said. "I'm going to give you what you need most. A chance to survive."

It was a lie. He had no chance, but her words had the effect she wanted. He lifted his chin, and his shoulders loosened.

He paused and continued rubbing the marble dust between his fingers. Then he asked, "Why are you doing this?"

She couldn't bring herself to tell him the truth. "Because you belong to me now. I can't let you keep putting the rest of my gang at risk."

"I suppose I do make it easy for the other miners to find and kill us."

"Forget them. Asif and the others would do you in first, if you can't figure out some way to navigate the dark."

He glanced in the direction of the snores. "So you'll teach me to survive them, then."

She looked that way too. She didn't answer him, but it wasn't much of a question anyway. They sat in silence a while longer, each other's company freeing them from the madness of their own thoughts.

Then he sighed and cleaned the marble dust off his fingers. He reached into his coat pocket and withdrew the book. Her eyes caught on the burgundy cover, trailing over the gold lettering. He ran his thumb over the cover, like it meant something special to him.

"My mother gave me this." His thumb brushed over the title. "'Beneath the Sands of Sorrow'—It was her favorite book. The only thing I have left of her, really."

Reema stared at the book, wanting nothing more than to feel the pages between her fingers. It was strange; she'd never once cared to pick up a book. That was something for the Bloodlined and the more educated of the Commonborn, and besides, why waste time reading words on a page when there was real life to live?

But his words still lingered in her mind.

"This was the woman who was supposed to be his everlasting love, whose soul had been made in measure for his. And now she was gone."

She hadn't known that simple words could make a person feel so much.

He held it out for Reema to take, and her heart skipped a beat.

"Take it," he insisted.

"But why?" she stammered.

"Because I know what you're doing. So take it as my thanks."

She started to reach out but stopped. It felt wrong to take it from him. He frowned and leaned forward, pushing it into her lap. He took her hands, warm against hers, and gently pressed them over the cover.

"I'm blind now, so it's not of much use to me anyway. And besides, it's too beautiful a story to stay hidden away."

She swallowed as she realized his hands were still pressed against hers. But she didn't move them away. The warmth of his hands felt ... nice.

He smiled, like he could read her mind. Then, he stepped back and flipped up the collar of his coat against the chill of the cave.

"Get some sleep," he said.

He started to turn away.

"Wait," she said, her voice soft and vulnerable.

He paused.

"I ... I forgot how to read."

When he looked back over his shoulder, she could sense the pity in him. "So you, too, are blind."

She didn't know what to say to that. She had never thought of herself that way, but she knew that when she opened the pages, she would see nothing of the world hidden behind the words.

She stood, approached him, and pressed the book back into his hands. She was all too aware of how their fingers brushed against each other.

"Keep it," she said. "You should keep what you love near your heart."

His fingers slid down to her wrist, and he kept her there as she tried to turn away. Before she could say anything else, he stepped closer and pressed the book against her chest, right over her heart. She wondered if he could feel her heart pounding through the cover.

He leaned in, his mouth by her ear, his warm breath

making her burn in a way that rage never could. He whispered to her, and butterflies fluttered in her stomach.

"I'll teach you."

She was breathless as he backed away, leaving the book in her hands.

"You help me, I'll help you. Does that sound fair, Reema?"

Shivers ran down her spine, and she wasn't sure if that was good or bad. But sundamned hells, the way her name sounded coming from him ... this was dangerous. This was playing with fire.

"Okay," she said before she could stop herself. A glance toward the tunnel that led to her sister's grave filled her with a wave of guilt; she should be maintaining focus on her goal, on the fact that they were so damned close to finding out if the myth of the Djinn was true or not. But she couldn't help herself. "The others can't find out about this, though."

"Why not?"

"They just can't," she said, her gaze darting toward the group of sleeping miners. It would completely undermine the rule she had over them. The last thing she needed was them truly believing that she had gone soft for the blind bastard. "I'll come up with a plan."

He smiled and dipped his head in acknowledgment. "I'll leave it in your capable hands, *boss*."

"Oh, piss off," she scowled, earning a deeper grin from him. "I'll find you later."

He tucked his hands away in his pockets, his smile lingering as he left her. Reema sat back down, staring at the book. She ran her fingers over the title, feeling its ridges.

Beneath the Sands of Sorrow.

So that was what it said.

A smile played on her lips.

CHAPTER
SEVEN

Reema led the way through the tunnels with her gang at her back. They brandished their pickaxes and shivs, wanting nothing more than to get revenge on the bastards who thought they could poach their territory.

The tunnel they'd been taking the day before might have been collapsed, but there were other ways to reach the territory. It was along one of these that Reema trailed her hand, feeling out the grooves marked in the walls. She tried to stay focused, but it wasn't easy—not with the unfamiliar weight of the book inside her tunic, and certainly not with Alaric following just behind her.

She winced every time he bumped against the side of the tunnel, knocking fragments of marble to clatter against the floor. Something had to be done about it, because the way echoes traveled through the tunnels, they were likely to get caught and killed before they could gain the upper hand. And the rest of her gang knew it, judging by the scowls and the hatred-filled looks.

Some of them were even directed towards her, and she couldn't blame them. She was the one who saved him, instead of letting him meet the end that every other disabled miner faced down in these cruel depths of the earth.

Reema paused, and the rest of the gang halted behind her. She ran her fingers over the groove in the wall again. It was different from the others—a marker she left for when they were close to her territory. She looked back and gave her gang the *look*.

Be ready to fight.

They rolled their shoulders and cracked their necks. The torchlight gleamed in their dark Commonborn eyes, the rage that bonded them together flaring to life with snarls and bared teeth.

This was Reema's gang, the men who lived for vengeance. Any miners who thought they could get the better of them were sundamned fools, and they were about to learn why.

Reema drew her shiv in case of an ambush and pushed forward, the torch held out in front of her. She waved it slowly from side to side, exposing every creeping shadow. It was quiet, almost *too* quiet. Every nerve screamed for her to run forward and slaughter her would-be enemies, but she had to be cautious. Otherwise, she risked the lives of everybody in her gang.

The shadows softened, shifting slowly into white marble. Reema's mouth parted and her stomach fell as the torch revealed yet another collapsed tunnel.

Curses echoed behind her.

"They closed this tunnel too," she muttered to

herself. She climbed the rubble and tested the rocks at the top, but she had a feeling that whoever was method-ical enough to collapse this tunnel had been thorough with it.

Reema turned back, bristling as she led her men through the mines. Every tunnel she took brought them to another mound of rubble blocking the way. As insane as it might be, she had a gut feeling that every single tunnel into the southern mines had been collapsed.

Her gut feeling was confirmed when they reached the final tunnel and found an even larger mound of rubble. She crouched before it, her hands curling into fists as her mind raced.

It was one thing to try and trap them in a tunnel by collapsing it, but collapsing *every* tunnel in the territory? What sense did that make? Why would they do that?

Her brows furrowed. The only thing she could think of was that they had somehow found out about the black marble. Could they know what she was trying to do?

Reema clenched her jaw, shaking with anger. Just as she was about to stand, she noticed something lying in the rubble. She yanked it out, ignoring the echoes of marble rocks clattering down the mound.

It was a broken pickaxe.

"There's another one," Asif said. He stepped forward and dragged out not one but two pickaxes.

Reema suspected that if they managed to clear the rubble, they would find three bodies to match. She couldn't give two shits about them; in her eyes, their deaths were the result of their own hasty efforts that caused the tunnel to collapse. No matter how skilled a miner might be, rushing the job could draw the earth's wrath. And deep in the mines, the earth showed no mercy.

She turned back to the miners, and the others saw the face of the Ifrit.

"Back to the cave. Now."

They had spent the day walking the tunnels, and she could feel the weariness in her bones. Whatever they decided to do couldn't happen today.

As Reema led the way back to the cave, she could not help but wonder how someone could have found out about the black marble. It was a tightly guarded secret, and she never shared it with anyone outside of the members of her gang.

How could someone know every tunnel that led to the southern mines? This place was a maze, with twists and turns ending in dead ends more often than not. Yet, someone had figured out every single pathway into her territory.

Who could have figured that out, and who had the power to make it happen so *quickly*?

Her thoughts took a dark turn. She forced herself not to look back over her shoulder at her gang. Was it possible that one of her crew was working with another gang lord? For some reason, that thought more than anything depressed her. This gang had become like a family to her over the years. Despite their differences, they had a bond that ran deeper than blood; they shared their traumas and a dying need to get revenge at all costs.

She wasn't sure what she should hope for: the

betrayal of someone she'd come to trust, or finding an enemy who was so ... capable.

Someone bumped into the wall again, causing a rock to drop onto the stone floor, the heavy thud reverberating on all sides. The members of her gang cursed, and Alaric muttered a quiet apology.

There was one man she could trust; one man who hadn't been in the mines long enough to know what was going on, what they were up to, let alone the paths that led to her territory.

That thought followed her through tunnels, and long after they made it back to the cave and discussed what to do next.

The only plan they could come up with to regain the upper hand was to build an entirely new tunnel straight toward the southern mines. If they tried to clear any of the rubble, they would be too tired to face what was on the other side. And Reema knew that if that happened, they'd be ambushed and meet their eternal end.

As they began to fall asleep around the fire, one by one, Reema worked with the pickaxes, binding them together with strips of cloth torn from her own tunic. The idea struck her in the final moments before they reached her cave, and she figured it might just be enough to keep him from smacking against the walls and announcing their location so easily. Of course, she didn't want to ruin her only set of clothing, but she had no choice. There was nothing else to bind the pickaxes. She'd have to tear the clothing off the next miner they found and take care not to stain it with blood when she killed him.

Her gaze flicked up to Alaric from time to time, noticing he hadn't fallen asleep yet. He seemed to be waiting, hopeful that she would come for him.

When Asif finally dropped off, his snores joining the other miners, she stood, the makeshift stick and a blanket under her arm, and went to Alaric. She touched her fingers to his shoulders gently enough so that he didn't startle.

A small smile played at the corner of his lips, but she wasn't in that kind of mood tonight. The butterflies she felt the day before had burned away before the flames of the Ifrit.

She leaned in and whispered in his ear, "Come with me."

His smile disappeared. He seemed to notice the change too. He nodded and carefully stood, reaching out to rest his hand on her shoulder.

With her guiding him, they went not to the spot they spoke before, but beyond. It wasn't safe to speak in the same cave where the others slept, not with what she suspected. Her blood roared in her ears with every step that took her closer to her sister's grave. She struggled to breathe as the tunnel opened up to a smaller cave, no larger than ten feet wide. The walls were painstakingly covered with fabric, taken from dozens of fallen miners: some she'd killed, some she'd found. It was all that protected her and kept the sound of her crying from traveling out into the rest of the mines during those early days that she grieved.

The only sound she could never stop was the soft trickle of water. Her eyes found it, where the water ran from a crack in the stones, pooling at the base of the grave she'd built. The grave was just as she remembered it, every detail exactly the same.

She touched a hand to it, and it was all she could do to not fall to her knees and cry out her sister's name.

She was gone.

"Where are we?" Alaric asked.

She shushed him and hung the blanket from two hooks embedded in the walls. She stepped back and surveyed her work with a satisfied nod.

"We can speak now," Reema said, her voice still hushed. It almost felt wrong to speak here, next to her sister's grave, but there was nowhere else to go. This was it.

She turned to see him reaching out in an attempt to feel his surroundings. He was stumbling toward the grave, his footwork unsteady.

"Stop!" Reema shouted, suddenly unsure if the blanket was hung well enough. But it must've been, given how her voice boomed into the silence.

Alaric abruptly halted, his mouth parting at the sudden loudness of her voice. He had never heard her shout. For that matter, *she* couldn't remember the last time she'd shouted or even spoken so loudly.

"Just … step back," she said, her voice as quiet as a whisper.

He stepped back without questioning her.

She waited for him to ask why, but he remained quiet.

"I told you I'd teach you to survive," she said, trying

to move past the fact that he had almost run into her sister's grave.

She stalked forward and shoved the makeshift walking stick into his arms. "First things first, learn to walk without bumping into every Angel-damned thing."

His hands felt along the stick, his brows furrowed in contemplation. He seemed to recognize it had been made from broken pickaxes by the metal stubs at the end of each pick. She couldn't get rid of them, so she had to tie around them when binding them together.

"Clever," he mumbled, as he took hold of the end.

It wasn't the most practical walking stick in the world: it was heavy and covered in splinters. But down here in the mines, surrounded by white marble and little else, it was the best she could do.

Gently, he slid the end along the ground, seeming to understand that he should try to feel out the surroundings before walking. A small smile came to his face as he started to feel out the edges of the cave, painting a picture in his mind of the space around them.

But Reema could only wince as the stick scraped against the stone floor. It was a bone-chilling sound that she knew would draw miners to them in the tunnels. If the other miners didn't kill them, her own gang would just to keep the silence.

Then Alaric began tapping the stick against the stone, drawing a groan from her.

She needed to tear another strip from her shirt, but she didn't want to tear more from the bottom. As it was, she'd already torn enough to expose the bottom of her stomach to anyone who laid eyes on her. That made her

uncomfortable enough, not because of her bare skin—
these were the mines, and there had been times in the
past when she'd been unlucky to have much to wear—
but because it revealed the top of the book tucked into
her waistband.

She stripped off her top and flipped it inside out. The
linen tunic had a thin inner layer that helped keep the
miners warm in the earth's cold tunnels. As much as she
didn't want to tear it away, she knew she'd need enough
fabric to mute the full weight of the walking stick, and
that fabric had to come from somewhere: either her top,
the blanket behind them, or the fabric covering the
walls. It felt sacrilegious to remove something from her
sister's grave, so that wasn't an option. And, well, the
blanket was worth far more than her top. It was what
kept the silence as they mined.

With the fabric torn, Reema went to Alaric and took
the stick from him without saying anything. She
wrapped it around the bottom of the stick, forming a
small ball, and tied it off.

A wandering hand pressed against her bare shoulder,
and she froze.

Alaric froze too.

They were both suddenly aware of how exposed
she was.

Though she knew he couldn't see her, she flushed a
deep shade of red as he slowly removed his hand. She
slipped her top back on and saw a sly smile.

She shoved the stick into his chest.

"Try that," she said, her voice strangely choked. She
could still feel the imprint of his hand on her shoulder,

the warmth against her skin. The butterflies appeared again, and her heart ached in a strange way she didn't understand.

Alaric lowered the stick. The sound of him finding his way around the small cave wasn't quite what she'd hoped for, but it was enough to keep them safe in the tunnels.

"You are a clever girl," Alaric said, clearly pleased with the result of the walking stick. "But I hope you don't plan on walking around topless."

"Keep your worries to yourself. I've got my top. I may be a bit cold, thanks to you, but I'll be fine."

Still, she wrapped her arms around her chest, realizing that the anger she felt earlier had dissipated, replaced by a want to feel his hand on her again. Why was she feeling like this? She knew nothing about the man.

Reema sat and watched as he continued to move around the small cave, gently tapping and sliding the stick against its edges, staying quiet except for when he began to near her sister's grave again. She knew he needed to feel out the cave, but she couldn't help the strained noise that escaped her.

He stopped moving.

"There's something here you don't want me to go near," he said.

Her voice was small, so frustratingly small. "Yes."

She thought he would ask why, but he didn't. Instead, he respected her statement and did his best to veer around the edges of her sister's grave. Waves of gratitude passed through Reema. She wasn't ready to talk about her sister, not yet.

A shout of surprise drew her attention back to him as he stumbled and fell into the small pool of water. It was only waist-high at its deepest, but it caught him by surprise and his head dunked beneath the surface as he fell.

Reema shot to her feet and went to him, pulling him out of the water. He tripped and fell on the stone floor, landing flat on his back. She couldn't help but laugh at the sight of him, lying there with his hair drenched flat against his face and his legs and arms flailing to the side. As strange as it was, there was something almost *endearing* about how pathetic he was.

He stayed there, not moving, not breathing.

"What is it?" she asked.

"Nothing," he said at first. Then he said, "That's the first time I've heard you laugh."

She sighed and shook her head, taking his hand and pulling him to his feet.

She handed him his walking stick. "Well, it's the first time in a long while I've seen something stupid enough to *make* me laugh."

"Glad to be finally of use, then," he said. He meant it as a joke, but his voice came out bitter, and he seemed to realize it. He brushed his hair away from his face and fixed his hold on the walking stick. He continued to walk around the cave, practicing with the stick.

"What is it you think miners do?" Reema asked.

"Mine," he said jokingly, trying to move on from the bitterness. But there was still a note of it in his words.

"Did you know Javid can't mine a block?" Reema said.

He frowned but said nothing.

"The brute has no sense of his own damned strength. Every time he tried to help, he cracked the rest of the marble block and we'd have to start all over. Now he's just there to guard us. And you know Omar and Ra'ad?"

He came to a stop.

"They're masters at shaping the earth. But between you and me, they fight scared. They're just as likely to hit you with their pickaxe as the enemy. Hadi? He hides it well, but he's got a bad knee that makes it difficult for him to run. He knows he'd be dead if we ever had to make a break for it."

"Asif?" he asked.

"He's piss scared of the dark."

He approached her, gently sweeping the makeshift cane from side to side until it touched her foot. He stepped closer, until he was just a breath away from her.

"And you?" he asked, this time in a softer voice.

Reema stared at him, wishing that she could see his eyes, wishing she could get a glimpse of what he was thinking.

"I am the Ifrit. I have no weaknesses."

The corner of his lip lifted. He didn't believe her. And neither did she believe herself. Her weakness was standing right in front of her.

"You're telling me all this to make me feel better?"

"No, I'm telling you because despite everyone's weakness, they've found a way to make themselves useful. You've got to do the same if you want to survive in this place."

"Are you afraid of the dark, too?" he asked.

"Every miner's afraid of the dark. The dark means death down here."

He nodded and turned away, but this time, he faced her sister's grave. Damn the deep, she wished she could see into his mind. The moment of silence lingered between them. Reema was unsure what to make of it.

"You have a piece of chalk with you?" he asked.

"Chalk? What do you want that for?"

He stuck his hand out. With a frown, she reluctantly dug within the folds of her linen and handed him the chalk she used to mark the tunnels. He placed the walking stick aside and crouched down.

"Come here," he said.

She stepped closer and crouched across from him. He drew a symbol on the floor, and Reema recognized it from the book. Somewhere in the back of her mind, a memory pulled: her mother's distant vague voice, whispering a sound that represented the symbol.

"We'll start with the letters. Once you get these down, it'll be easier for you to remember how they make up words, and how words make books." He tapped the chalk against the ground as if to emphasize his point. "This is how we start."

During the secret hours of the night, while the others slept, Reema relearned everything her parents had once taught her. To her surprise, Alaric proved to be a patient and gentle teacher. Under his guidance, she traced the contours of letters etched into the stone, each stroke drawing her closer to a world she had long forgotten. As the shapes connected and formed words, it wasn't just the act of reading that was slowly returning to her—it was the soft murmur of her mother's voice, the reassuring tone of her father as they guided her through each letter. Those whispers, long buried by the darkness of the deep, began to surface, filling her heart with a bittersweet warmth she hadn't felt in years.

There was something freeing about the lesson, something in the way it soothed the burning rage. For those few precious hours, nothing mattered except those small, simple letters. And when the lesson finally ended, she ran her fingers over the cover of the book, her heart fluttering as she read the title for herself.

"Be ... nea ... th, the, Sa ... nds, of ... Sor ... row."

"Look at that," Alaric said, picking up his walking stick and crossing the cave without stumbling. "Now we're both beginning to see."

CHAPTER
EIGHT

Opening a new tunnel was no easy task. It's not enough to simply take the pickaxe and start hacking at the wall. Beneath the earth, it's easy to get lost, to tunnel into a different territory rather than your own.

Before Reema's gang even picked up their pickaxes, they spent hours ensuring they had the right direction. They walked the mines, drew a mini map of the path they'd taken back to the cave, and made their best guess as to where they'd discovered the black marble.

The whole time, Alaric kept to himself, practicing with his new cane. None of the others gave him much notice even after seeing the cane, but Asif gave her a questioning look.

"Had to keep the bastard from making more noise, didn't I?"

His gaze narrowed, flicking down to her tunic, noticing the tears in the fabric and the goosebumps covering her skin from the cool air.

"You can't do everything to keep him alive. Eventually, he will die. You know that, right?"

Reema and Asif watched Alaric reach the edge of the wall, the rose quartz reflecting off the steel band over his eyes. Asif *was* right. She could do her best to help Alaric survive the mines, but she knew what was likely to happen. Somehow, someway, he would meet his end. Her stomach fell. She wasn't sure if it was worse to see him so helpless and hopeless or to see him actually trying, thinking he had a chance.

Alaric turned and moved back across the cave, closer to the edge of darkness. It was subtle, but he moved a pace faster than before.

"We should take him out into the tunnels, leave him there, and let the man find his end," Asif said.

"We can't."

"Why?"

"Because he's one of us, Asif. When I went back for him, I heard it in his voice."

"The rage?" he asked, taking another look at Alaric, studying him more closely.

The way his voice had gone cold stuck in her mind.

She nodded and said, "Take a look at him, look what happened to the poor bastard. Somebody's done that to him."

He grunted in acknowledgment. "Whoever did it had coin, that's for sure. You don't get that kind of work done cheap."

They continued to watch Alaric walk the cave, the muted tapping of his cane just barely audible under the sound of Javid starting in on the rose quartz that covered the cave wall. Reema tried not to think about the fact that they were destroying the beautiful place she'd left for her sister. They didn't exactly have any options if they wanted to take back the southern mines.

"Well, let me see his rage for myself," Asif said.

Before Reema could stop him, he grabbed the torch and crossed the cave. Alaric stopped as he heard Asif approach. He didn't flinch as Asif snatched the cane from his hand and tossed it aside. The wood clattered across the stone, drawing the attention of the other members of her gang. They paused and turned to watch.

"Is there a problem?" Alaric asked calmly.

"I'm getting tired of watching you walk back and forth, pulling your dick while the rest of us work."

Alaric raised an eyebrow, noticing the sudden quiet in the cave. He glanced toward the direction of the gang.

"I see."

Reema was about to interfere when he suddenly cocked a fist and drove it into Asif's stomach. A heavy *oof* pierced the silence, followed by sharp intakes of breath from Reema and the rest of her gang. Even Asif stumbled back a step, surprised by Alaric's strength.

Then a gleam flashed across his eyes, and he straightened. "Finally, the blind bastard shows us a little *something*."

Asif's meaty knuckles smashed into Alaric's face. His head snapped to the side, but he kept his footing. Alaric slowly looked back at Asif, his bottom lip cut and blood running down into his beard. Something heavier than the darkness draped over them, deepening the shadows and the chill.

Reema held her breath as the tension tightened in her shoulders.

Alaric took a step back and began to slide his coat off, revealing a filthy shirt covered in blood and sand dust from the surface.

Asif chuckled as he walked around Alaric, rolling his neck and cracking his knuckles. "You really want to fight me?"

Alaric held the jacket in his fist and listened for Asif's position.

Asif landed a heavy punch in Alaric's side, then skipped back before Alaric could swing at him. He landed another punch. He battered Alaric over and over, without Alaric managing to land a single punch back.

"You think you stand a chance against me?" Asif spat.

He kicked the back of Alaric's legs, knocking him down to his knees.

"The only reason you're still alive is because the boss took *pity* on you."

A punch smashed into the side of Alaric's head.

"Trust me, that pity? It wasn't because you're blind. It's because you're helpless and *weak*."

He threw another punch.

Alaric caught the heavy punch, and a deep growl rumbled through the cave. A chill ran down Reema's spine as Alaric stood, his coat still gripped in his free hand.

"I'm not weak."

He threw his coat over the torch. Darkness swallowed the cave as his coat smothered the light. The other members of her gang shouted as the shadows pressed in on them, held at bay only by the dying flames of the campfire crackling behind them.

Silence consumed them, disturbed only by the sound of Asif's ragged breaths. Then a second sound came: the muted tap of stick against stone. Somehow, Alaric had found his cane.

Alaric's low, calm voice cut through the silence.

"You're in my darkness now. Let's see who you are."

Asif roared in pain as the echo of hardened wood smashing against flesh danced along the walls. Reema could see nothing. She was just as helpless as the others.

A savage grunt pierced the darkness, followed by the clatter of wood against stone. Bodies hit the ground, primal growls echoing through the cave as bone-raw fists smashed blindly against flesh and stone.

Finally, as the remnants of the coat charred away, light burst forth, slashing across the cave. It revealed Asif, disheveled and bloodied, gasping for air as Alaric's hands gripped his throat. Alaric seemed intent on murder, blood dripping from his nose, cut lips drawn back over bared teeth. He seemed indifferent to his injured hand.

Asif glanced toward Reema and the other men watching, then growled. He broke through Alaric's grip and rolled him over. Now that the darkness was gone, he landed punch after punch. Reema and the others dashed forward, pulling Asif off Alaric.

Once they were separated, each breathing heavily, they all stared at Alaric.

His figure cast a long, ominous shadow across the cave as he stood. He drew a deep breath and straightened his back, his torn shirt hanging loosely. Reema noticed the wiry muscles that had been hidden before, but there was something else there.

"Are those whip scars?" Hadi asked, just as shocked as the others.

Alaric flinched, fixing his shirt as best as he could. He didn't answer.

"Fucking—"

"—hell." Omar and Ra'ad's voices echoed in the silence.

Asif shrugged them off and rolled his shoulders back. Still catching his breath, he wiped the blood from his face.

"So he is one of us," Asif said.

Reema grinned as the others exchanged nods of agreement. Asif picked up the torch, tossed the last burnt pieces of the coat aside, and clapped Alaric on the shoulder.

"Let's get this man some lentils."

For the first time, Reema felt some hope that Alaric might actually survive the mines for a while. It wasn't just the way he defended himself against Asif, but the way the others accepted him.

She expected to see him smile at Asif's welcoming, but instead, the shadows seemed to deepen over his face. His fists curled at his sides before he turned away, stalking to the other side of the cave without a word.

Asif blinked in surprise and looked to Reema. But she didn't have an answer for what had just happened.

"I'll talk to him."

Asif shrugged and returned to the campfire, shoving

the others as they teased him for how battered he'd gotten at the hands of a blind man. But it was done in good spirits, and he knew that. Truth was, all of them, Reema included, could never have expected what happened.

When Reema reached Alaric, he was sitting in the spot where they'd first made the deal. He was fixing the cane, straightening the ties; he'd hit Asif hard enough with it to loosen them.

She sat next to him, her eyes catching on the whip scars crisscrossing his chest.

"It was a good fight," she said.

He grunted, running his hands down the cane to check for any other damage from the fight.

"You're not upset by the outcome of the fight, are you?" Reema asked, following her gut. He seemed too upset for that to be the case.

He didn't answer her for a long minute. Then, in a near-shattered voice, he whispered, "'Let's see who you are.'" He tapped the steel band forged to his face. "The man who put this on me said that to me." He pulled apart his shirt and traced one of the scars crisscrossing his chest. "He said it to me with every stroke of his whip, after he'd told me I was worthless and weak."

Reema didn't show compassion. Not here in the mines, where every slave had a history painted with pain and trauma. But for some reason, she found herself reaching for him, placing her hand over his.

"You gave Asif all he could handle. You're *not* weak."

"That's not the point!" he snapped, his echoing voice drawing the attention of the other miners. Their stares lingered for a moment before they returned to their own conversations. "I know I'm not weak. You don't understand."

"Then make me understand."

"I became *him*," he said. "I used *his* words, felt *his* anger running through me."

"Who?"

He was quiet for a long time. The silence settled between them, and she couldn't help but feel that it was doing its best to isolate him, to drown him in a darkness deeper than the cave's. There was nothing she could do about it. It was up to him to overcome it.

Reema sighed and stood, resting a hand on his shoulder. "The rage you feel, it belongs to no one but you. It's yours, and just like the rest of us, it'll be what keeps you alive in this Angel-forsaken place. Come to us by the fire when you're ready."

As she walked away, she heard his answer to her question. His voice was so soft that she thought she misheard, but the way his words echoed around her, she knew she had heard right.

"He was my father."

CHAPTER
NINE

Alaric did not show up at the fire. Reema held out hope as they cooked the lentils that he would come, if only for the food, but he did not appear even for that. The crackling fire burned low, the men began to drift off one by one into sleep, and soon, only Asif and Reema were left awake. Neither of them spoke, yet it seemed they were both staying up for the same reason—the hope that Alaric would join them. But he did not. His silhouette remained exactly where she had left him.

When it got late enough that even Asif gave up hope for the night, he exchanged a look with Reema that said "maybe tomorrow" and went to sleep. Reema waited another hour still, cold despite the warmth of the fire burning nearby. She stood and walked through the cavern, struck by the beauty of the rose quartz shining on all sides, just beneath the flickering shadows. She passed by Alaric, knowing he could hear her, but she said nothing.

She arrived at the cave where her sister's grave lay

and stared at it. It was strange to think that the sister she so sorely missed lay just beneath this heap of marble.

She brushed her hand across the marble as though she could feel her sister one last time. But she felt none of her sister's warmth. There was only the cold, impassive feel of the white marble.

Reema sighed and took a seat with her back against the grave, pulling the book from her waistband. She traced her fingers over the title.

"Beneath the Sands of Sorrow."

She read it smoothly this time, a small smile playing at the corner of her lips. With a gentle touch, she flipped it open to the first page. There were so many letters that it felt overwhelming. How was she supposed to read all of *this*?

A cane brushed the blanket hanging over the entrance aside. Alaric entered and, without a word, he sat across from her.

Reema studied him, feeling again that strange sense of familiarity. She still couldn't place it. Her eyes drifted downward, catching on those scars crossing his chest. What kind of father could do that to a son? Her gaze trailed upwards to the steel band hiding his eyes. Reema might not have had an easy life, but she knew that her mother and father loved her and her sister. She could still hear her parents screaming for their slavers to come back, to give them their precious daughters. But her parents had been on foot, and their slavers had camels. They'd been taken over the horizon before her parents could even cross to the next sand dune.

"Focus on the first word."

Reema blinked, suddenly torn from the memories that had distracted her. "What?"

Alaric gestured in her direction. "I know there are lots of words on the page. But the thing about them is that they come one after the other. So just focus on the first one."

"Oh."

Reema glanced back down at the page and she did her best to ignore all the words except for that first one.

"Th … is, is, the, stor—" she got stuck.

"Story," he said.

She pursed her lips together, fixed her eyes back on the page, and started again.

"This is the story of Fai …" she paused. "What is that?"

"It's a name," he said. "Faisal."

Her finger trailed along the line as she read, "This is the story of Faisal and Tas … neem?"

He nodded. "That's your first sentence. Congrats. You're quick to remember."

She looked up at him. "The names look funny on the page."

"I guess they do. But when you stare at a word long enough, they all look funny, don't they?"

He found his way to the chalk they left behind in the cave and began to write. While he might be blind, he was starting to adapt, getting visibly more comfortable with navigating the space around him. He was putting the makeshift cane to good use.

"Alaric," he said, pointing to his own name, his fingers slightly smearing the letters as he brushed through them. Then he wrote again and pointed to it. "Reema."

Her mouth parted as she stared at her name. She closed the book and went to it, running her fingers over the letters etched on the stone floor.

"That's me?"

He nodded, sitting back and crossing his arms over his knees.

Reema stared at her own name, unable to tear her gaze away. It still blew her mind that something so complex as a *person* could be reduced to a few letters.

"Want to try?" Alaric asked, holding out the chalk for her to take.

Without a word, she took it from him and began to trace his letters, getting a feel for them. The R was the strangest letter of them all, but it was her favorite because it stood out from the —eema. It had *character*.

When she saw her name written next to his, she smiled, feeling an urge to write it all across the stone floor. She wondered if she had done that as a child, but try as she might, she couldn't recall ever writing *anything* at all. Maybe she never had.

She took up the book again, opening it back to that first page, and continued to read, if you could call stumbling your way through letters that. From time to time, Alaric stopped her and corrected her pronunciation, showing her why the combination of letters sounded different ways. It was confusing at first, but before long, she started to get the hang of it.

She managed to read only to the bottom of the second page before she had to stop, but that task alone had taken her the better part of an hour. She spent so long focusing on how the letters fit together that she felt the onset of a migraine. Yet, the thrill coursing through her veins was undeniable, a sensation rivaled only by her discovery of the black marble.

She closed the book with a self-satisfied sigh. She hadn't unraveled much yet; nothing about the mysterious 'she' that Alaric had mentioned earlier. However, she had gleaned enough about Faisal. He was a Commonborn, like all the slaves in the mines who were unfortunate enough not to have any of the Angel's ancestral blood in their veins. He lived in the city of Zareen, nestled somewhere in the lower half of the Market District, sharing a home with another Commonborn family. He appeared to be an aspiring clothesmaker, a man with dreams and aspirations seemingly ill-suited for a poor Commonborn man from Zareen.

"I didn't know you could get so tired just *reading*," she said.

Alaric chuckled, resting his back against the wall. He rubbed marble dust between his fingers. "When I was back home, I used to read every night before I went to sleep. There's nothing like falling asleep with a book on your chest."

This was the first time she could remember him mentioning a home.

"Where's home for you?" she asked.

He gestured toward her and the book. "Zareen. And you?"

"I came from a small village called Mirash."

"You don't call it home?"

"I don't know. Do you think you can really call a place home if you were only there for a short while? I mean, I've spent most of my life in these tunnels."

"If it's where your heart feels you belong, sure."

She glanced away from him, her gaze finding her sister's grave. "Then this *is* my home."

He leaned forward, intrigued. "Why's that?"

She couldn't bring herself to answer.

"You feel that way because of your gang? I've noticed how close you are to them."

She didn't answer.

"No? Is it because this is where you'll get your vengeance?"

"What?"

"Before, when you ordered Hadi to give me a bowl, you asked them who promised them vengeance. They said you. But it's not about their vengeance, is it? It's about yours."

She scowled but stayed quiet. What was she supposed to say?

He ran his hand through his beard, working his fingers through the tangles as he considered her. "Is it because of her?"

She froze. How could he know about her?

"I see."

Her voice was razor sharp. "What do you think you *see*?"

His brow lifted at the tone of her voice, and he raised his hands as if in surrender. "Nothing. Isn't that the point? Her grave is here and you don't want anybody to even lay an eye on her. That's why you allow me here, isn't it?"

"Stop asking questions," she begged, her voice on the verge of cracking. She hated how vulnerable she felt here, before her sister's grave. She hated how vulnerable she felt in front of *him*. Somehow, he managed to strip away everything that made her the Ifrit, the terrifying gang lord that everyone in the mines respected.

She waited for him to continue to push, but to her surprise, he did not. Instead, he stood to go. He stopped just before the blanket.

"Tasneem? She's got a sister too."

Reema's eyes stung with unshed tears as she watched him push aside the blanket.

"Her name was Hana," Reema whispered.

He stopped, looked back, and favored her with a gentle smile. "Beautiful name."

Then he left.

Reema broke, pulling the book close to her heart. She grieved her sister, tears streaming down her face.

She was gone.

She couldn't remember the last time she'd said her sister's name aloud. The cavern around her felt larger, emptier, the shadows lingering like mournful specters in the flickering light of the torch she kept. She thought of Hana—her laughter, her dreams, the light in her beautiful eyes—all buried now beneath cold marble.

Her grief surged again, overwhelming the burning embers of rage that had driven her for so long. The fire that fueled her vengeance seemed trivial, almost petty, when cast against the vast, unyielding sorrow of her loss. She realized, in this quiet, haunted moment, that her quest for revenge was as much about filling the void left by Hana as it was about seeking justice.

A shuddering breath escaped her, the cold air of the cavern mingling with the warmth of her tears. The very sound of Hana's name reminded her of how much she missed her, of how much she longed to hear her laugh just one more time.

Reema's fingers traced the title of the book through the blur of her tears, each letter a reminder of what she had lost and what she still carried within her. If Tasneem had a sister, maybe there was an answer for Reema within these pages, some way of understanding how she could begin to heal the cracks of despair within herself. For the first time, she was afraid that even once she earned her vengeance, she would still feel as empty and broken as she felt now.

She waited in the cavern's silence for the shattered pieces of Reema, the sister who had lost her other half to the slave master's cruelty, to draw back into the darkness, and for the Ifrit to return, because she knew that only the Ifrit could survive these cursed mines.

When the coals of her rage began to burn again, she tore down the hanging blanket, looking back just once more. It was strange. She thought she could still hear her sister's name, once a whispered token of the past, now echoing through the cavern like a hymn.

She kissed her fingers and pressed them to the marble walls. Then she dried her face and left.

CHAPTER
TEN

The next morning, Reema woke to the sound of clattering rocks. For a moment, her eyes flicked toward the entrance of the cave, fearful that some wandering miners had found their way to this sacred place. But then she realized the sounds were coming from the new tunnel they were shaping, and each member of her gang was still sleeping around the embers of their fire.

With a frown, she turned toward Asif, who wore a matching expression on his battered face. They each grabbed their pickaxes.

A distinct grunt echoed back toward them, and just as they were about to enter the tunnel, Alaric emerged. He had the blanket tied around his shoulders, full of rocks left over from the tunnel. His cane tapped against the stone as he made his way across the cave to an unused corner, and with another grunt, he dumped the rocks.

This time, the rest of her gang woke, glancing around with bleary eyes for the source of the sound.

Reema and Asif watched in stunned awe as he made his way back across the cave and into the tunnel. He turned to her with a grin and stroked his beard.

"Looks like he figured out how to make himself useful."

"Guess so," she said, her frown still lingering. She wasn't sure how to feel about him being little more than a beast of burden, but if that was the best way for him to survive the mines, then she supposed that's what he had to do.

"Get up, boys," Asif shouted, his voice booming off the rose quartz walls. He kicked Omar's leg, earning a muttered curse. "You hear that? That's the sound of a blind man putting you all to shame. Let's get to work."

"We haven't eaten," Ra'ad complained.

"You earn what you eat," Reema said stepping in. "Do as Asif said. Get to work. Sooner we get this tunnel built, the sooner we figure out what bastard took my territory from me, and the sooner we get it back."

He grumbled as he got up but made no further complaints. One by one, the members of her gang filtered into their tunnels with their pickaxes leaning against their shoulders. They left their other tools behind. The only purpose for this tunnel was to clear a way through, and as grueling as the work was, pickaxes were the only tool for that.

They fell into their roles: Javid at the point, using his brute strength to break through the marble, with Reema and Asif at his sides. They hacked at the sides, opening up the tunnel, leaving Hadi, Omar, and Ra'ad to focus on shaping support columns with the rubble to prevent any collapses. And throughout it all, the leftover rubble that the three of them couldn't use, Alaric carried out, as silent as he was blind.

Reema waited for him to sit, to take a break from it all and catch his breath. But somehow, he lasted longer than any of them. She suspected he would have worked through the entire day if she hadn't ordered him to take breaks now and then.

Between the grunts of exertion and the muttered curses, Hadi hummed a tune that kept them going. Soon, the twins joined in. Their voices in sync, it sounded ... nice. Normally, she wouldn't have tolerated it—the risk in the mines was far too great—but here they were isolated and protected from the sudden attack of miners in the dark.

When the long day had passed, and even Alaric's trembling muscles had given out, they gathered around the fire again. They'd made fast progress, but by her estimation, it would be some weeks yet before they pushed through the earth enough to reach her territory.

The fire crackled and burned. Omar and Ra'ad cooked the lentils. Javid lay back, resting his head against the wall, while Hadi drank from the water skins. Asif chewed on the last pieces of a date, his gaze fixed on where Alaric sat, replacing the binding around his injured hand. The work had reopened the knife wound, letting blood soak the bandage red. Reema couldn't help but notice how both of their faces were mirrored in bruises and cuts, though Asif had bruising down to his neck from being strangled.

When the food was cooked, Reema stood and took

the first bowl of lentils. She glanced at Asif and the others, receiving nods from each of them. Her heart pounded in her chest. It was time.

She went to Alaric and shoved the bowl into his arms. He glanced up at her. She could sense his surprise behind the steel band.

"This gang of mine is a family, full of men more likely to be warmed by hellfire than to ever see a shred of light from any of the heavens."

The men chuckled behind her.

"We might not have blood bonding us, but we've got something deeper: a shared rage and a desire for revenge. You've got that. I've heard it in your voice, and the others saw it when you fought Asif."

They muttered their agreement. There was no debate about that.

"But that's not enough to be part of this family."

She paused, letting the silence gather around her, heavy with anticipation. Then she leaned in, her face inches from his.

"To truly belong, your rage must become ours, and ours must become yours."

She scooped her hand into the lentils and held it before him, close enough for him to feel the warmth radiating from it.

"Eat from my hand, share with us your rage, and I will promise you your revenge."

The others held their breath, waiting to see if Alaric would take her offer. Reema's heart sputtered as it pounded in her chest, knowing that if he refused to share his secret, the others would attack and kill him. There could be no risking what they had at stake. The secret of the Djinn demanded that every man in this gang be dedicated to each other, not to themselves.

Alaric stared in her direction, sensing the looming danger. The longer the silence stretched, the darker the shadows grew around them. He slowly reached for her hand, his fingers lightly brushing the inside of her wrist. Her pulse quickened under his touch.

He brought her hand to his mouth and ate, his wet lips brushing across her fingers in a way that ignited a fire within her. Desire unfurled, leaving her wanting nothing more than to feel his lips against hers.

"I accept," he whispered.

Conscious that the others were watching, she cleared her throat and stepped back.

He rose, his steel-bound gaze sweeping across them all.

"You want to know my rage?"

He unbuttoned his shirt slowly, then let it fall from his shoulders. Reema's heart fluttered at the sight of him and the way the shadows danced between the contours of his abs, but it crashed to a stop as she caught sight of his scars—not just the whip marks from before, but a brutal tapestry of pain that wrapped around his ribs and shoulders. As if feeling their stares, he turned, showing them his back, a canvas of scars so deep they could draw tears from stone.

"My father enjoyed his whips, and he made sure to leave marks only where society couldn't see," he explained, his voice low and haunted. "But his cruelty didn't stop there or with making this for me."

His finger tapped against the steel band, the sound echoing in the emptiness of their hearts.

"Growing up, I was helpless to watch as he beat my mother. He broke her until she lost the will to live—she took her own life. And now, I'm stuck down here as he plans to ruin the place I call home."

He glanced in her direction, as if he could sense where she stood.

"I don't need revenge. I just want to do what I was too young to do before. I want to stop him."

He replaced his shirt and took his seat again. He held the bowl of lentils in his hands, and though he stared in its direction, Reema knew he was someplace far away from here.

Asif stood and went to Alaric, clapped him on the shoulder, and said, "You may not want revenge for yourself, but trust me, we'll get it for you."

The others nodded.

"I've been as angry as long as I can remember, and I'm older than anybody here," he said, stroking his beard as his face darkened. "My wife died in childbirth, left me with the most beautiful girl I'd ever seen. The slavers took me and left her on the doorstep of some piss drunk addicts." His voice dipped lower. "That was a long time ago. I have no idea if she's even alive now."

Hadi was the next to speak. "My mother gave me an old lucky coin, a relic that had been passed down through the family. The guards took it from me before they threw me down here. Angel knows what they did with it."

Omar and Ra'ad glanced at each other, then leaned

forward, the flames flickering in the reflection of their dark eyes. Their voices intertwined as they shared what happened to them.

"When we were boys, we were betrayed by an uncle we thought we could trust. He tricked us away from our home and sold us to the slave master to cover his debt."

Javid grunted, shaking his head. "One of them Blood-lined bastards raped a girl I loved, done something to her soul. She wasn't the same afterward. When I went to kill him, the guards caught me and threw me down here. He's still out there somewhere, free as a sundamned bird."

The fire crackled in the ensuing silence.

"And you?" Alaric asked.

Reema knew whom he meant.

"My sister and I had been stolen from my family by the slavers. By the time they brought us to the slave master, I had caused them enough hell that they were willing to be rid of me for any price. He murdered my sister, bought me for a soft penny, and threw the both of us down the Hole."

She could not forget the slave master's smirk, or the way his blue eyes glowed down at her.

"I don't even know his name," she said.

She looked up at Alaric and noticed the strange look on his face. Something about what she said had struck him to his core.

Asif's stomach grumbled, snapping them all out of the depths of their rage.

"Hadi, a bowl for my hungry second," she said.

"Yes, boss," Hadi replied, making a second bowl.

Asif grinned as he took the bowl from Hadi. He and the others fell into conversation, eased now by knowing that Alaric was well and truly one of them. Soon, they would share with him the secret of how they intended to get their revenge, but that wasn't a conversation for tonight.

"Welcome to the family," she said, her gaze lingering on Alaric.

He did not respond. Reema wished she could look into his eyes, see what he was thinking, but the steel band blinded her just as much as it did him.

"Eat, before it gets cold," she said before she found her own seat. Hadi passed her a bowl, and she began to eat. Seeing the smiles and laughter from the men around her, she wondered how she had ever thought that one of them could be capable of betraying her. Each of the men around her had as much reason for revenge as she did.

Her mind turned to the enemies she'd made over the years, wondering who could be capable enough to take her territory. But she came up empty. There were too many enemies, and yet, she could see none able to achieve it.

She lay down after finishing her meal, her body exhausted by the long day. She waited for the others to finish their conversations and go to sleep so she could sneak off for another reading lesson. But she was the first to fall asleep.

CHAPTER
ELEVEN

The days passed, spent in long and hard labor. They continued to make steady progress with the tunnel, forcing their way through the unyielding earth. Reema and Alaric rarely spoke to each other, so focused were they on the tasks at hand. But that was true of everyone. The only time any of them relaxed and chatted was at the end of the day, when their muscles had given out and their stomachs demanded to be fed.

They looked forward to those moments, but Reema had her eyes on a time much later, when the cave was filled with the quiet snores of her gang and she was free to sneak away to her sacred place to read with Alaric.

Alaric had been right. She was quick to remember how to read, evident by how much better she was getting. Pronouncing the words still took her full focus, flowing from one to the next. But the better she got, the smoother it became, and the smoother it became, the more the magic ensnared her.

The story of Faisal and Tasneem stuck in her mind

from the moment she woke to the moment she could flip open the pages.

He'd come across her in the narrow alleyways of Zareen, hobbling and desperately clinging to the folds of her dress. Faisal had always been the kind of man to keep to himself, but something about the innocence in her eyes drew him, made him ask if she was okay.

She was, except for the tear in her dress.

Reema could not help but be amazed at the alignment of the stars—how Tasneem, a woman who'd been so unlucky as to fall and tear her dress on the way to a meeting about some work, had been lucky enough to meet perhaps the only man who could help her in that moment of need.

He'd gotten on his knees to fix her dress. Those few minutes it took for him to sew it closed were all it took for him to fall for her. And her for him.

Page after page, Reema was drawn deeper into the story, her heart threatening to seize in her chest because of the words that stuck in her mind.

This was the woman who was supposed to be his everlasting love, whose soul had been made in measure for his. And now she was gone.

They met in secret in that alleyway, crossing paths every day for a month. Their love flourished, first with small notes from one to the other, then with thoughtful gifts. She'd bought him high quality threads that he could never afford, and with those threads, he'd made her a dress of his own design, so that wherever she went, he would always be with her. A brush of a hand, a whisper by the ear, and eventually, a kiss that sealed their fate.

They'd gotten married to the knowledge of exactly no one, beneath the light of a beautiful moon hung in a sprawling canopy of stars.

Reema clung to the book, strange tears welling in her eyes as she read aloud for Alaric. She could feel the love through the pages, could feel the mountain of pain heading her way.

She snapped the book shut, wiping her eyes dry. "I can't do this."

Alaric smiled sadly. "Because you know she will die."

"What happens?" she asked.

"Reema, you know what I'll say. Read and—"

"Find out," Reema said, completing his sentence. "Damn you and all the deep, just tell me. You've already messed things up by letting me know she dies."

Alaric shook his head. "I could tell you more, I could speak word for word what happens, but the point of the story isn't in the end. It's what happens along the way."

He tapped his cane against the floor.

"Keep going. I want to hear you read this next part."

Reema snarled and opened the book again, turning the page to where she left off.

"They kissed under the ethereal moonlight, and in that moment, the thread of love sewn between them knotted, tying them together forever. Faisal took her hand and led her through the night to his home, where peaceful quiet awaited."

Heat flushed through her skin, turning her red as she realized where this was going. She paused and glanced up at Alaric, noting the corner of his lips turning up. She had a feeling that if not for the cursed steel band over his eyes, he would have winked at her.

He tapped the cane against the stone floor again, signaling her to continue.

Reema cleared her throat.

"He led her to his bed, and again, he kissed her. This kiss was different from the one before. Rather than warming her heart and bringing a smile to her face, it burned like fire, stealing a whisper of a moan from her lips. His lips continued to brush against her, branding her with his love. For all his life, and for all of hers, the darkness in the night had been lonely. But now, with the heat of each other pressed against them, and their racing hearts beating together, they made that lonely darkness theirs."

Reema swore she could feel Alaric's gaze on her, piercing the steel band. As she read, the image of Faisal shifted in her mind, replaced by Alaric. She became Tasneem, feeling the strength of his arms around her, holding her close. Her breathing grew heavier, her heart fluttered instead of pounding against her chest. She imagined the warmth of his lips, from where he had branded her fingers, brushing across the rest of her.

She wanted to stop reading, but she couldn't bring herself to. She wanted this. Damn the deep, she *needed* it.

While she'd never coupled with someone herself, she'd heard others at it in the dark, their guttural grunts and moans echoing through the mine tunnels. Yet it had never sounded as magical as the book described. She sensed, though, that with Alaric, it would be different. It would be everything she imagined.

The words continued to pour from Reema like molten silver, smooth yet searing, capturing a moment that seemed to suspend time around them. "And in the quiet of his room, the world outside melted away. Only the sound of their breaths remained, mingling in the cool air. Each touch between them was both a question and an answer, a delicate exploration of years of solitude coming to an end."

Her voice trembled slightly. The space between her and Alaric felt charged, like an invisible thread pulled them closer with every word she spoke.

"He whispered her name, and it sounded like a vow," she read, her voice barely above a whisper, as if afraid to break the spell that the book had cast over them. "In that moment, they were no longer two separate souls, but one."

Reema paused and looked up at Alaric, her eyes meeting the obscured gaze of his steel band. For a fleeting moment, it felt as if he saw her, truly saw her. The corner of his mouth twitched, transforming his expression into something softer.

She exhaled a shaky breath and closed the book gently. The echo of their fictional embrace lingered in the air, her skin burning with the idea of what could be.

"Why did you want me to read that?" she asked, the words slipping out before she could stop herself.

He shifted slightly, leaning closer, the air between them thick with unspoken thoughts. His voice was husky and low.

"Because your voice does something to me," he said.

Her breath caught.

"It lulls me to sleep, you know?"

She scowled and threw the book across the cave at him, where it smacked against his chest. He laughed, felt around for the book, and held it in his hands.

"If you really must know, then I had you read that because it's important to know that there's more to life than anger and rage. There's beauty, too."

Reema's gaze lingered on him, studying the scars that peeked through his shirt.

"And pain."

He was quiet for a moment, then nodded.

"Plenty of that, too." He sighed and stood, crossing the room until his cane pressed against her leg. He bent over and offered her the book. "We'll stop there for the night."

"There's still some time left to read."

He shook his head, "It's a good place to stop."

She had a feeling she knew why. Things turned bad from here. They always did when the going got too good.

"Okay," she said. She glanced toward her sister's grave. She didn't know how much longer she had until they tunneled the rest of their way through the earth, but she knew that once that happened, things would go back to the way they were. She would focus again on her and the gang's revenge, and her sister would remain here, resting eternally beside a cave of rose quartz. "I think I'll stick around for a little while longer."

He nodded and started to leave, only to stop just before the hung blanket. It seemed like he was about to say something, but the words never left his mouth. He gave her a sad smile, and left her there.

The moment he was gone, Reema loosed an explosive sigh.

"Must've been a bit awkward for you, huh?" she asked her sister's grave. She couldn't tear her gaze from where Alaric had stood. "I'd say sorry, but I know you're not listening. You're dead."

She rested a hand on the marble slab covering her sister's body.

"Still, if you are listening to me somehow, just know ... I do miss you. A lot."

She glanced back in the direction Alaric had gone. She should go back, get some sleep.

"What do you say to one more page?"

Silence.

"Yeah, I was thinking the same."

She opened the book and flipped to the next page.

His heart broke.

As he stared into her dying eyes, watching that light fade into the eternal darkness, his heart broke.

Reema froze, dread draping itself down over her shoulders. They had just gotten married. Surely they hadn't reached this point already.

This was the woman who was supposed to be his everlasting love, whose soul had been made in measure for his. And now she was gone.

Rage consumed him with a fire that would rival even that of the seventh hell. He wanted revenge, to destroy the man who had robbed this earth of its most precious light. But he knew it would change nothing.

She was gone.

Her eyes raced across the text, her knuckles white as she clutched the book, hoping it might shield her from the pain. Yet, the emptiness in her voice as she sounded out the words made it clear—there was no protection from it.

How could he have known that letting her go in the dead of night to return to her family would be the last time he would hold her, that he would find her in the early morning, lying in the street among shocked merchants, broken and choking on her own blood?

He should have escorted her home, or convinced her to stay. Had he done that, this would never have happened.

It was supposed to be the happiest day of their lives. He was going to take her to a special garden, where she could see flowers in every color she could imagine.

She loved flowers.

Holding her limp hand, he was jolted by a scream that drew his attention to a Bloodllned woman standing at the crowd's edge. Her glowing hazel eyes mirrored the terror Faisal felt. But before he could figure out who she was, guards rushed in and tore him away from the body.

The other merchants knew him, and knew that he was not the one to injure this stranger. He was released,

but still, the grips of rage and grief held him tight, and
he had a feeling that they would never let him go.

Reema paused, drawing a shuddering breath. She ached for Faisal, hoped that he would find that bastard that killed Tasneem and do him in. She should stop, end the story here and pick it up tomorrow. But she couldn't.

This was his wife.

And yet, to the world, they were merely strangers. Numb, he watched the guards lift the body of the woman he loved most and carry her away, while the Bloodlined woman clutched his beloved's hand, choking on her sobs.

When it was gone, someone wiped away her blood from the paved stone. Everyone returned to their business, setting up their stalls and quietly, as if afraid to break the tormented silence, began calling out their wares. And soon, the crowds of Zareen began to walk the streets, unaware of how the world had shifted for the poor clothesmaker standing in the streets.

Faisal returned home.

The darkness that night was lonelier than ever before.

CHAPTER
TWELVE

The next night, Reema waited for Alaric to appear. She stood over her sister's grave, her mind fixated on how Faisal had found Tasneem. He was right. He should have never let her go, even if they were married in secret. Whatever consequences her family might have faced, they were infinitely better than the tragedy he discovered that morning.

That thought stuck in Reema's mind. Was there anything she could have done differently that would have kept the slave master from murdering Hana? The shadows gathered over her, the cold truth seeping down into her bones. She knew there was.

If she hadn't been so difficult with the slavers, perhaps they would have treated her like the other slaves they sold. Maybe then she would not have drawn the eye of the slave master. Maybe then, her sweet, poor Hana would have lived.

Her jaw muscles flexed at the realization. She touched a hand to her sister's grave.

"I'm sorry," she whispered.

"What for?"

She spun around. Alaric stood by the entrance, with his head cocked to the side and his makeshift cane in hand. How had he managed to be so sundamned quiet? She was disturbed by how quickly he was adapting to the mines.

"Does Faisal find the man who killed Tasneem?"

He drew a deep breath, then sighed. "You kept reading."

"Answer my question."

He considered her for a moment. "He does."

Reema took a step toward him, as if it could bring her close to the answer she desired. "And does he get his revenge?"

He was quiet.

"Answer me."

In a soft voice, he answered, "You'll have to keep reading to find out. As I said, it's about—"

"The journey, not the end, I know." Reema scowled, turning her back to him to stare once more at her sister's grave. She wondered if her sister's face would still appear as transcendent and beautiful as she remembered, should she pull aside the marble slabs.

She didn't dare find out, because a part of her knew the truth. Hana was nothing more than bones now. And she didn't need to see that.

"I keep thinking about her, you know," Reema said. "When she ... when she died, I thought that was it. I would never see her again. But truth is, I see her face every fucking night, haunting me as her body falls through the air."

In a small voice, so quiet that she wasn't sure if he heard it, she whispered, "I'm so tired of it."

The cane tapped through the silence and she felt his hand on her shoulder. To her surprise, he pulled her into him. It was strange at first, almost unnatural. She wasn't sure what she was supposed to do, but as his warmth enveloped her, it melted away the tension and the rage and the grief. Leaning against his chest, she could feel his heart—so steady, so *strong*. She waited for him to say something, to try and give some bullshit wisdom about how it would all get better. But he didn't. He held her, and kept the silence, and somehow ... somehow that was exactly what she needed.

Then the moment ended, and she stepped away from him. It was impossible to see his eyes, but she could feel the same pain radiating from him. She remembered what he said, about how his mother had taken her own life.

"Do you ever wish you could have done anything differently?" she asked.

"You mean to save someone's life?"

"Yes."

His lips pursed. "All the time."

Before Reema could say anything else, he gestured toward her and asked, "How far did you get?"

"He'd found her body and returned home."

"So he's seen the Bloodlined woman, then."

Reema frowned. "Who was she?"

"Read and—"

"How about you eat a bag of shit, Alaric?"

He smiled.

"What?"

"I do enjoy hearing you say my name."

She didn't know what to say to that. She cleared her throat as she sat down and pulled out the book.

"How about we get started?" she asked.

"By all means," he replied.

She flipped to the right page.

The days passed in numbness, until at long last, a burning sun appeared from behind dark clouds—the guards found him, the monster that had robbed the world of Tasneem's light.

As soon as Faisal learned the news, he raced to the prison. He stood at the bars and screamed for the guards to come, to let him have at the bastard who murdered her. They came, and with the weight of their fists, they calmed him, told him that the man's fate wasn't left up to him.

They left him lying in the blistering sand. But it didn't matter what they said, what they thought. He knew the monster's location, and he wasn't content to sit back and let fate guide the murderer to his end, or to the devil waiting for him in the afterlife.

A devil lingered here, in this life, one that desperately needed to meet him.

Faisal went back, and he began to scheme. As the weeks passed, he hatched a plan that neither a wise man nor an emberdusted addict would dare conceive: to infiltrate the prison and commit murder.

Reema grinned as she read, a dark thrill traveling through her veins. Her heart beat faster as she realized that she and Faisal had very much in common: they would stop at nothing to ruin the monsters who hurt the ones they loved.

The merchants he once called friends did not check on him, even though they noticed his absence. They were merchants, after all, and they saw opportunity where others did not. They took the space he usually set up his stalls for their own, as though he never existed.

And perhaps, he did not exist. Perhaps he had long ago been consumed by the darkness of his home, turned into such a shadow of his former self, that his own parents wouldn't have recognized him, even if they were still alive.

The only time Faisal came up for air from the drowning rage and grief was on the day of her funeral. He walked to the graveyard, each footstep heavy as he ever felt. When he arrived, he found a small crowd of people gathered.

There were Commonborns, people she worked with or friends that she had made. He knew none of them. And nor did he know the Bloodlined family standing closest to the body.

As he tried to draw nearer to the funeral, several guards appeared and stopped him.

Faisal was not a bad man, despite his plans to murder. But at that moment, he nearly found himself spilling innocent blood.

"Step aside."

*The Bloodlined woman he had seen before,
screaming at the sight of Tasneem's body, ordered the
guards away.*

*He stood before her, staring into those haunting
hazel eyes. And she stared back.*

*"My sister had a ring upon her finger," the Blood-
lined woman said. Her gaze flicked down toward his
finger, where he wore the only match to it.*

Faisal knew his grief showed through his face.

Sister.

*Tasneem had never spoken of her family, only that if
she were to agree to be with Faisal, her family could
never find out. He had assumed that it was because her
family had far too much coin to allow her to be with a
lowly merchant, but he had never dared believe that they
could be Bloodlined.*

"What?" Reema said, stunned that somehow Tasneem belonged to a Bloodlined family. "How is that possible?"

"Sometimes, the Bloodlined take on Commonborn children, raise them as their own. It is exceedingly rare, but I have seen it once."

"What a load of camel shit. No, you haven't."

"I have," he insisted.

She stared at him, trying to see through his lie. But it seemed that he spoke the truth. She struggled to understand.

"But why?" she asked.

He shrugged, "I can't say why they took on Tasneem. But the family I knew, they couldn't have children. They wanted one bad enough to take on a Commonborn."

Her mouth hung open in disbelief. "The Bloodlined aren't capable of that."

"Of raising children?" He laughed.

"No, of basic fucking decency," she said. It was true. The Bloodlined were at the peak of society, with all the wealth and power and status anybody could ever dream of, and it was all propped up by people like her; slaves hidden away in the mines to mine the marble to build their great big mansions.

Damn the deep, the *slave master* was Bloodlined.

"The Bloodlined don't know how to love a child, how to raise them to be good. How could Tasneem be raised by *them*?"

He leaned forward, grasping his cane in both hands.

"You don't believe the Bloodlined are capable of love?"

"Are monsters capable of it?"

He gave her a sad smile. "Very much so. My father, for all his cruelty, loved my mother once."

"He didn't. And do you know why?"

He stayed quiet.

"When you love someone, the way that Faisal loved Tasneem, you would *never* hurt them."

Her words died against the fabric-covered walls, leaving a damning silence stretching between them. Reema didn't understand how Alaric could possibly think any good of the Bloodlined. The very idea sparked her anger. A Bloodlined killed her sister, like her life meant *nothing*.

"Perhaps," he said. "I think that's enough for tonight."

Reema agreed. She slammed the book shut and rose to her feet. Without another word, she grabbed the torch and tore down the blanket from where it hung. She left him in the darkness, but it did nothing to him.

As she lay down and shut her eyes, she could not help but think how convinced he was that his father loved her mother. She hated to be the one to shatter that mirage, to expose the ugly truth, but someone had to do it.

She waited for him to come back, but he did not.

She struggled to sleep that night.

THIRTEEN

The challenge of shaping a new tunnel through the mines is that you can never tell exactly where you are. It's easy enough to make an educated guess if you know what you're doing, but knowing *exactly* where you'll emerge, and *exactly* when? Only liars and fools would claim to know that.

Reema's gang continued to work through the day as they had been, inch by inch making their way through the hard and unyielding earth. So it was a surprise when, this day, Javid's swing made a hollow sound.

The sound stopped them all in their tracks.

All thoughts of Beneath the Sands of Sorrow faded at that sound, abruptly forcing Reema back into reality; someone had the stones to try and force her out of her own territory, force her away from the black marble that carried her justice, and now she was close to finding out who.

"Asif, Hadi, ready yourselves in case there's someone on the other side," she ordered. It had always been a risk that one of the miners on the other side could've felt or heard the earth's muted groan as Reema and her men forced their way through it. But there was nothing they could do about that. "Alaric, get these stones out of the way, then you're at the back with Omar and Ra'ad. Understand?"

Alaric nodded.

"Good. Javid, I'll be behind you, in case any of those bastards are on the other side."

She drew a deep breath and looked at each member of her gang. They were all exhausted from a half day's worth of work, but she couldn't risk them turning back and taking time to rest. With a hollow wall of marble between them and their territory, the risk of another miner stumbling on a tunnel being made that led straight to her sanctuary was too great.

"Remember your rage, remember the man's next to you, and remember mine. *That* is what we are fighting for here. Not the territory, but the chance to have our vengeance."

The flickering torch cast dancing shadows across their grim faces. Alaric was stoic at the back. He hadn't said anything to her since the night before. But she couldn't think about that. Now was the time to focus on breaking through this wall and meeting the enemy.

Reema turned away from him and signaled to Javid.

They watched as his pickaxe slammed into the marble, dust flying into the air with each swing, the only other sound being marble chips and rocks scattering across the stone at their feet. Then, he broke through.

Javid widened the hole, and with Reema's help, they

broke away enough space for them to step through. Reema glanced both ways as the rest of her men filed out of the tunnel. She realized that they were only one tunnel over from the one that led deeper into the earth, where the black marble waited for them.

"Omar, Ra'ad, Javid, the three of you stay here," she said, doing her best to keep as quiet as possible. But she knew that they had made more than enough noise for nearby miners to know someone had broken into these tunnels. "Hadi, Alaric, Asif, you're with me."

"Are you sure about that?" Asif asked. "If we come across anybody, we could use their numbers."

She nodded. "I'm not risking anyone finding the way back to my cave."

"Why don't I stay with Javid then?" Hadi asked. "It'll give you another man in case you come across anyone, and you can trust that me and Javid have this locked down."

She glanced at him. It was a good idea.

"Fine. Omar and Ra'ad, you're with us then."

They shrugged as though it made no difference to them, while Hadi grabbed a spare torch and held it to hers. The fire roared to life, illuminating the tunnel enough to reveal Alaric at the edge of the shadows, tapping his cane to gauge the tunnel's layout.

Asif gave Reema a look that made it clear that though he thought that Alaric was one of them, he didn't expect him to survive whatever they were coming up against. Reema tried not to think about it. Truth be told, it would've been better to leave him behind with Javid and Hadi, where it was far less likely for him to get caught up in a fight. But she couldn't bring herself to do that; she wanted him close to her, where she could protect him.

Asif clapped Alaric on the shoulder. "Time to earn your blood stripes."

"Right," she said. "Let's get going."

She handed her pickaxe to Asif and gripped her shiv in her free hand, holding the torch in the other.

The darkness at the edge of the light was as oppressive as any Reema had ever encountered. Even Asif seemed to recognize it, his eyes glinting with a hint of fear. The thing about Reema and her gang was that they were always prepared for what they were going into. But now, they had no idea what enemy they were up against.

The tension in the air was palpable as Reema led her them deeper into the earth. The tunnel's walls closed in around them, the space pressing in on them from all sides. Reema couldn't tell if it was the walls or the ominous darkness that stifled their breaths. The only sound she could hear was the muffled, rhythmic tap of Alaric's cane.

Then, she heard a second sound, slowly emerging through the ominous silence: distant, sporadic clinks of metal against stone. It brought her to a halt, made her heart skip a beat as she realized that it was coming from deeper in the earth, where they'd found the first sign of black marble.

"No," she whispered, cold seeping into her bones.

"What is it?" Alaric asked, his voice just loud enough for a soft echo to pass through the tunnels. The sporadic clink of metal paused.

"Quiet!" Asif hissed, clamping his hand over Alaric's mouth.

After a moment, the work resumed, but Reema could not breathe a sigh of relief. The miners' efforts were exposing what *she* had worked toward for so many years.

She clenched her jaw and pressed forward. Her torch-light flickered, casting ghostly shadows against the jagged walls. The tunnel narrowed further, the darkness seeming to break their resolve with its oppressive fear. Reema's grip on her shiv tightened.

They were close now. She could tell by the pressure in her ears. But as the faint, rhythmic sound of pickaxes intensified, so did the unease twisting in Reema's gut. She could feel the others' tension—a shared thread of apprehension drawn taut with every step they took.

Just as their path converged into the final tunnel leading to the black marble, an unexpected flare of light around the bend brought them to a halt. Her pulse thrummed in her ears, shattering the sudden silence that enveloped her gang.

A dozen figures blocked their way, pickaxes and shivs and heavy marble rocks all held in hand. They stared at her with hot hatred in their gazes.

She recognised none of them.

Her lips drew back over her teeth. "And who in the sundamned hells are you?"

They remained silent.

"You're not going to tell me?" she asked. "Then you can die nameless."

"Reema," Alaric said. There was something in his

voice that raised goosebumps along her arms. "Do you hear that?"

She frowned, unsure of what he was talking about. But then, after a long moment, she heard it: the sound of a dozen more footsteps.

She watched as a group of miners made their way down toward them. Her breathing was tight as she realized that they were trapped with enemies on both sides.

Then the miners stopped, and a figure stepped forward.

"You," she breathed out, recognition and dread coiling within her.

"Yes, me," Salman said, his voice a smooth veneer over the threat his presence posed. "Did you think I wouldn't find out about the Djinn?"

He gestured toward the miners trapping her, and to the still rhythmic sound of pickaxe against stone.

"Every rogue miner I came across was quite interested to hear about that, about your ... intentions. Interested enough to swear themselves to me."

Reema steadied herself, her resolve hardening like the stone around them. She laughed, her voice harsh and sharp as she asked, "You think you know my intentions?"

His gaze lingered on her, "I do. I have it from the mouth of one of your men."

Her laugh came to a sudden halt. It was like he'd stuck a blade into her heart and twisted it. So someone *did* betray her. Of course they did. She scowled. She should have trusted her gut instinct.

She could not help but look over her shoulder and wonder if it was any of Omar, Ra'ad or Asif. But judging by the looks on their faces, they were just as gutted as she was. She turned back to Salman, and as she did, the Ifrit emerged, hot anger baring itself before him. She'd been a *fool* to ever think she could trust him.

But before she could say anything, Alaric stepped forward. He stood between her and him, his hands resting calmly on his makeshift cane. His voice cut through the tension.

"You'll let them go."

Salman's brow rose, and he chuckled, "I don't think so. The world would be much better off with them—and her—dead."

He dismissed Alaric with a glance and began to turn back. His men bristled, raising their pickaxes and shivs.

"You will let them go," Alaric repeated. Despite the softness of his voice, it was strong, firm, like he would not tolerate being disobeyed.

It was enough to bring Salman to a halt.

Salman turned back, regarding Alaric again with a scrutinizing gaze.

"And why would I do that?" Salman asked.

"Because I challenge you, as a gang lord, to fight me."

Reema's heart fell as Salman burst into laughter.

"I admire the bravado, truly, but that is not how things work down here in the mines," Salman said.

"Maybe not, but you won't refuse me."

"Why? Because you're blind? Trust me, there is no pity down here, and my men will not lose respect for me because I refused to waste my time fighting a blind man."

"But they will once they know who I am."

Salman chuckled again, his voice carrying through the tunnel to meet the continued sound of mining.

"Look at me," Alaric commanded, his voice low and dark.

Salman looked at Alaric, *truly* looked at him, studying him with a scrutinising gaze. His chuckle died as he recognized the same sense of familiarity that Reema had felt the first time she saw Alaric.

Alaric's presence pressed down on them all, dominating the silence with a power that suddenly seemed to ... fit.

"You *must* see it, don't you? My resemblance to my Bloodlined father?"

Bloodlined father? Reema's heart jumped up into her throat, choking all breath from her and stilling her heart. A dread as deep as she'd only ever once known crept through her.

Salman paled, his humoured smile disappearing.

"Yes, I do believe you do see it now," Alaric said, his lip curling as he straightened his back. "I am Alaric Damaris, son of Kaiden Damaris, the ruler over Sandspire and the man who sentenced each of you to these mines."

A collective sharp intake of breath echoed off the stone walls. Salman stared at Alaric, his face a mixture of shock and confusion. He could see it now, just as Reema could. Though they could see nothing of his eyes, she could see the resemblance in the sharpness of his jawline and the strong chin he carried.

His father was the one to murder her sister.

"Refuse my challenge and what respect is there left

for you in these mines?" Alaric continued. "You'll forever be the one who cowered from the blinded son of the slave master himself."

Salman clenched his jaw. The air was thick with tension. Reema could feel the rage boiling from Asif and Omar and Ra'ad behind her. She should feel the same, but instead, she felt ... hurt, like he'd grabbed her heart and twisted it.

Finally, Salman nodded. "Well, when you put it like that, you don't leave me much of an option, do you? I accept your challenge. But you will not win."

As Salman stepped back to prepare, Asif surged forward. She stopped him with an arm across his chest. He shoved aside her arm, but she pulled him back by his wrist.

He turned on her with an ugly growl. "Don't tell me you're *still* standing up for him. The son of the bastard who ruined us is standing right there."

"You think I don't feel it? The want to strangle the life from him, right now? I *do*. But he is our only way out of this."

"We can fight our way out."

"And we'll die. Everything we've been working toward will be for *nothing*."

His gaze fixed on Alaric. The hatred in his eyes burned as hot as any of the seven hells. With a reluctant huff, Asif gave in. He relaxed and stepped back in line with Omar and Ra'ad, each of whom were staring at Alaric with stoic looks of murder.

Salman emerged from his gang, his shirt removed, no doubt to keep it from being stained by Alaric's blood.

Reema wrung her hands, struggling to distill her emotions: there was an undercurrent of concern because, damn the deep, she felt *close* to this man. But a dark cloud had come out over it, a cloud so full of rage that she wasn't sure it would ever disappear. How could he not tell her who he was?

He knew how she would have reacted. If he'd told her, with her sister's grave right there, she probably would have lunged across the cave and choked him to death right then and there.

She would have kept it a secret too.

Her mind turned back to everything he'd told her, about all the cruelties he'd endured at the hands of his father: how he'd been whipped by a man who took savage pleasure in it, how his mother took her own life to be free from him. Her gaze settled on the steel band forged to his skull. Despite all the times she had wished to see the eyes behind them, to look into his eyes and discern his thoughts, and see the man who treated her with such rare gentleness and care, not once had she imagined they would be the eyes of a Bloodlined.

And now, he would die, and the light in his eyes would die a lonely death in the darkness that his father had forced upon him.

Salman stood across from Alaric. He dragged the tip of his pickaxe weapon across the marble stone, as if its loud scratching sound spelled Alaric's fate.

"Are you ready for your death?"

Alaric smirked then, drawing frowns from every miner around him, including Reema and Salman.

"You have a chance to fight the son of the slave

master himself, and you won't do it with your bare hands?" he challenged.

The miners around Salman grumbled, voicing their desire to do it themselves. It was clear that Alaric's smirk had gotten to them, judging by the look on their faces.

Salman glanced at them and motioned for silence. Reluctantly, they did. He handed one his pickaxe and shrugged, without an ounce of concern in his eyes. After all, what did he have to be afraid of? He was fighting a blind man.

"If you want to die that way, it makes no difference to me."

Alaric rested the cane against the wall, and took his place from across Salman.

Fighting in the tunnel was difficult, with marble walls pressing in from all sides. There wasn't much room to gather your step or to cock a punch, as only about four men could stand side by side at a time. That was ideal for Alaric, but still, Reema wasn't sure that it would be enough. Though she had never seen Salman fight, she'd heard enough to know he was dangerous in his own right; all of the gang lords were.

Alaric waved for Salman to come.

"Come and get your blood."

Salman grinned, a flash of admiration passing through his eyes. Then he charged.

CHAPTER
FOURTEEN

Salman's roar echoed through the mines, reverberating off the white marble walls, accompanied by the shouts of his gang. Spittle flew from their mouths, and their faces flushed red with anger, all wanting to see Salman paint the walls red with Alaric's blood.

This was a special day for them, and not just because they were getting their chance to put an end to the Ifrit of the mines, but because they were getting to witness the slave master's son's death.

The heavy sound of bone raw fists smashing into Alaric's jaw made Reema wince. His head snapped back, and before he could recover, Salman drove a punch into his gut that nearly folded him over.

Salman landed another punch, then another, and a kick to the chest that knocked Alaric back against the wall. Salman drove in, pummeling Alaric with punch after brutal punch to the ribs, the crack of a broken rib sounding out loud enough that it cut through the echoing shouts.

The gang's shouts began to quieten, their rage giving way to muttered confusion. So far, Alaric had not put up a fight. He simply endured every punch that Salman had to throw, not making even an attempt to dodge them.

And Salman had noticed it himself.

He paused, catching his breath as he straightened. His fists and chest were speckled with Alaric's blood.

"Why aren't you fighting back?" Salman asked with a deep frown. "You made a challenge, Bloodlined. What are you doing?"

Alaric straightened, leaning his back against the marble wall. He drew an arm across his mouth to wipe away the blood. The corner of his mouth lifted infuriatingly. While it enraged everyone around her, Reema understood its true nature.

It was fake, a mask to hide what he truly felt.

She could see it now, how broken he was. Through the years of torture at his father's hands, at the loss of his mother who could no longer endure it, not even for his sake, his soul had shattered in a way that not even Reema could know.

Her heart ached for him, despite everything.

Alaric pushed away from the wall, and for the first time, raised his fists, "I was giving you a chance."

Salman barked in laughter, his surprise evident in his eyes. "It's a shame that you have your father's blood running through you."

"Isn't it?" Alaric said with a genuine grin.

Then he lunged forward, catching Salman off guard with a wild punch. It connected with the side of Salman's shoulder, knocking him off balance.

Salman hit Alaric with a harsh uppercut that would have put most men to sleep, but Alaric simply took the hit in stride as he crashed into him. The two men fell to the ground in a tumble, their arms and legs entangled. Salman was doing his best to free his arm enough to get a good punch in, but Alaric had a tight hold on him, and was driving his elbows into Salman's neck to choke the air from him.

Salman finally broke Alaric's grip and punched him across the face. A loud metal ring echoed through the tunnels as Alaric fell back.

A loud curse escaped Salman's lips as he rolled away, holding his hand. When he released his hand, it was clear why. His hand was visibly broken, the fingers hanging loose as tears of pain came to Salman's eyes. He clenched his jaw.

"Enough of this," he said, stalking toward Alaric. "You've surprised me, Alaric Damaris, but your time is up."

Salman's voice cut through the humid air of the mines like a knife, the few flickering torches casting a sinister glow on his contorted face. Silence had gripped the miners around them, making it easy to hear the macabre drip of blood from his broken hand as it splashed against the marble.

Alaric stood his ground. His expression hardened. Blindfolded by the steel band, he suddenly resembled a cold, intimidating statue, like he was carved from the same marble around them.

Salman lunged again, his good hand leading with a

punch meant to end it. And to Reema—and the other miners'—amazement, he sidestepped.

He countered with a fierce backhand, the impact resonating audibly through Salman's skull. The gang lord stumbled, a new wave of blood trickling from his nose.

Salman touched a finger to the blood and looked up, surprised.

Alaric said nothing, and somehow, that silence was more fearsome. Despite the torchlight filling the space, shadows seemed to gather around him. The way he took a step forward in Salman's direction, the way his head tilted, it felt like he could see through the darkness his father had imprisoned him in. His fists were clenched, knuckles white from the force.

His calm, cold whisper echoed. "Let's see who you are."

The words hung in the air, and a chill ran down Reema's spine.

With a sudden burst of speed, Alaric closed the distance between them. He moved like a predator, each strike impossibly precise and devastating. He drove his knee into Salman's stomach, eliciting a guttural cry. Following up, he delivered a crushing elbow to the spine, sending Salman to his knees.

Salman swung wildly, but his broken hand made him weak enough that his blows left Alaric unfazed. He grabbed one of the flailing arms and twisted brutally, the sickening snap of bone causing the miners to flinch. Salman screamed, the sound of his voice almost inhuman.

The miners, once shouting for Alaric's blood, now watched in stunned silence. And next to Reema, Asif was breathless. They had seen brutality in the mines, things that most men would be too afraid to have nightmares of. But this was something else. This was born from not rage, but from the shattered soul of a man who'd endured a lifetime of trauma at the hands of an unloving father.

Blood smeared the floor, mixing with the white marble dust and the grime of the mine.

Salman collapsed to the ground, clutching his arm, his face masked with unbridled fear; something that none of them had ever seen from a gang lord like him.

Alaric straddled Salman, his face stoic and impassive. He pinned the gang lord to the ground, and coldly, quietly, he rained fists down like hammers. The heavy thumps echoed across the silence, each punch driven by years of suppressed pain and rage. Salman's face became a mask of blood and bruises, his struggles weakening with each blow.

Then, as abruptly as it had begun, Alaric stopped. His chest heaved with exertion, blood dripping from his fists, his beard, and the steel that covered his eyes.

He raised his fist one last time, ready to end the broken man beneath him and and secure Reema and her gang's freedom. But then he hesitated, like a spark of humanity had peered through the darkness.

He lowered his fist, stood up, and left Salman gasping for breath on the ground. Alaric stepped back, his own blood mingling with the sweat and dirt on his skin. He took a deep, shuddering breath, the cold air filling his lungs.

"You lost," he said. "They go free."

Salman's laughter was almost deranged as he answered, "That's not how it works down here."

"It doesn't matter. I won, I say what goes," Alaric said, his blinded gaze turning in Reema's direction. In a soft voice, he added, "She goes free."

Salman followed his gaze, landing on her. A dark chuckle escaped him.

"You have no idea who you're letting go. There's a reason why she's called the Ifrit."

Reema froze, goosebumps crawling across her skin.

"Do you even know what she intends to do once she frees the Djinn?" Salman asked.

Alaric tilted his head toward Salman, a soft frown playing across his lips.

"She—"

The steel point of a pickaxe buried itself into Salman's face with a distinct *squelch*, stealing the words away with a gasping wheeze. Darkness descended on the miners around them as Asif straightened, his hands on his hips.

"The bastard's dead," he said.

That fact was emphasized by the death rattle that escaped Salman, and the macabre sudden jerk of his hands and feet.

While the other miners stared in shock, still processing what happened, Asif grabbed hold of Alaric's arm and dragged him toward the crowd blocking the way out. Ra'ad and Omar followed after them. Reema stared at the body for another moment before she came to her senses. She grabbed Alaric's cane and followed.

She thought that the miners would hold, that they would descend on them with their pickaxes and shivs and readied fists. But to her surprise, they parted before them like grains of sand, pushing to the side to avoid touching the blind man who'd slaughtered their gang lord.

For once, they were in fear of someone more than the Ifrit. She could see it in their eyes, in how they averted their gaze from the silent monster who walked before them. And monster *was* the right term. Reema could think nothing else of what she had just seen, and if she had not seen the gentleness in Alaric's heart from their long hours of reading together, then she, too, would think of him as such.

Asif dragged Alaric forward, his torch holding the darkness at bay. The moment that they were free, they began to run.

It only took a minute for the miners behind them to come to their senses.

They outnumbered Reema's gang.

Let them go free?

Honor would say that they had to respect the challenge that Alaric had won, but these were the mines. There was nothing down here except for unharvested marble and the warm bodies of men soon to be cold.

FIFTEEN

As Reema and the others fled toward the tunnel leading into her territory, she couldn't shake the bad feeling that had settled in her gut, and it had nothing to do with the bloodthirsty miners chasing after them.

No, it was all about what Salman had said: he'd had a man in her crew, right under her nose the whole time, and she hadn't known it.

With Omar, Ra'ad, and Asif behind her, and Alaric being too new to even know her plans, that only left Hadi and Javid. And she'd left the two of them alone, standing at the entrance to her sacred place.

She panted as she turned the corner and sprinted through the tunnel, the light chasing away the dark only just fast enough for her to run. The flames flickered and roared beside her as she ran, barely audible over the echoing din of the miners.

"There!" Asif shouted, still dragging Alaric along.

Reema squinted, seeing a silhouette slumped against the ground.

Her stomach fell.

It was Javid, his wide eyes lifeless. He lay in a pool of blood that trailed far off into the dark behind him, like he'd dragged himself here. She growled as she clutched at him. A deep bloodstain marred his back.

Hadi had betrayed her, had killed one of her own. This gang was like family, a feeling that she knew each of her men felt. They were supposed to be brothers, and Hadi had stabbed him right in the back.

Javid. One of the first to join her after Asif. She remembered the day she had found him, standing over the bodies of three miners. He was starving, and pledged himself to her if she could just feed him. He had been loyal, reliable, a brother in every sense of the word. And now he lay dead, betrayed by someone they had trusted.

The echoes of the miners grew louder. They could not stay here. Gently, Reema brushed his eyes shut.

"We need to keep moving," she said, her voice thick with emotion.

They surged forward, her legs feeling like lead as she pushed herself to step over his body. His blood trailed in her footsteps.

The passage narrowed as they approached the entrance to her secret cave. Reema's thoughts raced, her fear spiking as she worried what Hadi had done to her sacred place.

As they neared the entrance, a sickening realization struck her. The tunnel was unnaturally quiet, the sound of pursuit fading behind them. It was too quiet.

She reached the mouth of their carved tunnel, her

heart pounding. The entrance was caved in, a solid wall of rubble blocking their way.

Reema let out an explosive shout, unconcerned with the miners pursuing them at that moment. All she could think about was the fact that she had no way back to her sister's grave, and who knew what Hadi would do to her cave. Her sacred place was no longer safe, and neither was her sister.

Again, she had failed her.

"Trapped," Omar muttered, his voice filled with disbelief. "We're trapped."

She knew what he meant. This was the only way out of the southern mines. It was only a matter of time until they were found.

Reema gasped in short, sharp breaths. Her mind raced, trying to find a way out of the nightmare. She glanced back at Alaric, who stood silently, his face unreadable. Her eyes then fell on Asif and Ra'ad, their expressions mirroring her own dread and confusion.

"Hadi made sure we can't leave," she said, her voice trembling with fury and sorrow.

"That *bastard*," Asif growled.

"What do we do now?" Ra'ad asked, his voice tinged with panic.

Reema clenched her fists, the reality of their situation sinking in. They were trapped, betrayed by one of their own, with no clear way out. The miners were surely closing in, and time was running out.

"We have to fight," she declared, though her tone suggested she expected it to go poorly.

"No." Alaric's voice drew their attention to him. "There's one other way."

"Quiet," Asif snapped, towering over Alaric. "I don't want to hear a fucking word out of your mouth, you Bloodlined traitor."

Alaric ignored him, his gaze facing Reema's direction. "I can distract them."

"What?" Reema asked, confused by what he meant.

"I'll go back, lead them away from you while you open this tunnel back up."

She shook her head, "Hadi would have collapsed all of the support columns. He was smart. The whole tunnel's probably done in."

Alaric's brow furrowed over the steel band as he thought. Then he said, "There's another way out."

Reema, Asif, Omar, and Ra'ad exchanged a skeptical glance.

"Think about it, think about how many of them there are. There can't be enough food for all of them. They'd need a way back up to the Hole."

He had a good point. With the rogue miners under his arm, there were far too many members of the gang to be fully supported by the few bags of lentils and dates that Salman had just earned from the captain.

"We've only got the one torch," Omar commented.

"I don't need one." He tapped his cane against the ground and walls, as if to prove his point. But Reema frowned. No miner ever went on their own out into the dark; it was as good as suicide. She knew she should let him go. He was the son of her mortal enemy, the man who murdered her sister. And if that wasn't enough, he was *Bloodlined*. That was reason enough for him to be cast out from her gang.

But despite those things, and despite his keeping that information a secret, she could not bring herself to speak the words.

"Fine," Asif said, releasing Alaric.

"I'll find you," Alaric said softly, as if he were speaking only to Reema, rather than to the group.

"Don't bother," Asif said. "We don't need a Blood-lined dog with us, especially not one the likes of you."

Alaric was quiet, like he was waiting to hear Reema counter Asif's statement.

Instead, her voice thick with emotion, Reema said, "We have to keep moving."

He nodded at her rejection and slowly, he began to back away into the darkness. They watched it swallow him whole, and soon, he was gone.

Asif started off, then Omar and Ra'ad after him. Reema stared into the pitch black, realizing that she might have just seen the last of Alaric Damaris.

She suddenly felt numb.

"Come on," Asif said.

She pursed her lips, waited a half-second longer for Alaric to re-emerge from the darkness, but he did not. She followed Asif.

"I'm going to kill Hadi when we find him, rip that fucker's arms from his body," Omar said.

"And his legs," Ra'ad said. "I want to hear him scream."

"Quiet," Asif said.

Reema halted as a shout echoed through the tunnels.

"I heard something. That way!"

Soon, the sound of the miners chasing after them faded to nothing, leaving them alone with the cold, empty walls of the marble around them.

They were free.

CHAPTER
SIXTEEN

Alaric had been right; there was a way out of her territory —a fresh tunnel carved by Salman's men. The tunnel was dangerous, with reinforcing columns threatening to bow and break at any moment. But Reema knew that the work of other miners couldn't amount to what she had learned she could expect from the members of her own gang. They were the best of the best.

She expected a few offshoots within the tunnel that would lead to Salman's territory, but to her surprise, she found none. It was a straight shot to the Hole, leaving him completely cut off from the territory that he had ruled for so many years. It seemed that the discovery of the Djinn was enough to do it, to have him renounce the entirety of the mines for the myth that lingered in that black marble.

It was a long trek through the tunnel, with the hairs on the backs of their necks raised, fearing the earth might cave in and end their miserable lives at any moment. Once they reached the cursed Hole, they stepped through the sunlight filtering down from above and passed down through the tunnels that led to Salman's old territory.

It felt like a day or more had passed before they finally found the tunnel that led to her sacred place.

They were solemn, all of them, from Omar and Ra'ad falling into unusual silence to Asif stewing in his anger.

Reema fully expected the secret entrance to her cave to be collapsed too. So it was with a surprise that she found it still open, and the barely audible sound of humming and a crackling fire coming from within.

Her rage sparked to life, and as fast as she was, she couldn't beat Omar and Ra'ad scrambling through the hole, or Asif from going in after them.

As she crawled through, Hadi's happy hums were cut short by a surprised shout. Then he began to scream, his voice dancing off the rose quartz crystals.

To Reema, it sounded like sweet music.

She was relieved to find that the cave was untouched, though she had been right about the tunnel they'd carved: it was collapsed, and the weeks they'd spent forcing their way through the unyielding earth were wasted.

Perhaps Hadi had been content to keep this beautiful, sacred place to himself.

As if Reema would ever let that happen.

Inside the cave, she was met with the sight of Hadi being mercilessly beaten by Omar, Ra'ad, and Asif. Hadi lay crumpled on the ground, his body jerking with each blow. His face was already swollen, one eye completely shut, and blood smeared across his features.

Omar drove his boot into Hadi's ribs with a sickening crunch. The sound of bone breaking reverberated through the cave, mingling with Hadi's guttural cries. Ra'ad followed with a savage kick to Hadi's back, the force of it lifting him off the ground momentarily before he crashed back down.

"Why, Hadi?" Ra'ad shouted, his voice a mixture of rage and betrayal. "Why did you do it?"

Hadi tried to speak, but all that came out was a garbled plea as blood bubbled from his mouth. Omar grabbed him by the collar and hauled him up, only to slam a fist into his face, the impact splitting Hadi's lip wide open. Blood sprayed, but Omar didn't stop. He delivered blow after blow, each one harder than the last, until Hadi's head lolled back, barely conscious.

"You were supposed to be our brother!" Omar roared, his voice breaking. "We trusted you!"

At the side, Asif heated a marble shiv by the fire, his eyes darkening. "Don't worry. We'll get the truth from him, even if we have to cut it out."

Reema stepped closer, her face a mask of hot fury as she realized that Hadi had been sitting by the fire, cooking all their lentils and eating it. The remaining dates were already gone. He'd been celebrating.

Hadi's eyes fluttered open, and he looked up at her, his gaze filled with a mixture of terror and pleading.

"Please ... Reema," he croaked, the words barely audible.

Reema crouched down, her face inches from his. "Javid was a brother to us, all of us. And you murdered him. Why?"

Hadi sobbed, his body wracked with pain. Asif approached from the fire, the marble shiv's edge blackened and the air around it warping from the heat.

Omar and Ra'ad seized him, yanking his head back by the hair, exposing his bruised and bloodied face.

Reema held her hand up, and Asif paused.

"Answer me, or I'll let Asif take his time with you."

Hadi trembled, his gaze flicking toward Asif's shadowed face. For a moment, she wasn't sure he would answer. But then, he spoke, "What you're trying to do with the Djinn, what *all* of you are trying to do, it's wrong."

Reema's eyes narrowed. "Wrong? Do you not remember your rage? The guards took the relic that your *mother* gave you. Didn't you want revenge on them?"

"I do. But not like this. Not in the way you're planning."

"So you choose to betray us? Why didn't you just talk to me?"

"Because I know you wouldn't have listened," Hadi shouted. "Your anger, it blinds you."

She snarled, itching to reach for Asif's burning shiv and to drag it across Hadi's throat right then and there. But she wasn't done with him yet.

"Why Salman?"

"Are you serious?" Hadi laughed, his voice delirious as he answered. "Because you let your guard down. I knew you'd be prepared if Mehdi or Renfri came for you, but not Salman. Besides, he's the only one I thought could outplay you."

Her lip curled, and Omar and Ra'ad yanked his head back further, drawing a whimper from him.

"One last question, then I'll let you go," she said.

Hadi's lip trembled.

"Did you break my rule?"

She knew he understood what rule she meant. The first time she'd brought them into the cave, she'd ordered them to never go down the short tunnel that led to the small cave where her sister's grave lie.

And judging by the look in his eyes, he had.

"Hand me the shiv, Asif," she said.

"You said you'd let me go," Hadi shouted, his eyes jolting wide. "I didn't know that was where *she* was buried!"

As Asif passed her the shiv, Hadi began to scream.

She lifted the blade, ignoring the radiating heat, and inspected it in the torchlight.

"I told you what I'd do to you if you broke it."

She buried the shiv in his eye.

His voice broke as his scream came from the depths of his soul, leaving only the sound of sizzling flesh. The stench twisted her nose, but she would not turn from it. She would watch as she extinguished the light in his one remaining eye.

Omar and Ra'ad's noses wrinkled, and they stepped back to cover them.

Hadi loosed another scream, loud enough to hurt her ears. She twisted the knife, silencing the scream forever. She rose and stared down at the body of the man who'd killed their brother. He was just as bad as the slave master who stole her sister from her.

"Take him from here and dump him. I'm done with him."

Omar and Ra'ad nodded, taking a torch and dragging the body out of the cave. She took a seat, too tired to even take stock of what remaining lentils they had. Asif sat across from her, folded his arms over his knees.

Neither one spoke, both burdened with the weight of the losses. Javid and Hadi had both been with them for years. Asif must be thinking about all the memories they had, the times they spent laughing with each other around the fire and the times they'd worked together. In other gangs, miners kept their secrets to themselves, knowing that though they had allies, they could turn on them at any moment. But here in Reema's gang, in the *Ifrit's* gang, it was supposed to be different. They were supposed to be a family, who shared a single vision of revenge that could finally give them a single peaceful night of sleep.

In the span of just this day, they had lost two members of their family.

Three, Reema corrected herself, because she knew that no miner who ever went into the dark ever came back to the light.

Alaric was gone.

CHAPTER
SEVENTEEN

Reema stood over her sister's grave. It was quiet. Her heart beat slowly, like it was ready to stop at any moment. She was so tired of how grief continued to claw at her heart and mind, of how she continually failed the people around her.

It went beyond the promise she'd made to Javid, that she would lead him to vengeance. It went beyond being unable to protect her sister from the slave master. It had everything to do with Alaric.

She had promised to help him survive the mines, yet she had willingly let him go into the dark, where no miner ever survived. It didn't matter how skilled they were. The earth had a way of making you lost, of breaking your mind beneath the pressure of the white marble walls that imprisoned you.

Reema bowed her head.

Two days had passed. She held the book in her hand, wanting nothing more than to continue reading Faisal's story to see how he got his revenge. And yet, she couldn't bring herself to sit down and open its cover.

It didn't feel right to read without Alaric.

She'd tried that first night. Sat down, the page open before her. But the words were impossible to read in the drowning silence. She realized she was too used to the muted sound of his makeshift cane tapping against the stone, to the sound of his breathing and soft chuckles. She was too used to his presence, and the way that his warmth filled this cave.

It was so cold now.

A tear slipped from her eye, and she quickly wiped it away.

Why was she feeling this way?

She should be *glad* that Alaric was gone. After all, he was the son of her greatest enemy and a Bloodlined bastard at that. There was no place for him down here in the mines, and certainly not within her gang. It was better that he was gone, better that she could focus on the vow she'd spoken over Hana's grave, to see justice doled out and to put the world back to rights.

So why did it seem like the darkness was so much heavier now? And why did it seem like her vow felt so ... empty?

Words played in her mind, echoing from the past.

"You don't believe the Bloodlined are capable of love?" he'd asked.

"Are monsters capable of it?" she'd answered.

At the time, she thought it was a simple question, with an answer that she was all too certain of. But now, she wondered if there was more to the question.

Wondered if he felt what she felt, hidden away beneath the excuses and the lies she told herself.

She shook her head and rested a hand on Hana's grave. "The world's a sundamned confusing place, Hana. I hope it's a whole lot easier up there in the heavens."

She paused, like she was waiting for Hana to comment. The silence lingered, like Hana was too far away to answer. And perhaps she was. Perhaps she always would be. If she were honest, Reema knew that she didn't deserve heaven's light. No, she was the Ifrit, and the Ifrit belonged in one place.

The seven hells.

With a heavy sigh, she left the cave.

She couldn't read tonight either.

EIGHTEEN

Reema stood guard in the tunnels. The last couple of days, she and the others had spent their hours bickering, debating what the next best course of action was. But then she had an epiphany, waking Asif, Omar, and Ra'ad with several heavy swings at the tunnel that Hadi had caved in.

There was a reason Hadi had been so relaxed in this cave and why he'd been so surprised by their appearance; nobody else knew about the tunnel, except perhaps Salman, and he was dead now. With the entrance caved in, who knew how long it would be before some miners chose to open up these old passages.

He was supposed to be safe here.

That realization brought some degree of excitement to the others. They got started right away on trying to clear the path back through the tunnel, and while it would be far easier than carving a new way through the earth, it still would require a significant amount of work.

The torch wavered in Reema's hand as she walked

back and forth in the tunnel, keeping an eye out for any wayward miners. There was, of course, the possibility that she had it all wrong and that other miners would be coming their way to meet Hadi. But she didn't think so. Hadi knew the value of this place, how distinct it was from the other caves in the mines. He wouldn't render it useless by telling everyone he met.

Still, better to keep watch.

Reema rubbed her eyes clear of the spots swimming through the darkness. Her mind turned to the book, its solid shape warm against her body, almost like it was begging her to go back to Hana's grave and flip open its pages. But now wasn't the time. She needed to—

A silhouette appeared in the darkness at the edge of her vision.

She came to an abrupt halt.

The figure was moving slowly, deliberately, accompanied by an eerie shuffling sound that sounded like it belonged to a spectre rather than a man. A chill ran down Reema's spine as the shuffling grew louder, closer. Her heart pounded in her chest.

"Who's there?" she called out, her voice steady but tense.

The figure stopped.

Her torchlight reflected back, blinding her for just a moment. She adjusted her gaze and saw that it was reflecting off a steel band. She gasped, the breath catching in her throat.

It was Alaric.

He was shirtless and covered in blood, with cuts and

bruises seemingly covering every part of him. His skin was pallid and his face was disturbingly gaunt.

Reema reared back in horror. The mines could be cruel, its harsh darkness and overwhelming silence making miners think they were seeing things. This had to be an apparition, summoned from the depths of her regrets and fears, because he was *dead*.

"Alaric?" she whispered.

"Reema," he said, with a deep sigh that sounded like it came from the depths of his soul.

Then he collapsed.

She rushed forward, catching his head before it hit the stone. He was solid. Real. She tapped his cheek, but he was non responsive. With a curse, she began dragging him back toward the cave.

"Asif!" she called.

Nothing.

"Asif!" she called again, dragging Alaric through the exposed entrance to the cave.

She heard Asif's voice, followed by the sound of running footsteps. The moment she appeared with Alaric, he froze, his jaw dropping. Omar and Ra'ad appeared behind him, and they too stopped, their eyes wide with disbelief.

"How in the sundamned hells?" Omar asked.

"Is he alive?" Ra'ad asked.

Reema held her hand over his mouth and felt the softest brush of air. Relief surged through her, followed by a rush of conflicting emotions. This man was the son of the one who caused them so much pain and suffering. She knew that the others must be thinking about ending him, if only to get a taste of the revenge they'd worked towards all these years. Would she stop them, if they tried? *Should* she stop them?

After all, Alaric was not his father. Hadn't he proven that much?

"Get him to the fire, patch him up," Asif said, his voice flat, as if he could hardly believe his own words. "This man is one of us."

Omar and Ra'ad exchanged a look, then shrugged and did as Asif said, taking him from Reema.

Reema and Asif watched them go.

"What about—" Reema began, surprised at his decision.

"He's the only reason we're alive," he interrupted. He ran his fingers through his beard, his brow furrowed with a look of contemplation in his eyes. "I don't want it to be true. I want him to be everything that his father is, so that I can do him in. But it don't feel right. Much as I don't want it to be true, he saved us."

Reema was quiet, her gaze locked onto Alaric's unconscious form. He *did* save them. And judging by the look of him, it had come at great cost.

"I keep thinking about why he's got that steel band on him, too." He paused.

"And?" Reema prompted, glancing at Asif.

"He'd said that his father made it for him. It seems more than just a cruel punishment. It feels like it's ..." he trailed off.

"A rejection."

He nodded.

"You think his father is disowning him?"

Asif pursed his lips and pointed to Alaric, "*That* is more than disowning. You don't put a steel band around a Bloodlined's eyes and throw him into the mines unless you're saying he's nothing more than a sundamned Commonborn."

Reema drew a deep breath. He had a good point.

Asif cleared his throat. "Maybe keeping him alive is exactly what the slave master doesn't want. And you know my opinion on that."

"Anything he doesn't want is good," she said.

He nodded.

Reema couldn't help but laugh. "Look at you now, sticking up for the blind bastard."

He scowled, shook his head, and waved her off as he went to help Omar and Ra'ad patch up Alaric. As much as Reema wanted to help, she knew her place. She was supposed to be on watch, and with Alaric appearing out of the darkness, beaten and bruised, there was no telling who might have followed him.

She went back out to the tunnel.

The oppressive darkness seemed lighter than before, as did the shadows over her heart. Reema's mind was elsewhere as she kept watch.

She wondered what Alaric had done to deserve his father's banishment from the surface world. It must have been something truly awful for his father to think of his own blood as valuable as a mine slave. Shouldn't that make Alaric one of them? Shouldn't he have just as much reason to free the Djinn as she did?

Her stomach rumbled, the sound making a soft echo in the dark. She pressed her hand to her stomach in an attempt to silence it, but it carried on for another torturous second before stopping.

She grimaced at the pang of hunger. She could only imagine how hungry Alaric must be, after two days spent lost amongst the dark. They were short on food after Hadi decided to cook through it recklessly. Water too, but she made up for that by carrying water from the small cavern where her sister was buried. Asif seemed surprised, but he didn't ask any questions. Omar and Ra'ad seemed to appreciate what it meant for her to be sharing *anything* from that sacred place of hers.

They'd had just enough lentils to last the four of them long enough to get through the tunnels, but that was cutting it tight. There was absolutely no way they could feed Alaric too, and with no quick access to her territory where she had some reserves hidden away, she knew they would either have to risk stealing from Renfri's or Mehdi's gangs, or deliver the captain a marble block.

As much as she didn't want to face the captain again, she feared she had no choice. She didn't have Javid or Hadi anymore, and that left them vulnerable. Her lip curled at the thought, but a warm feeling against her chest quickly buried it.

She could feel the book's presence, almost as if it was calling out to her, telling her that Alaric was back, that perhaps tonight would be a night for reading.

Perhaps tonight she would see Faisal get his revenge.

Alaric slept so peacefully. There was something almost ethereal about the way his chest moved up and down, and the way his foot twitched from time to time. He was still shirtless—they had none to give him—but he'd been cleaned with a wet cloth. Already, he was beginning to look better, a healthy color returning to his skin. Another day and he'd probably be back to himself. He just needed to rest now.

Reema watched him, unable to tear her eyes away, even though she was supposed to be keeping watch by the entrance to the cave.

Asif, Omar, and Ra'ad had gone off to mine a small slab of marble. They wouldn't have time to get a full marble block, but they needed *something* to take to Captain Hamza. They had to hope he was in a good enough mood to toss down enough lentils to get them by until they could get through to the black marble.

It was painful knowing that even as she sat here,

others were swinging their pickaxes at what she had spent years mining for. But she also knew that whatever progress they made, they wouldn't have broken through. In the myth the old man had shared with her long ago, the Djinn was locked away in a black marble prison so vast it was like the night sky had forced its way into the earth's heart. There hadn't been enough time to cut through enough black marble to get to something like that.

Still, the thought made Reema anxious.

Alaric grunted, his breathing turned fitful for a moment. She crouched next to him, daring to draw herself closer. Her lips tingled as his warm breath brushed across them. Not for the first time, she wondered how he managed to find his way back to her cave, how he managed to outrun the miners chasing him, how he managed to *survive*.

It was clear that the others wondered the same thing from the way they had stared at him in the early morning. He was the first miner to ever go into the darkness and return alive and sane.

"You were right," Reema said gently, brushing a strand of his hair back away from his face. "You aren't weak."

His lips parted, and for a moment, she thought he would wake. But he did not. Instead, he turned his head the other way.

Reema sighed and returned to her seat. She pulled the book out and ran her finger over the title: *Beneath the Sands of Sorrow*. She checked to make sure the others hadn't suddenly returned before opening its pages.

She preferred to read in the small cavern where Hana lay, for the privacy and the hope that Hana was somehow listening to her, but she didn't want to leave Alaric, and she wasn't willing to wake him either.

With a tentative voice and a tracing finger, she began to read aloud.

Faisal stared into the sister's glowing hazel eyes. He had never thought that the Bloodlined could love, but he saw a pool of grief in her eyes as deep as his own. He could tell she had questions from the terseness of her lips and the tension in her shoulders. He prepared to defend himself, knowing that Tasneem had held her family at a distance for a reason. But to his surprise, she motioned for him to follow.

She led him to the grave and stood next to him as the grief settled deeper into his soul. It seeped through him like black poison, drawing up every memory of a kiss, every whisper of a touch. He thought he knew what pain felt like, but he did not—not until that moment, when he stood at the foot of his beloved's grave.

Tasneem's Bloodlined father and mother were too deep in their tears to realize that a newcomer had arrived. It hurt to look at them, because they did not seem like bad people. In fact, the more he looked at those surrounding the grave, the more he wondered why Tasneem had kept him a secret.

A dark thought came to mind—perhaps she kept him a secret because she was ashamed of him. After all, these people were wealthy beyond belief, with all the power and status any man could dream of. He was not.

He shook his head. It didn't matter if she was
ashamed of him or not. She loved him, and he loved her,
and now she was gone. Those were all the facts that
mattered. He wiped away his tear and held his hand out
over her grave, letting it fall to meet the earth, to seep
through the ground and touch her departed soul.

"May the seven heavens be blessed by the light you
have to share, my love," he whispered.

Then he was gone.

Reema took a break, resting her voice for a moment
as she collected herself. She knew the kind of pain Faisal
had felt when he'd stood by that grave. She felt it when
she'd buried Hana. She still felt it to this day, though its
sharp edge had dulled over the years.

"Keep reading," a voice croaked.

Reema jumped at the sudden sound. Alaric still lay
there, same as before, but his breathing was different. He
was awake.

She put the book aside and retrieved the bowl of
cooked lentils she'd prepared for him.

"It's about time you woke up," she lied. In truth, she
thought he'd be sleeping much longer. There was no way
he'd have gotten any sleep out in the tunnels because if
he had, he wouldn't be sitting here now.

He sat up with a deep groan, and she passed him the
bowl of lentils. He didn't hesitate to dive into the bowl,
scooping it into his mouth like an animal, hardly stopping to breathe.

Reema watched him, unsure of what she was
supposed to say. So she stayed quiet.

When he finished, he set aside the bowl and leaned back against the marble wall behind them, his blinded gaze finding her. She wasn't sure how he did that. She wondered if it was the loud beat of her heart that gave her away or if he could feel her very presence.

"Keep reading. Please," he said.

Reema frowned. She had questions for him. But maybe she could ask them after another chapter. With a heavy sigh, she reached for the book.

Faisal wasn't sure how many days had passed. Hidden away in his numbing dark, he was unaware of how the sun rose and fell outside. As far as he was concerned, the only things that existed outside his front door were enough food and water to keep himself alive long enough to murder.

So it was a surprise when a knock came at the door.

He wasn't sure if he had imagined it, so he stayed put. But again, the knock came. He crossed the room and threw open the door to find that strange Bloodlined woman again. For a long minute, they stared at one another, unsure how to broach the silence.

"How'd you find me?" he asked.

"I remembered my sister saying something about a clothesmaker. I asked around."

He frowned. "There are countless clothesmakers."

"But only one who seemed to frequent the same areas of interest that my sister had," she said. She glanced past him into the darkness behind him. "May I come in?"

Before he could refuse, she pushed past him. It was

clear she found his home filthy. He didn't have to imagine why. It stank of grief.

She brushed a chair clean, sat, crossed her legs, and stared at him.

"Why did my sister love you?" she asked.

He blinked.

"She must have loved you very much to keep you a secret from us. She was always like that, even when we were younger; she kept the most important, precious things close to her heart." The woman leaned forward, her gaze flickering around the room in disgust. "I cannot pretend to understand what she saw in you."

He scowled. Who did this Bloodlined woman think she was, to come into his home and question their love?

He threw open the door. "Get out."

The woman stared at him for a moment, then retrieved something from her pocket. In the darkness, it was hard to see, but then it glinted against the sunlight outside, and he realized what it was: the ring he'd given Tasneem.

He rushed forward, only for the woman to snap her palm shut over the ring.

Her eyes were like fire when she spoke. "I want to know everything."

His rage bucked and howled. His blood rushed in his ears. He wanted to tear the ring from her hands and drag her out, toss her back into the sunlight so he could be left alone to grieve in his darkness. But something in the way she stared at him stopped him. A certain kind of desperation pulled at the shattered remains of his heart.

He was reminded that he was not the only one who had lost her.

He stared at the woman. "What is your name?"

"Amira," she said, lifting her chin. "And you?"

"Faisal." He nodded toward the ring. "If I tell you everything, it'll only bring up the memories, make it hurt all over again."

She lowered her gaze. "I want to hurt. At least then I'd feel something."

Her words dropped into the silence like a rock. They struck him true to the heart.

"My sister is dead," she said, sounding as numb as he felt. "I thought she was gone forever, that I would never hear her again. But then I saw this ring on her finger, and then I saw you."

She looked up at him.

"Tell me everything, I beg you. I wish only to hear more about the person I cared most about in this Angel-forsaken world."

He stood frozen, his heart torn as he fought his desire to push her away. This wasn't just some random woman knocking on his door. This was Tasneem's sister. Would she not want him to tell Amira of their stolen moments together?

As the silence stretched, Amira stood. She approached him, took his hand gently in hers, and placed the ring in it. Without a word, she went to the door.

"Wait."

She stopped and looked back.

"I, too, wish to hear more about the person I cared

most about in this world," Faisal whispered, suddenly feeling desperate himself. He realized there was still more of Tasneem for him to know, as Amira had grown up with the girl he'd loved. "Come back tonight. I'll light a fire to stave off the chill, and together, we can speak of her."

"Tasneem," Amira said.

He bowed his head. "Yes. Of my Tasneem."

A light shone in Amira's eye. "Thank you."

The door shut behind her.

As Faisal lay down in the bed he and Tasneem once shared, he couldn't help but think the darkness didn't feel as heavy and lonely as before.

Reema shut the book and stared at the cover for a long while.

"Will you tell me about her?" Alaric asked. "About Hana?"

It was a struggle to breathe, hearing her name from Alaric's lips. If it were anyone else, she would have raged, would have beaten them, and taught them that her sister's name was holier than the Angel's himself, and never to speak of it. But it was Alaric—the man who had somehow found a crack in her hardened heart.

"Hana was like no one I've ever met," Reema said, Hana's sweet face appearing in her mind. Where Reema's hair was dark, Hana's was light, and she had a smattering of freckles sprinkled across her face. The way she smiled and laughed ...

Reema squeezed her eyes shut, her hand going to her chest as her heart seized in pain.

With a heavy grunt, Alaric slowly moved next to her, and a moment later, a warm hand pressed over hers. She turned her hand over, joining it with his. She'd never felt comfort like this. And now, she wasn't sure how she would ever go without it.

"Hana had a smile that lit up the world everywhere she went. She had a laugh that sounded more like a cackle than anything, and you couldn't help but be drawn into it. And it always seemed like she was laughing. The only time she was ever serious was when she found herself on a tall sand dune, staring off into the horizon. She liked to watch the sunsets, because she said she loved to see the way the stars burned in the sun's dying light."

Her eyes misted with tears. They had been watching the sunset when the slavers came. Her last sunset had been torn apart by her screams and the screams of their parents chasing after them.

Reema thought then of the man who'd silenced that scream, who'd made sure her dear sister would never see another sunset again.

She was holding his son's hand.

She released his hand, wiped the single tear that dared to spill down her cheek, and stood. The fire crackled nearby, its heat washing over her, joining what burned inside: the incessant need for revenge, to see the world pay for what it had done to her sweet, helpless sister.

Alaric seemed to feel the shift in her because when he stood after her, his voice was low and quiet.

"Reema?"

"What?"

"What do you intend to do when you free the Djinn?" he asked.

Dark shadows descended over her as she faced him, his stare piercing the steel band around his eyes. She had wondered if Salman's statement lingered in his mind, that he did not know what she planned. She knew he carried the same rage she felt in his heart, but for the first time, she wondered if it affected him the same way it did her.

"Do you plan to bring her back to life?" he asked, taking a step closer.

Even though he could not see, she shook her head. As much as she wished to see her beautiful sister again, she knew this was not a world that deserved her. How many beautiful sisters out there had been stolen by those cruel, indifferent humans that walked the surface? She was not the only one to suffer.

No, she could not waste the wish gained by freeing the Djinn on bringing her sister back, no matter how much she wished to hear her laugh just once more.

"Do you plan to free yourself and the members of your gang?"

Again, she shook her head, staying silent.

The darkness deepened.

"Do you plan to kill my father?"

Her breath hitched, and she hesitated. How could she admit the truth to him?

He reached for her hand again.

"Tell me," he said. "I would understand if you do. My father has caused so much *pain*."

Her gaze caught on the whip scars crossing his chest.

"Your father is just the start."

"The captain and his guards?"

"*They* are just the start."

He frowned, his brows furrowing. "What do you mean?"

With a deep breath, she lifted her gaze to his, wishing she could see his eyes as she spoke her dark intentions.

"When I free the Djinn, I will wipe the world clean. I will free it of all the evil that walks its surface and allow it to start anew."

His lips parted in surprise.

"All those people who walk the sands above and dole out cruelty as easily as they take their breaths? They will die."

His hands fell from hers. He was stunned into silence.

"You would wish destruction upon the world?" Alaric asked, his breathing suddenly sharp and tight, as if he was struggling to comprehend that she, the woman who read to him every night, could be capable of such evil.

Reema wasn't a fool. Truth was, she knew there was evil in what she was doing. But she also knew there was so much more good, because the number of people with blackened hearts outnumbered the good. It was only by burning the world that something beautiful and good could rise from its ashes.

"You're surprised," Reema said.

"Salman was trying to stop you," he muttered to himself, shaking his head in disbelief. "He—they—think you're the villain."

"There's a reason they call me the Ifrit."

He stumbled forward, taking her hands in his again. "But you're *not* the Ifrit. You're not the villain. You have a good, kind heart, just like so many people on the surface do."

"Then why is there is so much suffering in the world, Alaric?"

He didn't have an answer for her.

She held up the book. "What do you think lies beneath the sands of sorrow?"

"I know what lies beneath it. And it is not this. It is not destruction and rage. That will only draw you in deeper. It will *drown* you."

Again, she pulled her hands from his.

"Drown me?" she seethed. "I hope so, if it means your father, all you Bloodlined bastards, and all the slavers drown with me."

You.

She'd said *you.*

She could tell he'd gotten caught on that, but he straightened his back and moved past it.

"And the people I care about on the surface? The city I love? You'd drown them too?"

Her silence was answer enough.

She would.

He turned, slowly walking away. As the darkness began to swallow him, she called after him.

"Will you try to stop me?"

He paused at the edge of the light. "No."

She blinked in surprise. "No?"

"We'll keep reading. I'll show you there's another way."

"And if you don't?"

"Then I'll remain by your side, watching as everything I care about burns to ruin."

His words echoed long after he disappeared into the darkness.

The fire crackled at the heart of the gang, casting their long shadows far across the cave. Reema ate the last scraps of her lentils, her stomach still grumbling. Alaric sat across from her on the other side of the fire, but she couldn't bring herself to look at him.

What could be in the book that he was so convinced would change her mind?

It was a thought that bothered her because for as long as she'd been in the mines, she had been defined by the vengeance she'd sworn to get for her sister, the same as all the men in her gang. All the remaining ones, anyway. She glanced up at the others. It was strange, feeling so few after so long. She missed Javid. And, strange as it was to say, she missed Hadi too.

Damn the deep. She shook her head and scraped the bottom of her bowl.

"Didn't think the day would ever come when I'd share a meal with a sundamned Bloodlined," Asif commented in a gruff voice.

Omar chuckled over a mouthful of lentils and pointed at Alaric. "Is he really Bloodlined if you can't see his glowing eyes?"

Ra'ad's eyes widened. "That's a good point, you know."

Alaric sighed. "I am still Bloodlined, unfortunately for us all."

Asif grunted.

"So, what's it like being Bloodlined?" Omar asked.

Ra'ad elbowed him in the ribs, drawing a yelp from his brother.

"What? I'm curious."

"We just said he isn't Bloodlined, didn't we?"

"Well—"

"It's a terrible bore," Alaric said.

"A *bore*?" Asif questioned. "I grew up in Zareen, got to hear the music coming down from the Peak District while we starved. It didn't sound like a bore."

"Oh, but it is. I was never much into the balls, the gossip, the need to lord above everyone else and prove myself better than them." He scooped the last of his lentils into his mouth and set his bowl aside. "No, I preferred my books over them all."

Asif's gaze flicked toward Reema and the book he knew was tucked in her waistband.

"These books, they any good?" Asif asked.

"I—" Alaric started.

"I wasn't asking you," Asif interrupted. "I was asking our fearless Ifrit."

Reema frowned and looked around the fire. "What?"

"We've noticed you sneaking off to read with him, boss," Omar said.

Reema scowled and pushed aside her empty bowl.

"At first, we thought the two of you were having a go," Ra'ad said.

Omar winked at Alaric. Alaric didn't see it.

"We were not," Reema said, her voice as dead as she could make it. "Bloodlined and Commonborn don't belong together, let alone coexist."

She could feel him facing her. She stopped herself from looking at him, from seeing the hurt and sadness that must have been etched across his face. She didn't need that because she could feel it in her own heart.

"The Queen is a Commonborn, and she chose to be with a Bloodlined," Alaric said. "I'd say they're coexisting just fine."

Each of them stared at Alaric.

"Queen?" Omar asked.

"Commonborn?" Ra'ad continued.

"You think we're stupid enough to believe *that*?" Asif spat.

"It's true," Alaric said. "Razhan gave up his throne to her, and in an effort to unite the people of Zareen and Sundara, she took the Bloodlined man she loved as her consort."

"And I piss golden nectar from the heavens," Asif said. "Enough. Point is, Reema, we've seen you distracted by that book."

Distracted.

Reema scowled and leaned forward, the shadows

gathering about her as she spoke in a low voice. "Are you suggesting something, Asif?"

He shrugged. "Just saying, something don't seem right. You're different. Softer. Like him."

"What makes you think I'm soft?" Alaric asked before she could respond.

"Because you were going to let Salman live—the very bastard who conspired against us. Why?"

Alaric didn't answer.

His silence infuriated Asif enough that he shoved his own half-full bowl aside and stood. His shadow stretched across the cave as his face contorted in rage and his eyes burned with firelight.

"The way you fight, you've got a ruthless edge to you. I saw that for myself when you tried to choke me to death. But him? *That* bastard? Why'd you hold back at the end? What's keeping you soft?"

Reema turned to Alaric. She was curious too, as to why he didn't finish the gang lord off.

"Because I'm not my father."

Asif frowned, his pointed finger slowly falling to his side.

"Or at least, I'm trying not to be," Alaric added quietly.

His words hung in the air for a long moment.

"You don't have it in you to be him," Reema said. "You're too ..."

She wasn't sure what to say as the others' gazes turned toward her.

"She means you've got a heart," Asif said, finishing her sentence.

She looked away.

"But that heart will get you killed if you don't wake up and realize where you are," Asif said, and though he spoke to Alaric, his words struck at Reema. "There's no room for that compassion down here. You spare someone like Salman, and the moment you turn your back, they'll bury their shiv in you."

"Every time," Omar and Ra'ad said.

"I need to know that if you're going to have our back, you'll do what it takes," Asif said. "You can't be merciful down here. *This* is the place to let yourself burn, to wield your hatred like a sundamned sword, because that'll be all that keeps you alive. You get me?"

Alaric didn't answer him.

Asif growled and rounded the fire until he towered over him, his fists clenched at his sides. "I asked you a question. Will you do what it takes to keep us alive?"

Alaric faced Reema's direction.

"Always."

Asif stood over him, as if he was contemplating Alaric's sincerity. It seemed he was convinced, because he grunted and returned to his seat and his lentils.

Reema could still feel the frustrating radiating from Asif, and he was right to be frustrated. Their gang was falling apart, two members down, and their territory was overrun by enemies. And as much as she wanted to deny it, she *was* going soft.

She clenched her fists, watching the firelight dance over her white knuckles, before she glanced up at Alaric. He was eating quietly, but the firelight casting sharp shadows across his face, but there was a tension in his shoulders that she couldn't ignore. He'd said he would do what it took to have their back, *her* back, but she had to wonder ... what if what it took was to let her wipe the world free of men like Kaiden Damaris?

The man who helped her read, who looked at her like she was something more than a fierce gang lord—could he really harden his heart enough to let her?

She shook her head, trying to free herself of the worry creeping in her mind. She did not want to know what would happen if he could not.

Reema felt the fire's warmth against her skin, but it did nothing to thaw the cold that had settled in her chest. She pushed the thoughts aside, focusing instead on the sound of the crackling fire, the rhythmic clink of bowls as the others finished their meals.

Finally, the urge to piss pulled her from it all. She stood up, needing to clear her head, and stepped away from the fire without a word, heading for the shadowed corner of the cave. She had almost reached it when she felt a hand grab her arm, pulling her to a halt.

She looked back and met Asif's dark, intense gaze.

"What do you want?" she asked, tearing her arm free.

His voice was softer than when he spoke to Alaric. "You can't have compassion either, Reema. Not with what we're trying to do. Not for him."

His eyes glinted with what looked like pity, like he knew what he was telling her. Reema swallowed as a pang wracked her heart. She gazed past him, watching as Alaric finished his lentils.

He was beautiful.

But she knew they could never be together. She had

room in her heart for one thing only, and that was the desire for revenge. Her sister deserved justice, just as the world above deserved a fresh start. Whatever feelings she had for him would only get in the way of that.

Her gaze hardened as she looked back into Asif's eyes.

"As I said, Bloodlined and Commonborn cannot be together."

He nodded slowly. Then he offered her a rare smile before he returned to the fire. Reema stood there, watching Asif return to the fire, his smile fading into the flickering shadows. The distant warmth of the flames did little to chase away the cold that settled deep in her bones.

She withdrew the marble shard she kept hidden away, her eyes locking onto the black speck staining its flawless surface. She closed her eyes, took a deep breath, and welcomed the cold emptiness that seeped through her. She was so close to justice for Hana. She could not falter now.

Tucking the shard away, she turned and walked toward the shadowed corner of the cave, the need to relieve herself almost forgotten.

CHAPTER
TWENTY-ONE

Reema and her gang were the first to arrive at the Hole again. She preferred it that way because, even though she despised wasting time waiting, she knew it was safer; nobody could ambush her there if she got there first.

She turned the marble shard in her hand over and over as she waited for the other gang lords to arrive. Behind her, Asif, Omar, and Ra'ad leaned against the marble slab they'd mined, and Alaric was testing out his new cane. Reema had made it from the pickaxes of two rogue miners who thought they could kill them on the way to the Hole.

It had been too easy to put them down. Asif had done most of the work, and he seemed glad to finally get his shiv wet with blood. It seemed that he had some pent-up frustration to work through.

Of course, she would have preferred that he stop stabbing them once they were dead. She needed a new top, as hers was torn from the last time she'd made Alaric's cane. And Alaric, he didn't even *have* a shirt now. Something had happened to him as he made his escape from the miners in her territory, but he declined to say what. She suspected she already knew. At first glance, it was easy to think of Alaric as helpless and weak. But she knew better now. He was a survivor.

Her eyes squinted up at the light filtering down through the Hole. Two white clouds floated across the endless expanse of blue sky. For that short while, with them being the only ones there, she thought it was beautiful. Peaceful.

That feeling didn't last long as she soon heard the sharp crack of a whip. Mehdi emerged into the Hole, his bloodied face twisted into an ugly snarl. Normally, it was his second who carried the whip, but today she did not see him.

Mehdi's gaze swept across the cave until it landed on her. "You."

Her brow rose. "Mehdi. Did you forget what happened the last time you got tough with me?"

The scar stretching from his brow down to the corner of his mouth was a strong reminder, but her jab only seemed to enrage him further.

"What are you doing?" he growled. His men came to a halt behind him, releasing their ropes from the white marble block and collapsing to the ground in exhaustion.

Reema frowned at the sight. Normally, Mehdi would not have tolerated such a display of weakness because he knew the other gang lords would see his vulnerability. After all, though his men didn't realize it, their numbers were the only thing that kept Reema and the other gang lords from ravaging him and his territory, the western veins.

"I'm waiting, same as you," she answered.

Mehdi's eyes narrowed, and he took a step closer. "You're a fool, Reema. You would doom us all."

Before Reema could respond, another figure emerged from the shadows. Renfri strode into the Hole, her gang trailing behind her, dragging a large marble slab. Her eyes were cold, and her expression was one of disgust as she looked at Reema.

"Of course she would," Renfri spat, her voice laced with venom. "Look at her. She's a monster."

"What are you talking about?" Reema asked, her heart skipping a beat. Did they know about the Djinn? She forced herself to remain calm, her mind racing to figure out how they had found out.

"We *know* what you're trying to do," Renfri said. "Have you thought even once about who the *fuck* feeds us? If everybody on the surface is dead, there's no one left to send food down. We'll starve to death."

"That won't happen," Mehdi said, drawing up his chin and staring down his nose at them, his eyes reflecting the fire back at her. "The Djinn belongs to me."

Reema's blood ran cold.

"You're as big a fool as her, Mehdi," Renfri said. She shook her head and glanced toward Reema again. "We could be *free* of this place. You know that, right?"

A shadow appeared above the Hole, blocking the light.

Captain Hamza.

He smiled, his lips clamped over the pipe in his

mouth. A cloud of emberdust smoke unfurled from his nostrils, rolling up to meet the clouds above.

"Tsk, tsk, tsk. Are we fighting already?"

More guards appeared on either side of him, gripping their swords too tight as usual.

The gang lords fell silent, tension brewing between them like a dark storm, as none of them wanted to risk Hamza finding out about the sundamned Djinn.

"Now, where is Zayd and that other one?"

"Salman," Reema muttered.

The captain pointed to her. "Yes, that's it. Salman. Now where are they?"

Reema exchanged glances with the other gang lords.

The captain bent forward, his hands on his knees. "*Where* are they?"

"They're not coming," Reema said evenly. "They won't be coming ever again."

The captain blinked in surprise, his eyes slowly widening in realization. "You killed them?"

Then he began to cackle. It was a harsh sound, like the grating of rocks against each other. It echoed down through the mines, and Reema knew she would hear it for the next week.

The tension in the air was palpable, every muscle in Reema's body coiled like a spring. She could feel the weight of Mehdi's and Renfri's gazes, the accusations hanging heavy in the air.

Suddenly, Captain Hamza's laughter came to an abrupt halt.

"So, which one of you dogs is going to make up for what they aren't bringing?"

There was no answer.

He scowled and spoke in a disbelieving voice. "So there will be a shortfall in marble supply this month."

Captain Hamza's scowl deepened, and he began to tut, the sound echoing ominously through the Hole. He motioned to one of his guards, who quickly handed him a sack of lentils. Hamza untied the sack and began to empty it slowly, letting the precious grains spill out, mixing with the sands outside the Hole.

"Tsk, tsk, tsk," he continued, his eyes glinting with malice. "Such a shame. Only half the supplies this month as punishment."

The guards followed his lead, emptying the remaining sacks until only half of the original contents were left. The miners watched in silent fury and help-lessness, knowing they could do nothing.

"Now," he said. "Mehdi, why don't you deliver me your slab."

At his word, the guards worked to lower the wooden platform. It descended through the air until it hit the cave floor with a soft tap. A hiss above drew Reema's attention to the gleam of unsheathed swords.

Mehdi clenched his fists, his face red with anger. "We cannot survive on half a bag, Captain."

Hamza shrugged. "Then you should feel *inspired* to meet the monthly quota. You slaves have been put down in the earth for one reason, and one reason only. *Deliver. My. Marble.*"

Mehdi opened his mouth to speak, but Hamza stopped him with a raised finger.

"Say something other than 'yes, Captain' and I'll reduce your bag by another half."

Mehdi's lips drew back over his teeth, and his veins strained against his neck. The words must have tasted like poison coming from his mouth.

"Yes. Captain."

His men pushed the marble block onto the platform, and the guards began to heave it upwards. A moment later, the half-bag full of lentils hit the ground, and a cloud of marble dust rose into the air.

Mehdi snatched it and began to stalk away, throwing a hatred-filled look over his shoulder at Reema.

"Renfri."

Renfri said nothing as she had her gang load up the block. She waited for the captain's humiliation, but instead, her half-full lentil bag flew down through the Hole. She caught it and scurried away before the Captain could think twice.

Hoping she would get the same treatment, Reema motioned for Omar and Ra'ad to load their slab up. But she was not so lucky.

"What is that?"

Reema froze, a deep, frustrated sigh escaping through bared teeth.

"That is not a block of marble, as demanded. It is *hardly* a slab."

Reema glanced up at the Captain, squinting against the light. "It's all we've got."

"It's all you've got?" The Captain seemed genuinely stunned at the day's poor results. He shook his head and grabbed her bag of lentils from the guard. "You're lucky to get a single sundamned grain."

He upended it. Reema was forced to watch as her bag was reduced to less than a fifth.

"Now, bring me—"

Hamza's eyes landed on Alaric. His brow furrowed.

"He's still alive."

Alaric remained calm and resolute, though he took one small step back into the darkness as though it would protect him from whatever Hamza had in mind.

"I can't believe it. *How* is he still alive? And what is that? An Angel-damned cane?" He shook his head in disbelief. He fit the pipe to his mouth and took a long drag from it, blowing the smoke down the Hole. "Unacceptable. I promised the slave master he wouldn't last."

He pointed the pipe at Reema.

"It's your lucky day, my beautiful monster," he said, his voice dripping with mockery. "I'm about to make you a deal you can't refuse."

"I'm listening," she said.

"Two full sacks of lentils if you kill him right now. A handsome reward for what must surely be a thorn in your side, don't you think?"

Reema's heart pounded in her chest. She glanced at Alaric, who stood motionless, waiting. The gang's eyes were on her, waiting for her decision. The promise of food was tempting, especially with the risk that they might starve before they reached the Djinn. But she knew she could not give in to Hamza's twisted game.

"No," she said firmly, her voice steady. "I don't think I'll be doing that."

Hamza's smile faded, replaced by a look of cold fury. "Maybe you misunderstood. It wasn't an option. Kill him. Now. And I'll think about still giving you the two sacks."

"Because he's Bloodlined?"

Captain Hamza's face paled. He glanced at the other guards, who exchanged looks of confusion.

Reema's gang nodded at her, letting her know they were with her.

"Alright, Captain," she said.

The Captain's eyes lit up.

She jerked a thumb over her shoulder. "I think the twins have something to say to you."

His gaze flicked toward them, and they dropped their linen trousers, grabbing their nuts.

"How about you come down and empty *these* sacks instead!" Omar shouted, while Ra'ad made grotesque noises to the side before they both burst into laughter.

The Captain hissed in rage and emptied their lentils onto the sands outside the Hole.

"We're done here, boys," he said to the guards, his gaze fixed on Reema. "We're wasting our time talking to walking corpses."

With a dismissive wave, he backed away from the Hole with the guards.

Reema watched him go, her heart heavy with the weight of their situation. The gang was silent, the tension still thick in the air. They were in a bad situation, and they all knew it. There were no more lentils or even dates back at the cave.

"Who would you like to do more, Asif?" she asked. "Renfri or Mehdi?"

The shadows were deep in the pits of his eyes as he answered, "Mehdi."

"Then we need to move," she said. "I want to catch him before he's back in the safety of his territory."

"What's happening?" Alaric asked.

As the others grabbed their pickaxes, Reema turned to Alaric. "We're going to do what it takes to survive. So keep up, Bloodlined. You don't want to get lost in the western veins."

Reema led her gang to the mouth of the tunnel Mehdi disappeared into, and with a deep breath, she entered.

CHAPTER
TWENTY-TWO

The western veins were far different from the rest of the mines. Where some sections, like the central pit and the northern quarry, had wider passages that accommodated large blocks of marble and groups of miners working them, the western veins had tight, narrow passages that required the blocks to be narrow and long. Their tunnels curved and twisted, making it a wonder that Mehdi was ever able to get any blocks out of there at all.

Reema supposed that anything was possible when you put a whip to a man's back. Give him a bit of pain, some food and water to soothe it, and he'll do whatever's demanded of him. Of course, it helped that Mehdi had a reputation for valuing the lives of his miners even less than the marble dust that covered the tunnel floors.

Reema squeezed between the walls, thanking the Angel for once that she was starved and skinny. The other members of her gang had a rough go of it, particularly Asif, whose shirt tore a little more every time he had to squeeze through a section of the tunnels. His body was covered in scrapes. But as bad as Asif had it, she suspected that Alaric had it worse.

He was panting, trying to keep his breath even as he squirmed through the tunnel, trying to keep pace with them. His wounds were catching up to him. She could tell by the way he was grimacing and grunting every time he bumped into the walls.

Reema couldn't focus on him, though. She had to make sure that she was leading them in the right direction, because if they got lost, then they weren't just at Mehdi's mercy. They were at the mercy of this cruel earth. They say that for as many veins as there are in your body, there are ten times more in this section of the mines. Squeezing through these tunnels, Reema believed it.

Behind her, Alaric cursed and fell, banging his head against the wall. The sound echoed painfully through the tunnel.

Asif hissed at Alaric in frustration. Omar reached back and yanked Alaric to his feet.

Shaking her head, she continued forward, only to come to a stop. The narrow tunnel opened up to what looked like a bridge, with a depth to the darkness that not even the torchlight could pierce. The bridge couldn't have been more than a foot wide.

"Angel's balls," Ra'ad gasped when he looked over her shoulder and caught a glimpse of the path ahead.

"Where do you think *that* falls to?" Omar asked, his voice as soft as Ra'ad's.

"Quiet," Reema whispered back to them.

She bit her lip. This was the perfect place for Mehdi to ambush them. There was limited space for them to fight, which for his weakened and injured miners was perfect. And the way back was torturously slow to pass through.

"What do you think?" Reema asked Asif in a voice no louder than a breath.

"Could double back, try and find the path they took to bring the marble block to the Hole?"

She shook her head. "This is the way that Mehdi took. I'm positive."

"How?"

She raised her finger, showing him a speck of blood she'd wiped off the tunnel wall from where one of Mehdi's gang had pressed against it.

He grimaced and began to run his hand through his long, unruly beard. "Have the twins head up front, and I'll go behind them. Can you keep that blind bastard in line and make sure he doesn't fall over the edge?"

Reema thought on it but could come up with no better ideas of what they should do. They couldn't go back. They'd lose Mehdi and his gang and potentially get lost trying to find him. The only option was to go forward, and the order Asif suggested was probably the best. The twins were good with tight spaces. And she was the reason Alaric was still around, so it made sense for her to keep an eye on him herself.

With a heavy sigh, she nodded.

Asif tied the end of his pickaxe around a loop in his tunic and slung it over his shoulder, choosing instead to draw his marble shiv. If Mehdi and his men chose to ambush them here, it was a better option.

She motioned for Omar and Ra'ad. "Get over here."

They stepped forward, taking care not to fall over the lip of the edge. Her foot bumped against a small marble rock, sending it over the edge. She froze, listening for the sharp echo of the rock clattering against the walls. But she heard nothing. The silence was even more eerie because it meant there was no bottom to it.

Goosebumps ran across her arm, but Reema buried any hint of the fear creeping through her. She was the fearless Ifrit, the ruthless gang lord of the southern mines that all others feared. These mines were her domain. She ruled them. They did not rule her.

She slid behind Asif, taking hold of Alaric's arm. She leaned in and whispered in his ear.

"We're about to cross a very tight and narrow bridge. We need to be quick about it, but if you fall, there's no saving you."

"That doesn't sound good," he said with a smirk, though she heard the gulp as he swallowed. He wasn't stupid. A blind man making his way across a foot-wide bridge wasn't exactly ideal.

"I'm serious. If you fall, I can't help you, because you'll pull me down with you."

His smirk disappeared and he nodded. "I understand."

She drew a deep breath. "Good."

She passed the torch ahead to the twins. The torch crackled, the shadows danced off the walls, gathering in the pits of their eyes. With grim determination, they began to cross.

First Omar, then Ra'ad behind him.

Asif waited for them to take a few steps ahead, giving them space to slide forward before he followed.

Reema went next, her hand on Alaric's wrist to guide him. She didn't dare look back, for fear of losing her balance. The wrapped tip of his makeshift cane tapped gently against the stone bridge. Normally, Reema didn't think much of that sound; it wasn't enough to draw attention in the tunnel.

But here, where the silence of the earth seemed to amplify every small sound, including the pounding of her own heart and the heavy breaths of the others ahead, it was painful to listen to.

Beads of sweat ran down her nose, tickling her face. She did her best to ignore it, keeping her arms outstretched to remain balanced.

The tension was suffocating, knowing that each step was a potential death sentence. It didn't help that the torchlight flickered, casting eerie shadows that played tricks on them and their already frayed nerves.

Suddenly, Alaric's foot slipped to the side, and he wavered dangerously over the edge. Reema's heart leapt into her throat as she pulled him back. She felt her balance start to waver but lowered her center of gravity and caught herself.

"You idiot," she hissed, her voice barely above a whisper. The fear in her eyes was mirrored back at her by the steel band around his skull. "You almost got us killed!"

He grimaced, steadied himself, and gripped his cane tighter.

She didn't wait for an apology. They had to continue inching their way across; otherwise, they'd get stuck too far back behind Omar and lose sight of the bridge's path. That was the last thing they needed: the stone path of the bridge disappearing into the pool of shadows on either side of them.

Every inch gained felt like an eternity, her nerves spiking even at the touch of her marble dusted dark hair brushing against her shoulders. Reema dared a glance forward and breathed a sigh of relief when she saw that Omar had neared the other side.

Just then, a chilling sound pierced the oppressive silence—a sharp crack from behind. Her blood froze.

"Reema!" Asif roared.

She searched the darkness ahead for some sign of Mehdi, but she could see nothing.

"Behind you!"

She spun around, her balance on the bridge dangerously wavering, and saw Mehdi standing at the mouth of the tight tunnel they'd come from. His torch flickered violently beside him, the scar across his face twisting as a slow, toothy grin appeared.

Two of his men were standing at the edge of the bridge, pickaxes in their hands. The steel tips of the pickaxes gleamed as they rose.

"Run!" Reema screamed. Marble dust sprinkled down on them from above.

Omar and Ra'ad's curses spilled through the air as they scrambled forward, the torchlight dancing back and forth, making it almost impossible for Reema and Alaric to follow Asif.

Three more miners appeared ahead, their bodies covered in whip scars.

Omar crashed into them, knocking one down into the void below. He dropped the torch, and sparks flew as it rolled to the edge. Ra'ad snatched it up before it could fall, only to feel the plunge of a shiv in his shoulder. By the time Asif made it across, Omar and Ra'ad had killed the remaining men.

But they weren't what worried Reema, and judging by the lack of care on Mehdi's face, it seemed he expected it. Those men were simply there to slow them down, to slow *her* down.

Bone-chilling cracks echoed through the disturbed silence, and a deep groan rumbled through the bridge. Her instincts screamed for her to rush, to make it across in time. But no matter how much she wished she could, she couldn't leave Alaric behind. She dragged him forward with reckless abandon.

Her heart dropped as the flickering torchlight allowed the shadows to creep back on her path, and she took a wrong step. She began to fall, only to feel Alaric's tight grip around her wrist. With veins strained against his neck, he pulled her back onto the bridge.

The bridge groaned again and fell another half inch as crack after crack echoed from behind them. Mehdi began to laugh because he knew he had them.

A slow realization came over her.

This was it.

This was how they would die.

Reema turned and faced Alaric, her heart strangely slow and calm, as though she was resigned to death. Staring at him, she suddenly wished that she could have felt his lips against hers. That she could have felt the warmth of his skin against hers. That despite his Blood-lined heritage, she could have once, just once, felt his gaze upon her.

But that, too, his father had stolen from her.

He surprised her by raising a hand to her face. "Reema, I—"

The bridge broke.

The stone beneath their feet gave way. The world tilted and rolled. Her book fell from her waistband and plunged into the deep. Alaric clung to her, but they were helpless as they fell into the void.

And as they fell, his hand slipped from hers.

TWENTY-THREE

When Reema opened her eyes, she was greeted by a darkness so complete it shrouded even her own hand from her vision. It wormed its way into her chest, choking the sound of her own breathing, drowning her in such profound silence that she couldn't help but wonder if she had died.

Was this what the hells were like? Not the burning flames that drew screams tearing at the throat, but rather this maddening, consuming *nothingness*?

Then the pain came.

Reema was no stranger to pain, but even she could not stifle a gasp and whimper as it sliced bone-deep, coursing from her ankle up to her hip. She reached down, trying to feel out her injury, but it was impossible to discern anything in the suffocating darkness.

A wave of terror washed over her.

She patted the ground frantically, searching for a torch that she knew did not exist. Even if by some miracle it did, she wasn't sure she knew how to light it from down here in these cold, cruel depths of the earth. Her breathing became erratic as her hand settled on something too fragile to be stone. A soft clatter echoed gently around her. She picked up a fragment and drew it close to her face.

She had long since learned in her years spent in the mines that bones had a very distinct smell. It was an odd, earthy scent, tinged with just a hint of the decay of the brain that had rotted away inside.

The bone fragment fell from her trembling hands.

She told herself it was a figment of her imagination, that she was hallucinating. But as she continued to feel around, her hand brushed against another skull fragment. Her fingers traced the exposed, rotted teeth. Her thumb ran along the curve of the eye socket and across where a nose once was.

A scream pierced the void, swallowed whole by the cavernous darkness enveloping her. It took a moment for her to realize that the scream had erupted from her own lips as she discovered she was lying in a bed of countless souls who had met the same fate—fallen from the bridge, just like her.

Then a scream followed hers, so deafening that she was forced to clamp her hands over her ears. Each shift she made sent a cascade of bone fragments sliding down around her. She glanced around in a panic, trying to see some sign of the woman who'd screamed back at her. But there was nothing. No one.

The scream that followed hers was *her own*.

And that could only mean one thing. In these depths that she was trapped in, there was no exit, no place for her scream to escape, no place for *her* to escape.

She would die down here.

Madness tugged at the edge of her consciousness, its siren call begging her to open up her mind. It was not the first time she had heard its song. There were many times she had come to the edge of madness. But never before did she lack confidence in her ability to draw back, to find herself. Not until now.

A soft clatter echoed. Reema looked up. Another clatter followed.

Someone—some*thing*—was coming for her.

A voice slithered through the emptiness, a soft whisper that sent chills down her spine.

"Reema."

She scrambled back, ignoring the sudden sharpness of pain in her leg. Her mouth parted, her heart pounded, and a fear as terrifying as she'd ever felt surfaced in her. The voice spoke with such softness that she could not help but feel a sense of familiarity in it.

"Hana?"

The clattering stopped.

She raised her voice, trying to push herself to her feet. "Hana, is that you?"

"No."

The answering voice was nothing like Hana's. It was deep, low, and husky in a way that made her heart throb. It was full of sadness and despair over a pain that was not his.

"It's me. Alaric."

She breathed a heavy sigh of relief, and she hated

herself for it. She wasn't sure why she was so glad that it wasn't her, or why she'd been so afraid that it could've been her. Maybe because if it was, her sister would have had something to say about the monster she had become after all these years in the mines, about the cruelty that had settled in her heart and turned to stone as cold as the ones that surrounded them.

A hand brushed against hers, its warmth instinctively pulling her closer. She stepped into Alaric's arms and breathed him in. He smelled like blood and sweat, but she didn't care. And it seemed that whatever she may have smelled like, he didn't care either. His arms looped around her with a tightness that told her he, too, was afraid he'd lost her.

"Are you hurt?" she asked.

"Somehow, no. The bones must have softened my landing. Are you okay?"

She winced. "I'll be fine."

"Not often you get to thank the dead like this."

Reema grunted. "You'll get to thank them closer soon enough. We'll be dead."

He started to speak until he felt her hand on his face. She pressed a finger to his lips and silenced him.

"Don't say a word," she said. "Did you hear how my scream echoed? There's no escape from down here. No way except to climb up and—"

She winced as another wave of pain passed through her leg.

"You're blind and I'm injured. That's not going to happen. We're going to die."

Alaric took her hand in his, and though she could not

see him, she could picture his face in her mind: stubbornly defiant, that sundamned smirk playing at the corner of his lips like he knew something she did not.

Something sprinkled down over her face. She flinched backward, blinking it from her eyes as she wiped her face clean.

"What was that?" she asked, frustration and a hint of panic creeping into her voice.

"Your magical wish, sprinkled with my very own special marble dust," he said.

She frowned. "This isn't the time for jokes, Alaric."

"And who said I'm joking? I have a deal for you, Reema. Ask me what it is."

She pursed her lips. "What is it?"

"I'm going to help you survive this place."

Something about the way he said that lit a candle in this deep, unyielding darkness, giving her hope. It was foolish, to dare to hope. But she could not help herself. He made her want to hope for something better than to die a meaningless death amidst a bed of bones.

"And what will I do for you?" she asked.

His warm breath brushed across her ear. "The unthinkable."

Despite how filthy she felt, covered in marble dust, blood, and Angel knows what else, she felt her skin flush as a wave of heat burned in her core. It screamed for him to do it, to take the next step that she, the fearsome Ifrit of the southern mines, was so afraid to take.

She felt his presence, drawing nearer to her, even though they already stood chest to chest. his warm breath spilled across her face, and she could sense that his lips were but inches away from hers. Somehow, even in this Angel-forsaken place, he knew where she was.

"What is that?" she asked, her voice breathless.

"When we're free of this place, and we're safe, you're going to read me anything I want."

Her mind turned back to Faisal and Tasneem's wedding night. Her hand instinctively went to her waist, only to feel its absence. And that, more than anything, left her with a chill that made her shiver.

His hand trailed down her arm to where her hand lingered by her waist.

"I don't have the book anymore," she said. The lump in her throat was difficult to swallow past. "I must have lost it in the fall."

Then, in a much smaller voice, she apologized, perhaps for the first time since Hana died.

"I'm sorry."

There was a quiet moment of hesitation, and she could feel the pain of loss in it. But then a soft palm pressed against her cheek. "Don't be sorry. I will have you read me something from another book. But do not think I'll torture you any less."

She scowled and brushed away his hand, missing its warmth the instant it was gone. "You think I'm sorry for *you*? I'm sorry for myself. I won't get to see how Faisal gets his revenge."

It was a lie. She was sorry for him because his mother had given him that book. And now it was lost forever.

He chuckled. "Lucky for you, I've memorized it."

"The whole book? Word for word?"

"As I said, it was my mother's favorite. I'd always

worried that my father would take it from me, burn it, and make me watch. So I made sure it was something he could never take from me."

She struggled to comprehend how so many words could fit in a person's mind, but somehow, she didn't doubt him. Alaric had shown her that he was capable of so much more than she could have imagined.

A moment of silence passed.

"So, does Faisal get his revenge?"

"Listen, and—"

"Find out. Asshole."

"Let's find the way out of here. You okay to walk?"

She tested her leg. A heavy gasp escaped her lips when she put her full weight down on it, but she found that if she leaned on him, it was manageable. He wrapped his arm around her waist and supported her.

"You don't have your cane," she said.

"We'll be okay."

They started forward, every step knocking aside fragments of miners who'd broken in the fall. It was luck that she hadn't, but it was something more that the both of them had survived. Maybe it was fate. She hoped so. Because if that was the case, then there was something great in store for them. An end that meant something. An end that meant justice.

A skull cracked underfoot, the sound echoing back at her with ruthless claws, tearing into her thoughts and drawing forth a panic she hadn't known since she'd first been thrown down the Hole.

Alaric pulled her closer.

"Don't be afraid of the dark."

She could feel the lost souls of the miners around her almost laughing at the comment.

"Why shouldn't I be?" she asked.

"Because it's just you and me down here. This darkness is ours."

The panic dissipated. The pain faded away. She smiled.

"Read to me, Bloodlined. Let me hear your voice."

TWENTY-FOUR

Alaric cast a spell over her, his voice entrancing her the same way it had the first time she'd heard him. At first, she thought it had something to do with the Angel's blood running through him, but she knew that was a fool's thought. It had nothing to do with the Angel, and everything to do with him.

Beneath the Sands of Sorrow was the world his mother loved, the world *he* loved, and there was proof enough in the way the words spilled forth with confidence, passion, and... something else that drew her in, made her want to never stop listening to him.

She clung to him as they stepped over the bones, as they squeezed through narrow tunnels that clawed and scraped at them. The darkness they were trapped in, the darkness he led her through, was but a whisper at the back of her mind as he recited the book to her.

Amira returned that night.
Faisal opened his door to her, his brown eyes

meeting her glowing hazel ones, both filled with the same desperation to hear more of the one they loved and both feeling the same fear of the pain that would surface through their cracked hearts from the resurgence of their memories.

He stepped aside. He, like her, knew that even one more moment with the mere idea of Tasneem was worth the breaking of the heart all over again.

She took a seat at his table.

He sat across from her.

It was a small battle of wills, to see who would submit to the other and who would be the first to suffer the pain. They sat in silence for what felt like an eternity, him staring at her with Tasneem's ring rolling back and forth in his palm. And she stared at him, as still as stone.

In the end, he was the one to break. Maybe it was the warmth of Tasneem's ring in his hand, he wasn't sure.

At first, his words were tentative. Slow to come, like the sucking of moisture from grains of rice. He told her of the first time that he and Tasneem had ever met, and of how he'd walked the same alley hoping to bump into her again the next day.

He hadn't planned to give up the depth of what he felt for her. Hadn't planned to fall into his words, stumbling over them in a rush as they poured forth from him like the sands of a sandstorm. He tried to stop himself, to guard his heart, but he couldn't—not even when he arrived at the night of their marriage.

Not until he reached the moment of Tasneem's death.

Then it was all silence.

Such cold, painful silence.

He looked up into Amira's eyes. Trails of tears had marked their path down her cheeks. She reached over the table and touched his hand but said nothing, because what was there to say?

Faisal suddenly realized that his candle had long since burned itself away and that daylight was creeping through his shuttered windows.

"Do you need to go?" he asked.

She frowned. "Go?"

"It is daylight."

Amira glanced to the side, like she too was surprised at how much time had passed. She stood, went to the window, waited for a long minute. Then she ripped the board away from the window, spilling light across his chambers.

"Then let us pretend that the sunlight belongs to my sister. Let's pretend we can bask in it, like she's not dead."

It was the strangest thing to say, but as he opened his mouth to object, he felt the sun's warmth across his skin. He dared to close his eyes, dared to imagine Tasneem's warm hands against his face.

When he opened them, he found Amira sitting across from him with a smile.

"Let me tell you of my sister."

Alaric came to a halt, and Reema bumped into him, the sudden contact yanking her out of the world he'd woven around her in the darkness.

"What is it?" she asked.

"There's a wall in front of me."

A chill ran down her spine as her heart began to slowly fall. The candlelight of hope he'd lit in this overwhelming darkness was beginning to flicker.

"I told you we were going to die down here," she whispered, pursing her lips in frustration. She knew she shouldn't have trusted him. *She* was the one who knew the mines, not him. "My scream echoed *back*."

"And it was quieter."

"What?"

"Your scream. It was quieter, like some part of your voice escaped this place."

"Yeah, it could have escaped from where we fell."

"No ..." He released her, and a spike of panic speared through her heart. She clutched back out for him again, only to find him kneeling down. She could hear his hand patting against the marble stone wall, like he was searching for something.

Then he cursed.

"What is it? What did you find?"

"There *is* a way out, but it's not a good one."

"Damn the deep, Alaric, just *tell* me."

He straightened and reached out for her hand, connecting them once again. "There's a slit at the base of the wall. It's small, just wide enough for a person to squeeze through. Well ... wide enough for you."

She paled at the suggestion he was making and squeezed past him. Biting her lip against the pain, she got down on one knee and felt along the wall. He was right. There *was* a gap, and she'd probably fit, but it'd be with the weight of the earth pressing her down into stone. And there was no telling if it was really a way out. Alaric could still be wrong about that.

Still, there *was* a reason this place was called the western veins. It was said that just as the veins of the body lead to every limb and every organ, so do the western veins of the mines. She knew there was a seed of truth to it, but something like this ...

"Reema."

She froze, turning her head slowly as if she could see him through the dark. The way he spoke had a certain kind of finality to it, as if he was about to say his goodbyes.

"I—"

"No," she hissed.

"You know that I can't fi—"

"Then I'll *drag* you through it, if that's what it takes," she said, her body tensing as she rose. She gripped his hand so hard that she could hear him draw a sharp breath. "I'm not letting go of you, you sundamned bastard. We're getting out of here together."

He started to speak again, only to stop when she squeezed his hand even tighter. The warmth of his sigh kissed her face.

"And to think I was about to spoil the ending for you."

"You were going to tell me how Faisal gets his revenge?" she asked. "Why not just tell me now? You know, just in case?"

He chuckled. "Listen and—"

"Oh, fuck off and die in a hole."

"I've tried that. It's not going so well."

Something about the way he said that made her laugh. It was small at first, but then it began to bubble up through her until she could not help but wipe the tears from her face as her voice boomed back at her. She could not remember a time she had laughed so hard since witnessing Hana's death.

She could sense Alaric's smile. She wanted to say something about it, but the truth was, it was just nice to know that there was still a smile or two to be had in these dark depths.

"Well, boss?" he asked. "Are you ready?"

She shook her head, then realized that he couldn't see her, just as she couldn't see him now. "How'd you get used to it so quickly?"

"Used to what?"

"The darkness. Not being able to see anything."

"I had a stick. It helped. Of course, it's gone now, but it was enough to give me the confidence to figure it out. The stick was helpful, but it was only ever an extension of myself, you know? My arms are still here, and I can still feel the walls around me. It might take a little longer, require a little more effort, but I know I'll find my way. That *we* will find our way."

Her lip curled, any trace of laughter fading away. Somehow, she had a feeling that he wasn't talking about his makeshift cane anymore.

"You think I'm misguided," she said.

"No. I think you're lost."

"Don't worry. When I do what must be done, when I get the justice Hana deserves, *then* I'll be found."

He didn't say anything.

Her leg throbbed painfully enough her to take a seat. She could feel the gap against her lower back, like it was daring for her to enter. She ignored its call, leaning her head back against the marble and breathed.

She was asleep before she knew it.

CHAPTER
TWENTY-FIVE

Something gently tapped her shoulder.

Reema jerked awake, hissing as a sudden sharp pain coursed from her leg up through her hips and back. Curses spilled from her mouth, only to be met with Alaric's apologies.

"I didn't mean to hurt you," he said.

She gripped her leg. It was swollen. She could feel it now, like she had a deep bone bruise. This wasn't going to go away easily. With a deep growl, she forced the pain into a small box in her mind and slammed the door shut. This wasn't the time or place to let something like that bother her.

"How long's it been?" she asked.

"I don't know. Not long, though."

"Did anything happen?" It was a stupid question. They were stuck someplace no miner had ever seen and lived. The enveloping silence was proof enough that nothing had happened. "Ignore that. Are you ready?"

He grunted. It seemed he wasn't exactly at ease about what they were about to do.

It occurred to her that he had never had to squeeze through a tough place like this before. Though not *quite* this tight, she had experienced something close enough to know what it would be like.

There's something especially terrifying about how the earth sits on your chest, and there is absolutely nothing you can do about it; there is no pushing it off you, no scrambling away. You start to panic, start to hyperventilate, and before you know it, you're trying to force your way through the earth.

That's how you die.

There's a dance that you have to take with the earth, where slowly, ever so slowly, you slide your way through it. You don't think about the tightness of your chest, how difficult it is to breathe, or how if you get stuck, that is where you'll die of thirst and hunger, trapped in the folds of panic until your very final moment.

Reema pictured Alaric trapped in the gap, his terrified voice screaming for her to help him. It had happened before, in the past, with other miners. Rogue miners she used to roam with before she forged her path as a gang lord. The image of Alaric breaking like that was hard to stomach because it was impossible to imagine, and yet, she knew that if he got stuck, that was exactly what would happen.

Alaric, despite his quiet strength, was at his core, human.

And like all humans, they break when pushed hard enough.

Reema drew a deep breath and pressed a hand to his arm. She could tell by the sound of his breathing that he was nervous, and her willing touch made him even more so.

"I'm going to hate this, won't I?" he asked, his voice full of empty humor.

"You will," she said. "But at some point, it'll be over and done with. Whatever you do, don't panic, okay?"

"I don't panic," he said.

"Good."

She waited a minute, feeling a strange magnetic pull toward him. Her stomach fluttered with butterflies. It took her a moment to realize why. His breathing was heavier, and she wondered if it had to do with the thought of crawling between the cracks of the earth, or if it was because of how close they were standing.

She swallowed past the lump in her throat. She licked her lips, running her tongue over the cracks. She knew that if she waited but a heartbeat longer, he would pull her into his arms and kiss her.

And that would be the end of her.

That would be the end of Hana's justice.

She turned away, digging her fingers into her palm. A curse slipped through her lips, and it had nothing to do with the pain in her leg as she lay down next to the wall.

"Don't panic," she told him again.

Then she pushed herself into the earth.

Marble dust spread across her face, smooth at first until she wedged herself deeper into the earth. The smoothness gave way to jagged rock that clawed at her cheekbones. Her breathing tightened as the earth pressed against her belly, leaving her no room for her lungs to expand. She realized that every time she had ever done this, she had been able to at least see a shadow of the path she was going down. This time, she did not have even that.

A wave of panic passed through her, rising like the winds of a sandstorm, before she buried it with solid conviction.

She *would* get through this.

She stretched a hand forward, running her hand against the ceiling and the floor she was forced to fit between. As much as she wanted to use the hand to help shift her body, she needed to make sure that the path forward was safe, that she wasn't going to get stuck like she warned Alaric about.

A heavy grunt brought her to a halt. She wanted to turn her head back, to look and see if Alaric was okay, but even if she could see through the dark, the earth would not allow it. There was no room to even turn her head.

"Are you okay?" she gasped, remembering how difficult it was to speak.

Alaric growled in response, his voice rumbling through the dark like a demon's. He pressed himself through the earth. The eerie scrape of steel against marble echoed. She could hear his sharp intake of breath every time the marble dug into his bones.

As they made their way through the earth, time ceased to be a concept. All they knew was the pain of marble scraping against their skulls, the continual sound and echo of Alaric's steel band scraping against the stone, and the pain and suffocated breaths. It was miserable, but they knew they could not stop.

Reema had always known that the earth was a living, breathing thing. But it had never proven more true than there, stuck between a crack in the earth, feeling the weight ever so slightly shift just enough for her to pass through, only to press down again onto Alaric, drawing pain-filled gasps and grunts.

In an effort to escape the torture, she allowed her mind to go elsewhere. She thought of Amira and wondered if she felt Faisal's rage. After all, she, too, had lost Tasneem.

The more she thought about Amira, the more she felt a strange sort of kinship. It was strange to say, given that she was a Commonborn and Amira was a Bloodlined fictional character, but it was also true. There was a thread that bonded them—they'd both lost their sisters to the black whims of horrible men. She suddenly wanted to know more about Amira.

When she paused to let her muscles rest for a moment, she gasped to Alaric, "Do we find out more about Amira?"

"What?" he asked, clearly taken by surprise at the sudden question.

"The Bloodlined sister."

He grunted, and Reema's skin crawled at the long, eerie scrape of metal against stone.

"Yes," he answered.

Satisfied, she kept pushing into the earth, and into the pain that followed.

Space.

Reema froze, the tips of her fingers lingering in the open space. She moved her hand around, trying to find where the earth was, but she found nothing. Adrenaline and relief both passed through her, rejuvenating her efforts to be free of the sundamned gap.

"Alaric. We're here."

He was wheezing now. It was hard to listen to, but it was good. It meant he was still alive and still close behind her.

"Go," he whispered, his voice no louder than a breath.

Reema squirmed her way through the rock, her desire to be free making her a little reckless, earning more than a few scrapes and cuts against the stone. But she didn't care, because the moment she pulled herself free of the gap, it was like the heavens touched down against the earth. She drew a deep breath that left her close to tears.

A grunt drew her attention back to the gap, and she reached for him. Their fingers locked together, and she helped pull him free. He didn't say anything, but the way he pressed himself into her chest let her know he had thought he was going to die trapped under the earth.

They sat like that for a while, holding each other, savoring the feeling of being able to draw a full breath. Their bodies seemed almost hesitant to breathe that deep, like they thought they were still trapped. Eventually, they relaxed, the tension evaporating into the cold silence around them.

"I never want to do that again," Alaric said.

"Whatever happened to all your bravado? That you were going to show me how to survive this place?" she asked.

It took him a moment to realize she was teasing him. Hells, it took *her* a moment to realize it too. Was this flirting?

Before she could process that thought, she realized there was something seeping through the darkness, softening it enough that she could see the very faint outline of... something. She frowned as she realized it was coming from him.

"What is that?" she muttered, reaching out.

Her fingers brushed against the edge of the steel band, and she froze. The tiniest hint of glowing light danced across her fingertips.

"What is it?" he asked.

She touched her fingers to the edge of the steel band. Her mouth parted. It was hard to tell, so slicked with blood from cuts across his temple and cheeks, but the band was damaged.

There was light leaking from it.

A sudden urge passed through her, and before she knew what she was doing, she tried to dig her fingers underneath the band. He pulled back with a startled curse, no doubt feeling the pain of every cut and scrape he'd endured. She tried to yank it off to see his face, but the sundamned band wasn't budging.

"What're you doing?" he asked, grabbing her wrists and pulling her away from him.

"The band, it's damaged."

He drew a deep breath. Then he let her go.

She tried again, doing her best at first not to hurt him, but soon abandoning that in favor of simply trying to free him. She wished she could say that it was because it would help them get free of this place, to find a way out. But that wouldn't be true. It was because she had a heart-aching desire to feel his eyes upon her.

For all her efforts, though, she made no progress. She released him with a frustrated shout and sat back. Both of them panted—her from the exertion and him from the pain he felt. They sat there for a while, steeped in disappointment.

Then he spoke, his voice soft and hopeless, "Maybe someday."

"Maybe." In an attempt to turn his mind away from the band, she asked, "How did you manage to escape the miners? Back in the southern mines?"

The silence between them dragged. Just when she began to doubt that he would answer, he spoke.

"I thought it'd be easy. After all, I could just take any tunnel I wanted, get lost and it wouldn't matter. They had to keep track of me." She heard the brush of his finger running along his ragged beard, and the sound of marble dust flaking out of it. "For the most part, that was true. But there were a few stragglers who I couldn't shake."

"What happened?"

Somehow, she sensed his blind gaze on her, heavy

and disturbed, and the darkness around her shifted into something *else*.

"I killed them."

She chewed on the inside of her lip. She'd seen him angry, knew that his rage was just as great as hers, and yet, every time he came to the cusp of spilling blood, he stopped. She struggled to imagine him taking that final, soul-shattering step.

"How many?" she asked.

"Five."

Her eyes bulged, and she gaped. "Five?"

"It was easy enough once the torch went out."

She didn't know what to say. She thought back to when she'd left him in the northern quarry, helpless against Zayd's miners. She was sure that he was going to die if she didn't step in. But she wasn't so sure of that now.

"I couldn't see their faces, but I imagine them, you know. Everywhere I look, they're right there, looking back at me."

She shifted her leg, her mind turning back to the first person she killed. He hadn't even done anything, except make the mistake of looking somewhat like the slave master.

"I warned them to stop, that I wanted to let them go." He released a heavy breath. "Turns out I'm more like my father than I thought."

Reema frowned. "You're nothing like him."

"You didn't see me. I was ruthless, Reema."

"Still."

"What about when I was fighting Asif, or when I

fought that gang lord, Salman? You heard me use his very words: let's see who you are."

Reema reached for him, her hand clasping over his. "Trust me. I know more than anyone the difference between you and your father."

He was quiet at that.

"Your father did not warn my sister before he murdered her. He wore a smile the whole time, like her life meant nothing." She squeezed his hand. "You *warned* those miners before you fought them."

He was quiet, but he was listening to her. His hand turned over, so that their palms were against each other, so that their fingers could interlace.

Reema winced against her throbbing leg and pressed forward against him, resting her free hand on his chest. His heart was beating so hard, so fast.

"Do you know why I haven't cut you up and left you for dead?"

"I have an idea," he whispered.

Goosebumps rose all along her arms as his other hand pressed over hers, so that they could both feel his heart race. Reema knew that if she pressed her hand to her own chest, she would feel it racing in sync.

"You're compassionate. You're merciful. You like to read, for Angel's sake. What kind of bad man *reads*?"

He grumbled, but he could not come up with an answer.

"So listen to me, you fool."

She leaned in, until she could feel his breath brushing across her lips.

"You are a good man."

His forehead pressed against hers. It felt like her heart was going to beat out of her chest.

"And you? Do you believe you're good too?"

She smiled sadly. "No, I know I'm not. I would not have warned those miners before I slaughtered them."

"We disagree there."

Her brow rose. "You really think that the infamous Ifrit would have warned them?"

"I think there is more to the Ifrit than she lets on."

Her heart tumbled and skipped a beat, her breath hitching in her chest.

She inched forward, drawn by the inevitable pull of him. She wanted to kiss him, wanted to get a taste of the beautiful soul that lingered within the tortured man in front of her. But at the final moment, she hesitated because she knew that if they did kiss, there would be no going back. She had to stay focused on her sister. There was nobody else who could avenge her.

Reema drew back.

Alaric's hand snaked forward and grabbed her wrist. She froze, her heart dead still in her chest. The butterflies danced in a frenzy as his hand trailed up her arm to her chin. Then his thumb brushed across her lips, wiping away the marble dust, the soft inner part of her lip brushing across his thumb.

"How about I keep reading for you?" he asked as his hand fell away. "Where were we?"

Why had he done that?

She couldn't tear her mind away. She knew he liked her, but she hadn't known that he wanted her as badly as she wanted him until that moment.

"Amira was about to tell Faisal about Tasneem."

"That's right. Are you ready?"

A wave of exhaustion crashed down on her as the adrenaline from his touch drained away. With him sitting next to her, she lay down, resting her head in the crook of her arm. She knew that soon she would barely be able to keep her eyes open. But she wanted to hear the story.

"I'm ready," she said.

Instead of words, she heard the distinct sound of shuffling. She frowned, about to sit up and ask where he was going, only to feel his chest press against her back. His arm looped over her, drawing her closer to him.

"Sorry, I'm cold," he whispered in her ear.

She smiled. It was a bold-faced lie, and a terrible one at that. But she could not deny that the warmth against her back felt incredible, and that the warmth blooming in her chest felt even better. He spooned her in the deep dark, and with his lips by her ear, he read to her.

The days passed in a blur as Amira and Faisal spent every waking moment together. They ate their meals together and they walked together. Amira told him every memory she had of Tasneem, from the moment her parents took her in to the final day she saw her.

Faisal laughed when he had heard of Tasneem running through the house as a child, escaping from the servants with her clothes on her head. He cried when he heard how much Tasneem enjoyed sitting in their garden because he was reminded that he never had the opportunity to share that moment with her.

For every memory he shared, Amira seemed to have dozens more.

At first, Faisal thought Amira was simply sharing stories of her sister to fulfill her half of the deal. Then one day, as he looked at her smiling and laughing in the sunlight, he realized she was getting as much enjoyment out of it as he was.

And so, the days turned to weeks, and the weeks turned into a month.

But, as all beautiful things do, they came to an end.

Amira shared the very last memory she had of Tasneem, and they stopped in the middle of the road late at night. He turned and looked into her eyes, and she looked back into his.

This was where their deal ended. This was where he would walk away, take the flame burning in his chest, and deliver Tasneem's murderer his ruination.

But for some reason, he could not take that first step. He could not leave Amira because, over the many hours they spent together, he realized somewhere along the way that her company was ... nice.

It softened the darkness pooling inside him. It made him want something more than just revenge; it made him want to step into the daylight.

He swallowed, gave her a soft smile, and asked, "Shall we keep walking?"

It would be wrong to say that the smile Amira gave him was the most beautiful he had ever seen, because that belonged to Tasneem. But it was something else, something just as special.

She dipped her head and together, they walked the

road, late at night, caring nothing of the onlookers who wondered why a Bloodlined and a Commonborn would be walking together.

Neither said a word to the other.

It was just as well because, for the first time in a long while, both were content to enjoy the silence.

Alaric stopped reciting, and the silence rushed in to swallow them. She was on the edge of consciousness, about to slip into a realm that had once been filled with the endless nightmare of her sweet sister plummeting lifelessly through the Hole. But somehow, she felt the nightmare wouldn't be waiting for her tonight. Between the soft echo of his words and the warmth of him pressed against her back, she felt protected.

He interlaced his fingers with hers and pressed their hands against her belly, drawing her closer. They lay there in silence. His breathing was deep, like he too was falling asleep.

For as long as she'd lived in the mines, Reema thought the Bloodlined and the Commonborn could never coexist. And yet, here she was, with one against her back. As unthinkable as it was, somehow it didn't matter that he was the slave master's son.

"You don't believe the Bloodlined are capable of love?" Alaric had asked.

"Are monsters capable of it?" she had answered.

Her consciousness pulled the words from memory, dancing through the darkness with the softness of his words echoing in the background. A thought escaped her consciousness, slipping through her lips and kissing the air.

"Maybe we are," she whispered, answering her own question.

But his breathing had already deepened. As his chest rose and fell, she found herself pressing back into him. It wasn't long before she too was asleep.

TWENTY-SIX

"Tell me Amira joins Faisal's plan for revenge."

Reema clung to Alaric's shoulder as she followed him through the earth, trusting him to navigate the tunnels with both hands.

Neither had said a word about how they'd gone to sleep, and certainly not about how she'd woken to a certain pressure against her ass. In her dreams, it felt nice, but her cheeks had burned when she realized what she'd been pressing against all night. Alaric himself seemed embarrassed; it didn't take him more than a couple of minutes to get them up and going.

"Why would you think that?" he asked.

"Because I know what she must be feeling. Someone *murdered* her sister."

He paused, and she bumped into him. "Are you saying that you have something in common with a Bloodlined?"

She scowled. "I'm not saying that. But that's where

the story is going, right? Amira learns about Faisal's plan for revenge, and they go gut the bastard together."

Alaric muttered something, but it was lost in the echo of a rock clattering to the ground. Reema couldn't wait for the day they found their way back to the habitable part of the mines. It was hard enough not being able to see, but to struggle to hear against the echoes of their own sounds?

"What was that?" she asked.

"I said, of course that's the story you want to hear."

"Am I right though? That's what happens?"

He sighed. "I take it you're ready to hear more of what happens in the story."

He bumped into the wall and cursed, the color of his language surprising even her. It seemed he was getting impatient with being down here. Maybe he'd thought that they'd be free of the western veins by now.

She chuckled as she limped after him. "Come on, blind man. Prove me right."

In a soft, low voice, he continued.

Love.

It starts slow, builds moment by moment, until it springs on you all at once and then it's too late.

You're trapped.

"Wait a sundamned second," Reema interjected, unable to help herself. "You're telling me that Faisal fell for Amira? For Tasneem's *sister*?"

"Surely you saw it coming."

She didn't, and she wasn't sure what that said about her.

"This was the woman who was supposed to be his everlasting love, whose soul had been made in measure for his. And now she was gone," Reema recited. "*That's* how he felt about Tasneem. So *how* could he go for her sister?"

Alaric chuckled. "I'm surprised. Word for word. That's good."

"It's got to be the grief," she muttered, thinking aloud. "Grief makes people do stupid things. That's it, right? It's not *actual* love."

"Grief does many things. But it can bring people together too, in very real ways. And when people spend lots of time together, it's easy to fall in love. Take us, for example."

She froze, her hands slipping from his shoulder. She scrambled forward before losing track of him.

"What are you saying, Alaric?"

She could almost feel that stupid smirk spreading across his face. "I'm not saying anything, my hostile little Ifrit. Just that it's scenarios like these, *moments* like these, that the book is talking about. Moment by moment?"

She shook her head. "I don't buy it."

"Then listen to the story."

He continued to recite for her.

"Trapped" was a good word for Faisal. He did not mean to fall for Amira. He did not mean to kiss her, to feel that existential click of the heart. But he did. And he went home and cried.

He drowned in emotions: betrayal, for that was what he had done to the memory of Tasneem; despair, for not even the ember dusted addicts could be so foolish as to think that something could exist between Blood-lined and Commonborn; and perhaps most of all, rage, because he knew he could not have Amira so long as his heart was so filled with hatred for the monster that robbed him and Amira of Tasneem.

Faisal shut himself in his home once more, boarded the windows, sharpened his knives. He stoked the flames of his rage, let the devil rise up in him again so that he may have the courage to meet the murderer and end him for Tasneem, for himself, for Amira.

Knocks came at the door.

Every day, they came.

He did not answer. He hid, buried his breaths. Ignored the glowing hazel eyes attempting to peer through the cracks of his boarded windows.

When the day came that he was ready, there were no knocks. He was grateful for it too, because when he stepped out the door, cloaked in his grief and rage, he was all too aware it was unlikely that he would return.

He walked across the sands, heading for the prison where the guards kept the murderer. He tried not to think about how Amira would suffer if he was caught and sent to the gallows to be hung.

He buried that thought deep within the recesses of his mind.

There was room for only one thought, he told himself.

Revenge.

Reema thought that she'd be excited when they arrived at this point in the story. And while there was a certain dark part of her that grinned at the realization that Faisal would soon have revenge against the monster who had taken Tasneem from the world, there was another part of her that was left ... sad?

She struggled to process the emotion. Why should she feel sad? Faisal said it himself: it was foolish to think that Bloodlined and Commonborn could be together.

Except, what was it that Alaric had told her and the other members of her gang when they'd laughed at him?

"Alaric?" she asked.

"Yeah?" he stopped the story.

"That Commonborn queen and her consort, that wasn't a lie?"

"I would not lie to you, Reema."

"What was her name?"

"Nisha."

Her eyes narrowed at how quickly he answered, like her name had been sitting at the tip of his tongue. "You say that with some familiarity."

He shrugged. "I did not know her well, but the first time I met her, she left an impression."

"An *impression?*" Her blood ran hot, threatening to explode as her fingers curled into fists.

"Yes, an impression. She needed my help to enter the king's ball so that she could rob him."

She scoffed with disbelief. "So let me guess. You escorted her into the ball?"

"I did, and then I passed her off to the man she was in love with."

A quiet moment passed.

"Did you like her?" she could hardly believe what she was asking. She knew she sounded like, as though she was a spiteful, jealous bitch. But in that moment, she did not care.

Alaric abruptly halted, turning to her with surprise, like he'd suddenly realized what he had been saying. He grabbed hold of her shoulder and lowered himself close enough so that she could feel his presence mere inches from her face.

"I wondered that myself. I did admire her. After all, I had never met a Commonborn thief from the Glass District who could be bold enough to believe herself capable of robbing the King of Sundara."

She fumed as she listened, and for a moment, just a moment, there was a rage that burned hotter than her hatred of the slave master. She wanted to drive her fist through him, through *herself*, for being so foolish as to allow herself to be vulnerable with him, to give him this opening into her soul that he was so frivolous with in the world.

"But you deserve the truth."

She paused.

"I'm a romantic, Reema. I believe in that existential click of the heart. And there's only one person I've had that with." His finger brushed against hers. "It wasn't her."

Her mouth went dry. Her heart stopped. "Oh."

Dark clouds spread across the sky.

"What?"

"The story," he said, taking her hand and placing it on his shoulders. "We're not done."

She stayed quiet and listened.

They blotted out the sun as he strode across the city of Zareen, murder in his eyes, murder in his heart. He wore Tasneem's ring around his neck. It branded his chest, leaving a small mark where the sun heated the metal and irritated his skin, like it was some sign of the damage that lingered within.

He reached the prison, met the guard at the gate.

With the weight of Faisal's coins heavy in his pocket, the guard guided him inside, through the gate and into the hallway filled with cells. Shadows gathered over his eyes. His footsteps were loud, louder even than the shouting prisoners who pressed their gaunt faces against the bars.

His heart raced, thrumming to life in the most painful way. Every step he took, he remembered Tasneem. And yet, every step he took, he remembered Amira too.

What would she think of him when she found out what he had done? Would she be grateful, angry, disappointed? He had never dared to tell her of his plans, fearing those very reactions.

He shut his mind off, allowing his hand to drift toward his dagger as they neared the murderer's cell. He had to stay focused. He could worry about what Amira thought after the matter was done.

Then he heard the sound of sobbing. It was so out of

place in this murderer's row, that he nearly tripped over himself.

The guard guiding him snickered as he came to a halt in front of the cell. Faisal hesitated, but he steeled himself and followed.

In the far corner of the cell sat a man with black-shadowed pits over his eyes. Tears rolled down his cheeks as his face twisted in ugly grief. Why was he crying? Faisal was the one who lost someone, not this man.

Did he know Tasneem somehow?

He frowned, stepped closer. He studied the man's face, waiting for the moment of recognition to click. But no matter how long he stared, that moment of recognition did not come.

"This is him? You're sure?" Faisal asked the guard in a soft voice.

The crying man paused, glanced up with fearful eyes. His eyes shifted from the guard to Faisal and back.

"Are you here to take me to the gallows?" the man asked. "Is it finally time?"

"Shut your sundamned mouth, scum," the guard spat.

The man flinched back.

The guard turned to Faisal, "Oh, it's him alright. Saw them bring the bastard in myself. You want in?"

Faisal turned to the murderer and stepped closer to the bars. Frustratingly, his rage was tentative, disturbed and confused by the man's sobbing. This was nothing at all like he envisioned. He had pictured a man with dark, gleaming eyes and an ever-present smile. He had pictured a monster.

But instead, the man before him looked ... ordinary. Like any stranger off the street. His grief was raw, palpable, almost making Faisal's fury feel misplaced.

Faisal's lips pursed, the anger still burning within him despite the confusion.

"Why are you crying?" he demanded of the man.

The man's sobs quieted for a moment, and he looked up at Faisal with red-rimmed eyes.

"I ... I made a mistake. A terrible mistake," he choked out. "I didn't mean to ... I didn't know ... Please, believe me. It was an accident."

Faisal's heart pounded in his chest. He had come ready to strike down the evil soul that had taken Tasneem from him. But now, faced with this broken shell of a man, he felt his resolve wavering.

Faisal closed his eyes, remembered Tasneem's lifeless eyes, remembered how she lay in the street, her blood seeping from her.

"Let me in," he told the guard.

The guard sneered and turned the key.

The cell door swung open with a loud creak that echoed through the long corridor.

"I was never here," the guard said.

Faisal nodded. Once the guard disappeared, he entered, drawing his dagger.

"You said it was an accident?" he hissed.

He backhanded the man, and the flames of his rage burned like an inferno, rising up to swallow him whole. They urged him onward, begging him to take his revenge.

Faisal began to beat him. He could not stop the tears

that flowed down his cheeks or the spittle flying from his mouth as he realized he was yelling.

When he was done, the man lay flat beneath him, his nose broken and his eye swelling with an ugly bruise. Blood dribbled from the corner of his mouth.

"I'm sorry," the man whispered.

Faisal surged forward, pressing the dagger against the man's throat. This was it. This was the moment he had spent so many nights dreaming about. His beloved would soon be able to rest easy, knowing that her murderer had received the justice he deserved.

He knew that he should end the man now and take his leave. The guards would never know who killed him, as Faisal would be long gone and the guard he'd paid off wouldn't risk ratting on him. But even if he did, Faisal knew the guards wouldn't care. This was a murderer. He was meant for the gallows anyways. As far as they would be concerned, someone had simply freed up a cell sooner than expected.

But something stayed his blade; a need so sudden and desperate within him to know why.

"Why did you do it?" Faisal asked, his voice lower, more controlled.

The man's lips trembled as he answered. "It was dark. I thought she was someone else, a thief who'd robbed me the night before. I just wanted my coin back, and I ... By the time I realized my mistake, it was too late."

Faisal bared his teeth, the salt of his tears dripping down to stain the cell floor.

"I loved her," Faisal said.

The man shook his head slowly. "I'm sorry. I ..."

He descended into his sobbing again, catching Faisal off guard. The man's words echoed in Faisal's mind. There was genuine regret in his voice.

Faisal stood, backed until his back hit the wall. His breathing was ragged. He felt a whirlwind of emotions —anger, sorrow, confusion. His breathing quickened until he was hyperventilating. He clutched his chest. His heart hurt.

Before he could stop himself, he found himself sprinting away, the sound of his pounding footsteps lost in the roar of blood in his ears. He needed to be away from here, needed to be alone.

Reema frowned as the last vestiges of Alaric's voice faded into the dark. When Faisal had been led down the corridor by the guard, she couldn't hold back a dark grin. She'd expected a great moment of triumph. But instead, she found herself just as conflicted as Faisal.

"Tell me he goes back," Reema said.

"Back?"

"To finish the job."

Alaric paused in the tunnel ahead of her. "Would you?"

"Of course I would," Reema said without hesitation. She buried the rising doubt beneath the image of her sister's body falling through the Hole. "Even if the man made a mistake, he still murdered Tasneem. He deserves to pay."

"You don't think he's paying right now? With all his suffering?"

"Suffering? Tasneem was *dead* in the streets. He hasn't suffered enough."

She could sense Alaric nodding in front of her.

"And Faisal?"

"What about him?"

"Don't you think he's suffered enough?"

She frowned, unsure of what he was getting at. "What are you saying?"

"What do you think happens when Faisal is standing over the murderer's body? Do you think that all the pain and suffering he's feeling just goes away?"

Reema scowled. "It won't go away, but it's not about that."

"You think that's what innocent, quiet Tasneem would want?"

Her nostrils flared, and her brows furrowed as she formed a response.

"I didn't say that. It's about what she deserves. Who else can give her that but Faisal?"

Alaric was sad when he answered. "Reema, Hana is dead."

She flinched, her eyes widening at the sound of her sister's name coming from his lips.

"You think I don't know that?" she asked in a shaky voice.

She jabbed a finger against her skull. "I think about her every single fucking day. Every night, I have night-mares about how lifeless she looked as she was tossed down the Hole. Every night, I see your father smiling as he takes her life. I know she's dead. I *know*."

"Then you know that she feels nothing, wants nothing, *deserves* nothing." He reached out for her, and Reema drew away, but he caught her wrist and pulled her closer. He wrapped his arms around her in a warm embrace. His whisper brushed her ears. "But you, you're alive. You deserve happiness, love, a world free from the hatred you hold in your heart. And if Hana were alive, she would agree with me."

Reema could not refute what he was saying, even as her tears burned down her cheeks. Her teeth ground as she tried to hold back the grief, but in the deep darkness, a vision of her sister's face appeared nearby.

And she looked so disappointed. So *sad*.

Reema beat her fist against Alaric's chest. He took it silently, endured every blow of hers. And when she stopped, he leaned forward again, and whispered to her.

"Life is for the living. Not the dead."

He turned then, gently placing her hands on his shoulders, and continued to stride forward through the dark. She stewed on his words, trying to defend herself against them as they sought to break through her walls.

She wouldn't let this Bloodlined bastard's words be the thing that stopped her from achieving what she had focused on for so many years. She was the Ifrit, the harbinger of justice, the only person who could wipe the world clean of all its evil and cruelty. If she stopped, then men like his father would continue to rule the surface. And those like her sister would continue to die.

TWENTY-SEVEN

The hunger, the thirst, they were starting to get to Reema. She was weaker, and her footsteps grew heavy with exhaustion. She knew that Alaric had to be feeling the same, because they were not going as quickly as they were before.

It felt like an eternity as they passed through the darkness, squeezing and crawling through the veins of the earth. She wasn't ever sure what she expected to find, but now, she was starting to realize that perhaps this would go on forever. The mines were but a glimpse into the vast underbelly of the earth. For as far as the deserts of Sundara stretched, it was nothing compared to where they were now.

In truth, Reema did not want to hear any more of the story Alaric told. But it was all that kept her from the demons of her own mind, from the hounds of madness that barked and wished ruin upon her.

So, as painful as it was, in a small voice, she asked Alaric to continue reading.

He obliged, his voice shaky and weak. His stomach rumbled, even as the words spilled from his lips.

Faisal did not run to the darkness he knew but to the light he needed. He shoved his way through the Market District with tears streaming down his face. He dodged the patrolling guards of the Peak District and soon arrived at Amira's home, its white marble glinting in the sunlight.

He pounded his fist against the door, calling for her.

When the door swung open, he met the gaze of an older man, a Bloodlined with brilliant green eyes— Tasneem's father.

A woman appeared at his shoulder. He knew this must be Tasneem's mother. He recognized her from the funeral.

Then the man spoke, "You must be Faisal. Amira has told me much about you."

Faisal blinked, suddenly worried about what she had been telling him. He backed away a step, but Tasneem's mother rushed forward, her hand outstretched.

"Please," she said, her eyes desperate and tinged red with grief. "Stay."

Faisal's gaze flicked from her to Tasneem's father and back. "I ... Is Amira here?"

The man pursed his lips. "Do you intend to take her from me too?"

Faisal's heart twinged in pain. As much as he wanted to speak, he found it impossible. He dipped his head in respect, and began to back away, remnants of grief and pain ravaging him.

"Stop!"

He paused, looked up at the mother.

"Come in," she said, her face more determined than before. She glanced at the father. "You must forgive my husband. He is still ... he still feels her loss. But if you are here for Amira, then I ask you to come inside."

Faisal was suddenly conscious of the bruises on his knuckles and the blood spattered across his clothing.

"I should go."

"No, you will not," she said, her voice turning to iron. "You will come inside, and my husband will behave."

The father growled as his harsh gaze fell on her, but she brazenly met it.

"You know what Amira was like before him," she said.

The father's gaze flicked toward Faisal. With a resigned sigh, he stepped aside.

"Come in," she said. "I'll fetch Amira."

Faisal waited with the father in the entrance of their home, surrounded by a level of wealth that he could never hope to achieve in his lifetime. It did not take long for Amira to appear at the top of the stairs.

The sight of her took his breath away. It had nothing to do with how stunning she looked in her simple house robe. It had everything to do with the way her glowing hazel eyes met his and the joy he saw in them.

That joy turned to concern as she saw him. She descended the stairs and, without a word to her father, pulled Faisal into another room, shutting the door behind them so they could speak in private.

"What happened?" she asked as she turned to face him.

Faisal stood, unsure how to answer. Then he broke down into wracking sobs. He desperately wanted to be free from the sorrow, from the endless rage that seemed to consume him from the inside out.

She held him, not caring that her family was just in the other room.

"You went to see him, didn't you?" she asked.

His tears stopped, and he lifted his gaze to meet hers.

"You were going to kill him?" she asked.

He trembled. How did she know?

She led him to a place where they could sit. She held his hand in hers.

"Did you think you were the only one who wanted to avenge her? When the guards found the murderer, I saw him."

She shook her head. "My sister died because of an accident, but I knew that made the man no less of a murderer. I was prepared to pay the guards to take him into the desert and let the sun bake him alive."

"What stopped you?"

She gave him a sad smile. "I found you."

Faisal sat with Amira for some time. They spoke, cried, and laughed until eventually, Amira formally introduced Faisal to her parents. He had dinner with them, talking again about the woman they all loved.

By the end of his visit, when he stepped out the front

door into the cool desert night, he realized he did not
hurt so much.

He contemplated that thought as he walked home,
hands in pockets. He followed the same alleyway that
Tasneem must have walked every day. And when he
found the place they bumped into each other, he stopped.

He looked up at the stars.

One shone more brilliantly than all the rest, almost
as though it were winking down at him. He drew a deep
breath, and for the first time, he allowed himself to
think, 'what if?'

What if he did not let himself become so consumed
with revenge?

What if he did not let himself become a murderer?

What if he simply ... let go?

It felt as though a heavy weight lifted off his heart.
He drew another breath, this time deeper than before.
The air felt fresher, cleaner. The shadows surrounding
him backed away, and the moonlight kissed his brow.

The shining star shone brighter.

There was a lull in Alaric's voice as he paused, giving
himself a breather before he squeezed through the tight
marble walls ahead. The questions 'what if' rushed back
into her mind, attempting to set their roots. Reema
squeezed her eyes shut in an attempt to block them
away.

But try as she might, she could not stop one question
from slipping through.

What if she did not let herself become consumed by
revenge?

It was a foolish question, because what was there to give her purpose? It wasn't like there was a whole life she could live, where she could set up shop as a sundamned merchant and sell some wares. There was no safe place for her to return home to, where she could someday have children. There was only the deep mines, filled with men who'd shiv her and bury their pickaxe in her gut if given the chance.

She needed to survive. And revenge? That was purpose enough for her to continue living.

Her eyes caught on the softest part of the darkness, where some small hint of the light from Alaric's glowing eyes leaked through his steel band. Perhaps she was wrong. Perhaps there was another reason to live, a reason that she knew Hana would approve of. Perhaps she—

She stopped herself, clenching her jaw.

As long as the slave master lived, as long as *his* father lived, she could never rest. Because with every man, woman, or child tossed down the Hole, she would be reminded that she could have stopped it.

Reema followed Alaric through the gap, wincing as her chest scraped against a jagged piece of granite that jutted out from the wall.

"You okay?" Alaric asked, his hands finding her shoulder.

"I'm fine," she snapped.

She hated that when she was with him, she felt as Faisal had felt, where the darkness did not feel so heavy. Standing before him, with him guiding her through the pitch black, she knew that she would have been better if he'd never been tossed down into the mines.

"Why did your father throw you down here?" she asked, her words spilling over each other.

"I helped legitimize a Commonborn's claim to the throne. He told me if I cared so little about the Blood-lined, then I could rot in the mines with the Common-born." His finger tapped against the steel band. "This was his last present to me. He wanted to make sure I knew I wasn't Bloodlined anymore."

"I don't understand. He was so cruel to you. Don't you want to rid the world of people like him?"

There was a short pause before he answered.

"Before my father passed me to the captain, he made me a promise. He told me he would cleanse the world of the Commonborn, starting with the city I love."

Reema felt a chill crawl up her spine at Alaric's words. The coldness in his voice was the distant yet distinct echo of his father's ruthlessness. Her heart sank as she realized how closely her own desires for vengeance mirrored the very man she despised.

What would Hana think, if she were alive?

That thought gutted her. She felt the sharp sting of tears behind her eyes. Reema's hand trembled as she reached out, blindly seeking support from the walls of the cavern. The rough stone grazed her fingertips. The darkness seemed to press in closer, suffocating, like it was eager to swallow her whole now that she was giving in to the sorrow.

But then she felt the warmth of Alaric's hand in hers.

It staved off the dark and the guilt, anchoring her in safety.

"Come," he said. "Are you ready to hear what lies beneath the sands of sorrow?"

She could not bring herself to speak. He took her silence as a sign that she was listening.

The murderer was due to be hung in three days' time.

Faisal found himself at the prison gates, passing another fistful of coins over to a guard. In the blink of an eye, it was whisked away, and he was being led down murderer's row. The prisoners were quiet this time, but then dawn hadn't yet come. The only sound that passed through the bars of their cells were the snores of troubled men.

But there was one man who did not sleep.

The murderer lay awake on the stone floor, his eyes bloodshot as he stared off into the distance. Faisal motioned for the guard to leave them. He studied the man this time, noticing the unruly beard that now lined his jaw, and all the cuts and bruises he'd left him with from the last time he visited. He appeared the same as any of poor souls from the Glass District, but upon closer inspection, Faisal could see nothing of the signs of a life led in hardship. He must have grown up on the lower half of the Market District, like Faisal himself.

Faisal cleared his throat.

The man jerked in surprise. His gaze spun to where Faisal stood, and they locked onto his.

"What's your name?" Faisal asked.

"Kamran," he answered, saying nothing more.

"The woman you murdered, she was everything to me. She was who I first thought of when I woke, and who I thought of when I went to sleep. I dreamed of her, of growing old and having children of our own." Faisal paused. "That can't happen now."

The murderer stood, walked to the bars. They were close now, mere inches apart. Two men on different sides of a tragedy that changed the entire course of their lives. Faisal could still feel the vestiges of his rage urging him to reach through the bars and end the man. The tension made it difficult to breathe.

"Will you kill me now?" Kamran asked.

Faisal stared into his eyes. There was a pool of guilt there so deep, he knew the man must be drowning in it.

"No."

Kamran drew a surprised breath.

"That's not why I came. I came ..." Faisal struggled to get the words across. He struggled until he saw the hope in the man's eyes. "I came to forgive you."

Kamran rested his head against the bars. He cried then, not because of the guilt that had wracked him but because of the relief.

"Why?" he asked.

Faisal had asked himself that very same question since that moment in the alley. There was no answer that made sense, except ...

"Because I'm tired of hurting. I want to be free to live my life, and killing you doesn't do that."

A wave of peace washed over him.

The pain softened.

"Thank you," Kamran said.

He nodded and released a shaky breath, fighting back tears. Then he turned away.

He left the murderer behind to face his fate.

He stepped out of the darkness of the prison and into the sunlight.

This time, the shadows did not follow him.

The last of Alaric's words echoed through the darkness, hanging from it like stars in the sky. She listened to them, over and over.

This time, the shadows did not follow him.

This time, the shadows did not follow him.

This time, the shadows—

She clamped her hands over her ears, attempting to silence the persistent echo, only to hear them resonate within her mind. Throughout her life, the shadows hadn't just followed her—they had consumed her. Tears burned behind her eyes as anger and grief and desire gnawed away at her.

Reema's frustration mounted, the desire to tear at her hair, to scratch away the ceaseless thoughts overwhelming her.

Alaric came to a stop, realizing that she was no longer attached to his shoulder. He turned and faced her, that faintest hint of light the only thing she could see in the blackness.

She could sense the pity radiating from him. Somehow, he understood the struggle she was going through. He reached out for her, and gently removed her hands from her ears.

"Reema," he said, his voice soft, the warmth of his breath brushing across her skin, leaving a trail of goose-bumps. "Do you understand what lies beneath the sands of sorrow?"

She breathed deeply, her nostrils flaring as she fought for control. Facing him, she felt his sincerity and suddenly wished she had never met him, never stood at this agonizing crossroad between her sister's justice and her own deep-seated desires.

"Forgiveness?" Her voice cracked, her heart pulling towards him, twisting with pain. She knew what she desired, but she knew that to want that, to want *him* was futile. As long as men like his father ruled the surface, as long as this unrelenting rage burned within her chest, she knew that there would forever be that divide between them. "I will not accept that. I can't."

His finger touched the bottom of her chin, lifting it ever so slightly so that his breath touched upon her lips instead.

"It's not forgiveness."

She was breathless as her thoughts went quiet. She could think of nothing but how close they were. The air around them was tense, like nothing else mattered except for this moment. Her heart seized, as her eyes locked on the silhouette of his lips. She wanted him to kiss her. She wanted him to take her. But this was the son of her enemy, a man with the Angel's own blood coursing through his veins. There were a thousand more reasons that the divide between them existed, a divide that could *never* be crossed. And of all those reasons, there was perhaps one that mattered most: she could never go back if she did cross the divide.

Ignoring the sudden pain in her chest, she began to turn away from him.

But he did not let her.

Before Reema could fully turn away, Alaric's hand caught her wrist, spinning her back toward him with a swift, compelling motion. In one fluid movement, he pressed her against the cold, rough marble wall, his hands planting firmly on either side of her, caging her with the undeniable strength of his presence.

The suddenness of his actions, the intensity in his eyes—everything pushed her pulse into a frantic rhythm that thrummed in her ears. His body was mere inches from hers, his breath warm against her face, stirring strands of her hair. The darkness surrounding them seemed to draw tighter around them, thick with tension and unspoken desire.

Without another word, his lips found hers, the kiss igniting a fire that dwarfed her burning rage. It was consuming, relentless, his mouth moving over hers with a passion that bordered on desperation. There was nothing gentle about it—it was a claim, a fiery melding of their desires that obliterated the divide she'd hoped to keep between them.

Alaric's kiss deepened, his body pressing her further into the marble. Her hands dug into his shoulder, into his hair as she pulled him closer. She moaned as his kisses trailed down into her neck. Her body shook. The inferno traveled down to her core.

Every touch, every movement was charged with an urgency that left no room for the past, for vengeance, or for any other sundamned reason. All that mattered was this kiss.

As suddenly as it had begun, Alaric pulled back, his intensity matched by the heaving of his chest. The air was suddenly cool against her burning skin as they both caught their breath in the thick silence that followed.

"Life. *That's* what rests beneath the sands of sorrow."

Reema swallowed hard, struggling to contain her pounding heart within the cage of her chest. Her tongue flicked over her tingling lips, like she could still taste him.

Alaric's voice trembled with urgency. "When you learned who I was, I knew you couldn't love me. I'm Bloodlined, the son of the man you despise most. But I want you to experience *life*. What you're trying to do will destroy you, and the thought of a world without you? It ruins me, Reema."

The lingering silence was as heavy as Reema had ever felt. The raw honesty in his words made something within her shift. But try as she might, she could not bring herself to speak.

She could feel him deflate as he wordlessly took her hand, guided it to his shoulder, and silently turned to lead them through the darkness.

Reema followed. Though she was quiet, her mind was anything but.

For the first time, just like Faisal, she allowed herself to think 'what if'?

What if she lived for herself, and not for Hana's revenge?

Her eyes locked onto his back.

What if she did love Alaric, despite all that he was?

CHAPTER
TWENTY-EIGHT

The tingling in her lips had long stopped. The warmth that Alaric had given her had gone cold. But the inferno he lit within her still burned, hot enough that it scorched her mind. Try as she might, she could not free herself from the question that branded itself into her.

What if she did love him?

She'd been so consumed with that thought, that she failed to notice when Alaric had stopped. She bumped into him. Collecting herself, she waited for him to turn, to explain why he had gone so silent.

But instead, she noticed a mounting tension in the air.

"What is it?" she asked.

"The walls. They feel different."

She frowned and reached out with her free hand.

The white marble walls of the mines were never as smooth as they were when they were finally used to build the homes of the Bloodlined across Sundara. They were dusty and unrefined, with jagged, rough edges. So when she reached out and ran her fingers along the walls, she was surprised to find that they were as smooth as glass.

She touched the wall in multiple places, muttering to herself. Could there have been something that burned these walls to smooth them? Was that even possible?

"Have you ever seen anything like it?" he asked.

Seen.

She glanced toward him, and the hint of light escaping from behind his damaged steel band. She grabbed hold of his arm and yanked him toward the wall.

"What're you doing?" he asked, trying not to struggle as she maneuvered the spilling light closer to the wall.

"I'm looking," she said.

She leaned in. She expected to see white dusty walls, but to her surprise, it was still difficult to see. It was like the walls themselves had absorbed the darkness around them, embodying it like they—

"Sundamned hells," she breathed.

He tensed. "What is it?"

With trembling fingers, she quickly dug into her pocket and withdrew the black-specked shard. She held it next to the wall, and sure enough, the black marble was a perfect match to the walls surrounding them.

Reema's pulse quickened as she stumbled to another side of the wall, then further down. Everywhere she touched, the marble was smooth as silk, and she knew it would be as black as night.

A surge of excitement coursed through her veins.

"We did it," she whispered, more to herself than to Alaric.

Reema grabbed hold of Alaric's hand and pushed forward, the pain from her injured leg now an afterthought against the adrenaline surging within her. A grin spread from ear to ear as she guided them, her hands against the walls. She could feel it now; the tunnel was directing them in one direction, a thought proven true the further they got when no other tunnels appeared.

There was one section where she thought she heard the distant but distinct sound of a pickaxe striking marble. She ignored it. They were far too deep in the earth for anyone else to be here, unless the rogue miners had managed to mine deep enough through her territory. But by the time they broke through the final wall, it would be too late.

"You said we did it. What did you mean? We found the way out?" There was a quiet dread in his words, a sad hope that they had avoided the dark path he knew they were headed down.

But she was deaf to it, because cheer spilled into her voice. "No, we found something better. We found the black marble."

He stiffened as she pulled him after her. As fast as she went, she could feel the tug on her hand, the desire to stop and go back, to find another way out of this sundamned place. But she didn't want to be anywhere else.

After all these years spent carving her way through the mines, running her gang, she'd finally done it.

The walls suddenly shot out in both directions, the tunnel opening up into something far wider. Reema sensed they were in a gargantuan cave. The air changed —it was cooler, like ice touched her skin, tinged with a strangeness that raised the hairs on the back of her neck.

She took a cautious step deeper into the cave, then another.

Light suddenly flooded the cave, blinding her after being trapped in darkness for so long. When her eyes finally adjusted, she removed her hands.

A shiver traveled down her spine.

Balls of flame floated above them, hovering in a way that could be nothing but magic. They cast their ethereal light across the cave, chasing away the oppressive darkness and revealing the enormity of the cavern.

The light illuminated a breathtaking sight. In the center of the cave, encased in a massive block of translucent white stone, was the Djinn. His form was distinct yet blurred, the edges of his body flickering like he was made of smoke or flame. It was impossible to tell, with the stone imprisoning him shimmering with an otherworldly glow. Reema realized that intricate symbols were etched all along the top of the stone.

Reema's heart pounded with a mix of awe and triumph. She had found it. After all the years of searching, the endless days and nights fighting to survive just to mine through marble, she stood before the Djinn. The sight was almost overwhelming.

She released Alaric's hand, ignoring his whisper as she stepped forward. The tension in the air was palpable, a silent hum that vibrated through the cavern, through their very bones. Every instinct screamed at her to be cautious, yet the allure of the Djinn's power was irresistible.

The floating flames intensified, casting long, eerie shadows that stretched across the cavern floor. The symbols around the stone pulsed with a steady rhythm, almost like a heartbeat.

She stepped closer to the block, wishing she could see the Djinn's face. Her hand hovered just over the translucent stone. There was cold radiating out from the block, like it was made of ice.

The shadows began to dance along the walls, and the floating flames began to flicker, each pulsing in tune with an ancient rhythm. Her pounding heart began to match its tune.

Reema of Mirash, the great Ifrit beneath the earth.

She froze. The words hissed through the air around her.

I feel it in your heart. A justifiable rage. A fair rage.

"Reema," Alaric said, his voice echoing heavily around them. He heard the Djinn too.

Reema ignored him. She drew a deep breath and squared up before the stone.

"You know me?"

The chilling sound of laughter blew around her, like the howling desert wind.

Know you?

Reema's breath hitched as the floating flames around the cave suddenly roared, their light intensifying and shifting. Moments from her past materialized in the fire.

On one side, she saw herself falling through the Hole,

her mouth stretched wide in horror. She saw her sister's body plummet after her, the strands of Hana's hair floating, her lifeless eyes staring off into the distance.

Reema stepped back, her heart pounding against her chest. She struggled to breathe as she turned and saw herself learning to shape and carve her way through the earth. She noticed the flickering silhouettes of the bodies of the miners lying behind her, and how *angry* she looked.

Elsewhere, she saw the shifting flames show her stacking marble blocks atop Hana's body.

Her eyes burned with unshed tears as her gaze locked onto Hana's face. She looked so peaceful, as though she'd wake at any moment. But she never would. Not even as Reema placed that final block.

She glanced in another direction, seeing the flames depict her early days in the gang. She watched as she fought tooth and nail to earn her place, her knuckles bloody and her enemies pissed scared.

For as long as you have been in these mines, I have watched you. We share this in common, Ifrit. We both seek vengeance and justice to right the wrongs done unto us.

Her fists clenched at her sides. Everywhere she looked, she was reminded of the weight of her suffering, each memory a visceral reminder of the life she had endured.

A memory played in her mind, sharper than she could ever remember. She could see every detail of the sands she knelt upon, could smell the stench of fear coming from Hana next to her, and could taste the iron tang of blood misting the air as Alaric's father, Kaiden

Damaris, murdered her sister. She could feel how the world suddenly felt *wrong*. Her heart shattered anew, the pain as fresh and raw as the day she had lost Hana.

"Reema, please," Alaric's voice was a desperate plea, cutting through the haze of memories and emotions. He reached for her, his touch warm and grounding, but she shook him off, stepping closer to the Djinn's strange prison.

"If that's true, then you'll know of the old man who told me about you, and how he told me that you had the power to do anything I wish. Is that true?"

Free me from this cursed prison, and I will grant you the vengeance you seek, should you wish it.

"I have waited so long," she whispered, her voice trembling with a mixture of determination and desperation. "I agree to your terms. I need your power. I need to end this suffering, to make them pay."

The Djinn's silhouette within the translucent stone darkened, like he was gathering his power. She noticed then an outstretched finger, almost as if he were pointing in a direction.

She looked, and saw a small pickaxe resting against the wall. It was no regular pickaxe though—it shone with a strange kind of light that made her wonder if it was one of the Angel's relics.

She clenched her jaw and gave a sharp nod, starting toward the pickaxe. All around her, she could feel the Djinn's power pulsing, feeding off her rage, her grief, her unquenchable desire for revenge. Her only regret was that the other members of her gang couldn't be here to join in the triumph they'd spent so long hunting for together.

Alaric stumbled after her, his hands drifting helplessly through the air as he sought to find her. But she stayed out of reach, her footsteps echoing like the beats of a drum.

She wrapped her hand around the pickaxe's handle, feeling the thrum of incredible energy. For a moment, she wondered who had left it here—who would imprison the Djinn but leave such an easy way to free him?

But was it really that easy? Miles of hardened marble stood between the Djinn and the surface. Maybe they had underestimated humanity's capacity for cruelty, never imagining that children, men, and women would be condemned to slave away in these dark depths.

As she lifted it, she sensed that when swung, the pickaxe would shape marble as she needed, no matter how much strength she put behind it. This was the perfect tool to shatter the Djinn's prison.

She stalked toward the block, shadows gathering in her footsteps like a cloak.

Alaric was a few feet away when he stopped.

"Reema!" he shouted, his voice booming off the walls.

She stopped, looking at him over her shoulder.

"If you do this, everything I care about will come to ruin."

He does not understand.

She turned back toward the Djinn.

The world is already in ruins.

She neared the block and took up her stance. The pickaxe rose, and as though it sensed her intentions, the thrum of power began to accelerate, sharpening until she could feel it vibrating in her hand.

"I wasn't talking about the world. I was talking about her."

She had already swung.

Mid-swing, she heard Faisal's voice in her head, as though it had sprung from the pages of a book.

"What stopped you?" he had asked.

She gave him a sad smile. "I found you."

Out of the corner of her eye, she caught a glimpse of Alaric standing there, and in that fleeting moment, a vision of a possible future with him unfolded: moments filled with laughter and smiles shared between them, the hours they'd spend reading next to each other, and how they'd make love in the night, transforming the darkness into something they owned, not something that owned them. She saw herself living life with him, free from the sorrow and rage that ruled her existence.

Her swing faltered, and though she tried to stop herself, the momentum was too great. The tip of the pickaxe scraped against the side of the stone, thrumming with the power of her intention.

She held her breath.

Nearby, Alaric held his.

Nothing happened.

She breathed a heavy sigh of relief, only to freeze a moment later as a soft crack echoed through the earth, deep and hollow. She watched in horror as the crack spread, and she knew that it was too late.

She had freed the Djinn.

CHAPTER
TWENTY-NINE

As the soft crack reverberated through the cave, a profound silence descended, as if the earth itself held its breath in the wake of the Djinn's release. The fissure in the Djinn's prison spread like a spiderweb. Each new line that marred the surface pulsed with a foreboding energy, and the silhouette within the block began to burn.

Reema stood frozen, pickaxe still in hand, her heart hammering against her ribs with a ferocity that matched the throbbing power emanating from the block. The symbols etched atop the stone began to emit a piercing light, as if they were trying to keep the Djinn contained.

But they could not.

The atmosphere in the cave thickened, charged with a palpable tension that made it almost impossible to breathe. The ground beneath their feet began to tremble. Dust and small pebbles danced upon the cave floor as the rumble grew into a deep roar. Reema realized with cold dread that the roar belonged to the Djinn.

Suddenly, with a sound like thunder cracking across

the sky, the block shattered. Chunks of the translucent stone exploded outward, filling the air with a sudden rush of heat. As the debris settled, the Djinn emerged from his confinement—a towering figure made from what seemed like the very essence of the seven hells.

He leaned his head back and breathed a deep sigh that swept through the cave, as though he'd been trapped for centuries. The cave was now fully illuminated by the flames running off the Djinn's body, the heat radiating out in palpable waves that forced Reema back a step.

He lowered his gaze, burning with an unnatural fire, to Reema's, and he smiled.

A deep fear settled into Reema.

She had made a mistake.

He spoke, his voice scraping across her very bones. "I am pleased with you, my Ifrit."

She swallowed hard.

He extended his hand, the fingers tipped by ruthless claws that gave Reema the idea that if he wanted, he could flay the very skin from her.

"Wish for your vengeance, and I shall grant it."

"No!" Alaric's voice pulled their attention toward him.

The Djinn growled, his lips pulling back to reveal a thousand terrifying teeth.

Alaric straightened, his chin lifted as though he stood a chance against this monster born. But he wasn't speaking to the Djinn. He was speaking to *her*.

"The blind human cannot see the darkness in your heart; the darkness that his father planted," the Djinn said. He advanced a step, the heat boiling off him singeing the tips of the hairs along her arm. "You can right the wrong. But you must simply *wish.*"

Reema trembled, caught between the life she saw with Alaric and the chance to put an end to all the cruel men to walk the face of the earth.

Let me help you.

The Djinn's words slithered into her mind, tempting her with the promise of making her choice easy. His gaze locked onto Alaric.

Reema felt a surge of terror grip her heart as the Djinn raised his clawed hand and conjured a ball of fire, preparing to unleash his power upon the man who had stood by her side, who had taught her to read, who had tried to show her another way instead of forcing her to stop releasing the Djinn.

In that agonizing moment, time seemed to stretch, and Reema's mind raced back to the question that had haunted her: What if she did love Alaric, despite all that he was? The thought had been a fleeting whisper before, but now it roared to life. She felt a sudden existential click in her heart, the answer wedging itself deep within her core. It was a truth that resonated with every beat of her heart.

She loved him because of all that he was.

The memories of their shared laughter, the comfort of his presence, the lightness he brought into her world of darkness—all coalesced into a singular realization. She couldn't lose him.

The Djinn's hand descended, and with a fierce cry,

Reema sprang forward, propelled by a force more powerful than she'd ever known.

She swung the pickaxe into the Djinn's chest. It hit with a loud *hiss*, and instantly, a roar permeated the earth, shaking the cave so violently she feared it would collapse.

She stumbled back toward Alaric, her eyes fixed on the hole she'd made in the Djinn's chest. It should've been enough to kill him, but to her horror, the flames crackled, surging up and healing back over the wound.

She bumped into Alaric, and instinctively, their hands interlocked.

The Djinn's gaze spun to hers, boring into her with such fury that she could not help but take a step back. He advanced toward them, his snarl stretching from ear to pointed ear. The searing heat coming off him evaporated the beads of sweat rolling down her brow.

"You think you can do what the Angel could not?" His voice slithered through the air, assaulting them from all sides. "I am immortal. I am the *infernal*."

A cocoon of fire roared to life around Reema and Alaric, the heat burning away the air. They began to choke, unable to gather a single breath. They both fell to their knees, clutching at their throats.

The Djinn stood over them, his chin lifted as they were bowed before him.

"I should turn you to ash, Ifrit. But you were the one to free me. So I grant you one more chance. *Wish* for the revenge you have sought all these years."

A tear slipped from her eye. She screamed as it instantly boiled and left a trailing scar down her cheek before evaporating. Despite the fact that Alaric, too, was suffering, she felt his hand on hers, trying to anchor her, trying to offer her his strength.

But Hana's death flashed through her mind. Twice now, she had failed because she was too weak, too help-less. And twice now, she was the reason that someone suffered, from bothering the slavers enough to put her and Hana before the slave master to being the one to release the Djinn so that he could harm Alaric and bring the ruin she so desired to the world.

She ground her teeth together, frustration rising up within her. She wished she could go back on what she'd done. She wished that she could simply—

She rose, an idea turning over in her mind.

"Okay," she wheezed on the last vestiges of her breath. "I'll make my wish."

His terrifying smile widened.

Even though she was at her weakest moment, when she lifted her gaze to his, it was as hard as the marble stone walls surrounding them. Blood and marble dusted fingernails dug into her palms.

"I wish you back to the seven hells you spawned from, you Angel-damned bastard."

The Djinn staggered back, his eyes wide with fear.

Reema rose to her feet, fighting back the waves of dizziness rolling through her. Black spots swam before the burning light of the Djinn's form, but still, she fixed her gaze on the monster.

"Do not forget, Djinn, we made a deal. I would free you, and you would grant me a wish. So, you will *obey* me and do as I say."

He withered under the weight of her gaze, and she could feel his power retracting in on him. Next to her, Alaric heaved a deep breath.

Just when she began to allow herself a victorious crack of a smile, his power surged. He burned like the sun, waves of sheer heat rolling off him. She held her hands over her eyes to protect her vision, but still, dots swam across the darkness of her eyelids.

When the blinding light subsided, he was standing before her, trailing the claw of his forefinger down her chin. She hissed in pain as smoke trailed upward and the stench of burnt flesh filled the air.

"You humans are just as foolish as the day I was imprisoned. Did you already forget the terms of our deal?" His voice was a rasping whisper, each word scraping across her nerves.

She couldn't bring herself to answer as the Djinn forced her back down to her knees. Somewhere in the back of her mind, her injured leg screamed for relief.

"Free me from the prison, and I would grant you the vengeance you seek, if you wished for it." His claw continued further down the side of her neck. "I made no promise to grant any other wish."

She closed her eyes.

"Would you wish ruin upon the world?"

The fate of the world hung in the silence that followed, hers to shape, hers to burn. But she could see herself in the monster standing over them. Hana would never have wanted that for her.

"No."

The Djinn smiled, a cold, triumphant curve of his

lips. He straightened, and with a wave of his hand, the cocoon of fire disappeared. Reema could finally draw a breath, but the air had never tasted so poisonous.

"I know what rests within your heart, Ifrit. The words may fail to cross your lips, but rest assured, I will bring this world back to its knees."

Reema's heart pounded with fear and determination as she met his gaze.

"The Angel will come back. He'll stop you," she said, the words sounding empty in her own ears. She had never been much of a believer in the Angel—not with all the cruelty that existed in the world. But she knew that there was no mortal on earth that could stop this being.

The Djinn threw his head back and laughed, a sound so terrible it reverberated through her very soul.

"The Angel is dead," he declared, his voice a horrifying mix of mockery and triumph. "There is no one to stop me."

His gaze shifted from her to Alaric.

"I had hoped that the Angel would be the one to see me ravage this world. But as you carry his blood, you will suffice."

His claw tapped against the steel band that blinded Alaric, heating the metal hot enough that Reema could hear it sizzling against his skin. His scream raked across her bones, pierced her heart as she watched him suffer. But as his scream reached a crescendo, a sharp crack echoed through the cave. The metal band fell and clattered against the ground.

Alaric's hands went to his face, hissing as he burned his hands touching his face.

"Alaric Damaris, Son of Sons, Sons of Daughters, Daughters of our fallen Angel, do not linger in this darkness. I would not want you to miss seeing the city you love burn as I sit upon the Seat of the Desert."

The Djinn glanced once more to Reema.

"Farewell, Ifrit."

With that, the Djinn turned and left the cave, his form flickering like a mirage before vanishing into the shadows. The oppressive heat faded with him, leaving behind a chilling emptiness that gnawed at Reema's insides.

Her stomach fell through the floor, numb as the enormity of what had just happened crashed over her. Her gaze lingered on where the Djinn had disappeared.

How many people would die because of her?

How many would suffer?

She was a monster, every bit as bad as the Djinn himself. She could hear the screams tearing through the air from ravaged, burning towns. She could see the bloodshed, the mounds of ash of ruined men. She could see the desert that she hated reduced to something worse, something that would break her heart.

Arms encircled her, Alaric's warmth chasing away the chill that had gripped her. But his embrace was tighter than usual, almost desperate. She could feel his heart pounding against her back, his breath hot and uneven.

"Look at me," he said, his voice low but tense.

Slowly, she turned and looked at him.

Under an unruly beard and a bruised face scarred with

the burned outline of the steel band that had covered his eyes, a handsome man stared back at her. His eyes were like she had never imagined. They were brown, glowing with a mixture of emotions—anger, disbelief, shock at what she had done—but above them all, there was something else.

"I see you," he said.

For a moment, Reema was lost in those eyes, the world narrowing to just the two of them. The pain and regret that threatened to break her melted away under the compassion and love in his gaze, but she could see the tightness in his jaw, the flicker of anger he was struggling to control.

"I see you," he repeated, this time softer, knowing how close she was to shattering.

She tried to pull away, but he caught her, drawing her back before she could. Then, without a word, he leaned in and kissed her.

The voices screaming in her mind fell silent as his lips gently brushed across hers. This kiss was nothing like the one before, so full of passion and desire and need. This kiss was something far softer, deeper. It was a declaration of his love. It was a promise that etched itself into her soul, promising that no matter what, he would stand by her side, just as he had all this time. She leaned into it, the pain of all her wounds, both physical and mental, disappearing in the taste of him.

When he drew back, she felt her heart beating again, strong and calm and steady, as though it had been anchored by him. The storm that had threatened to overcome her had passed.

"What did I do?" Her voice was quieter than it had ever been.

Alaric shook his head, running his hand through his disheveled hair with a heavy sigh. Anger flared within him, but he forced himself to push it aside. There would be time for anger later, but right now, Reema needed his strength. "It doesn't matter. It's done now. Besides, you're asking the wrong question."

"What do you mean?"

"We need to focus on what we do next."

"What we do next?" she asked with disbelief. "With the Djinn free, everything's doomed. He'll burn the world to ash, and who's left to stop him? You heard what he said—the Angel is dead."

He frowned, the wrinkles etched in his face deep as he became lost in thought. The silence between them stretched, until she could take it no longer.

"What is it?"

"The Angel was killed by *someone*."

"And?"

"I think I know who." He brushed a stray lock from her face, his touch gentle and reassuring. "And if I'm right, she will help us."

"She?"

"The Commonborn Queen. I don't have the faintest clue as to how we stop the Djinn, but I think she might."

Her breath hitched, a glimmer of hope piercing through the despair.

For as long as she lived, she had wanted the world above to fall to ruin, to wipe it free of the evil that walked it. But for all that time, she had been blinded by rage and grief. And now she, too, could see.

She had to find a way to set things right.

"Then we'll need to break our way out of the mines."

She retrieved the pickaxe relic and leaned on him, her still injured leg sending throbbing pains up through her body. They made their way out of the cave and into the darkness. But they had a way forward now, without needing to feel their way through the dark. The glow of Alaric's captivating eyes offered them just enough light to see.

The Djinn had left a burned path through the tunnels. When they reached the spot where they had last heard the distant sound of mining, they found a hole blasted through the wall.

With a look at each other, they made their way through, cautious of stumbling across the Djinn again. But to her surprise, they found themselves surrounded by the bodies of rogue miners. Their corpses lay burning like coal, faces stripped of their flesh and the mouths of their skulls stretched in an eternal scream.

She averted her gaze because, as much horror as she had seen in the mines, this was something else. She realized with a jolt that they were in the tunnel where she had first seen the hint of black marble, where this had all started.

Needing to recover, they silently made their way back to Hana's cave.

It was a long, quiet walk.

CHAPTER
THIRTY

Reema and Alaric stood outside the entrance to the cave. They stopped when they heard the low murmur of voices coming from inside the cave. A cold anger burned in Reema as she realized some miners might have found their way into the cave. After all, they hadn't been around to protect it, and they had left the entrance exposed. She tried not to think about the possibility that they had gone and disturbed Hana's grave.

Reema's stomach suddenly rumbled, and she quickly put her hand to it to silence it. But the voices inside fell silent. She glanced at Alaric.

He lifted a shiv that he'd lifted from a body they'd come across. She had hoped the miner had some lentils, but it seemed whoever killed him had taken anything worth keeping. And if they weren't careful, someone would do the same to them.

They waited for the miners inside to come out and discover them, but the conversation inside resumed. She shook her head. Fools.

She motioned for Alaric to continue, knowing that, as much as she wanted to lead, she was a risk with an injured leg. He steeled his gaze and crawled through the entrance. Reema started to follow before she realized something was wrong.

Only *one* voice was speaking now, instead of the multiple they had heard before.

A roar echoed through the cave just ahead of her. Reema's skin prickled in fear. She scrambled through the entrance to save him from the miners, only to feel the cold edge of a marble shiv at her throat. Her heart stopped dead in her chest.

"Hold on," a familiar gruff voice said, laced with surprise.

Reema's eyes widened in shock as she recognised it.

"Asif?" she whispered, daring to turn her head slightly.

He pulled the shiv from her neck, his mouth gaping in disbelief. For the first time ever, she heard him stumble over his words. "W-what … how? How in the sundamned *hells* are you alive?"

A yelp echoed from the side, and she looked to see Omar and Ra'ad flat on their ass. Alaric stood over them with a smug grin, his glowing eyes bearing down into them.

Asif was speechless, but the twins weren't.

"The blind bastard's glowing!"

To her—and Alaric's—surprise, they scrambled up off their feet and embraced him, before rushing her and nearly tackling her off her feet. They too couldn't hardly believe that she was alive.

Asif began to laugh, his voice a mixture of relief and joy. She thought she even heard a tremble in it, like he was close to crying. *Asif*, close to crying. She would shake her head if she didn't feel the same way herself.

"We saw you fall!" Omar said.

"And her pickaxe is glowing ..." Ra'ad breathed, his eyes wide in awe as he stared at the pickaxe in her hand.

Reema grimaced, "It's a long story."

Asif nodded, "Get the lentils going, boys. The boss is back."

They shot back to the fire, their excited chatter filling the cave without care that it might echo out into the tunnels.

Asif's voice softened. "I thought that you were gone, that Mehdi had gotten the better of us for once."

She put a hand on his shoulder. Asif was one of the toughest miners she'd ever known, but she also knew that he had a soft spot for her. Thinking she had died, she knew it had to be tough on him. He would have blamed himself for the failure.

"I painted the walls with Mehdi's blood. Killed all his men too."

"I'm still here," she said.

He drew a deep, shaky breath, settling himself. He breathed out, nodding. Then he leaned in, his brows furrowing. "Did you feel the mines shaking? I'm worried that—"

She put a hand up. "I know. I'll tell you everything."

Asif paused, his brow lifting. His gaze flicked down to the pickaxe, contemplative. Then he nodded.

"So. Brown eyes, huh?" Asif said, turning to Alaric. "I pictured them to be a bit prettier than that."

"Yeah, well, you're about as ugly as I imagined you," Alaric responded, his gaze locked on Asif's.

Silence lingered between them for a moment, disturbed only by the sound of Omar and Ra'ad on the other side of the cave. She looked from one to the other, worried.

Then Asif burst into laughter and drew Alaric into an embrace, "Come here, Bloodlined."

Alaric grinned over his shoulder at Reema.

Asif clapped Alaric on the shoulder as he released him, "Thanks for keeping the Ifrit alive. I was worried what I'd do without her. Now, let's eat!"

The tension in her body eased as Alaric helped her to the fire after Asif. She breathed a sigh of relief as she took her seat and the smell of lentils filled the air. But there was still a knot in her chest, a worry about what her gang would think when she chose not to take the revenge they sought.

When they finished eating, she set her bowl aside.

With the eyes of her men on her, she told them how she and Alaric fell deep into the western veins, their fall softened by the bones of fallen miners before them. She told them of how Alaric guided them through the darkness. She could see from the way that they looked at him that he had earned their respect; miners were afraid of the dark, and the members of her gang were no exception to that.

The energy in the air changed when she told them of how they stumbled into the black marble prison. They leaned forward, the shadows gathering in the pits of their eyes.

"He was there, wasn't he?" Omar asked, his voice tentative, but carrying an undertone of excitement.

Reema nodded, her face grim, the knot of worry tightening in her chest.

"So it is done, then?" Asif asked.

She fixed him with a firm look. She shook her head. She could hear the grinding of his teeth.

"What happened?" he growled.

"I didn't wish for revenge," Reema said, her voice steady but laced with underlying tension.

Asif's expression darkened. "You freed the Djinn, and you let your chance—*our* chance—for revenge slip away? Why?" He glared at Alaric. "Because of him?"

"Yes," she said, her voice strong and her gaze unwavering. "I was wrong before. The world doesn't deserve ruination. That won't bring us peace."

"Peace?" he seethed, his voice rising to a roar that echoed through the cave. "Since when have we ever wanted peace?"

"Since I fell into the deep," she screamed back, standing up. "I came close to death and realized I wanted to live. I want us all to live."

The silence weighed between them, heavy with the disappointment in their stares.

"So you're giving up on revenge?" he asked, like there could be nothing worse.

"I didn't say that. I said the *world* doesn't deserve its ruin. But the slave master still does."

Her gaze shifted from Asif to Omar and Ra'ad.

"Your uncle that betrayed you still deserves to be ruined."

Omar and Ra'ad exchanged glances.

Her gaze returned to Asif. "The slavers who ripped you from your daughter, the Bloodlined who raped Javid's girl, even Captain Hamza—we'll have our revenge on all of them. I promised you that as your gang lord, and I made that promise in *blood*. You *will* have your revenge. But not like this."

A heavy silence filled the air, thick with tension. Asif's eyes bored into hers, searching for any sign of weakness or doubt. Finally, he spoke, his voice low and intense.

"Your rage is ours, and ours is yours. Tell us what to do."

Reema nodded, a silent message passing between them. She looked to the others, who nodded back, their expressions resolute.

"We're with you," Ra'ad said, his voice more serious than she had ever heard. "Whatever it takes."

Relief washed over Reema, loosening the knot in her chest. She sat down again, listening to the soft crackle of the flames.

Then she smiled. "It's time for us to leave the nest, boys."

"Are you saying we're breaking out of the mines?" Ra'ad asked, his eyes flashing with excitement. They had joked about it from time to time but were never serious. They all knew what they sought was buried here, behind black marble walls. But things were different now.

"We've got blood to spill and an immortal Djinn to kill. Can't do all that from down here, can we?"

Omar and Ra'ad cheered, stomping their boots in tune with their echoes off the white marble walls. Asif didn't join in, but he did smile. She could tell with one glance that he was apprehensive, almost afraid to see sunlight again. Who could blame him? After being stuck in the mines so long, it felt like that was where they belonged. She had told Alaric long ago that the mines were her home, and she had meant it.

They spent the next several hours working through a plan to break free of the mines. Once they settled on one, the members of her gang slowly fell asleep, one by one.

Reema waited until their snores danced off the rose quartz walls. She limped away with a torch in hand, doing her best to keep silent as she made for her sister's grave.

Walking through the tunnel felt strange. This path once burdened her with overwhelming grief and dread, suffocating her. But since Alaric had begun helping her to read, the journey felt different.

Reema's steps echoed softly through the tunnel as she made her way to her sister's grave. The oppressive darkness no longer suffocated her; instead, it felt like the gentle embrace of an old friend. She couldn't help but feel that the place had changed—no, more than that, she had changed.

The air felt warmer, more welcoming. Each step carried her closer to a place of solace rather than sorrow. A sense of peace settled over her.

She entered the cave, the flickering torchlight casting

dancing shadows across the walls. The rose quartz decorating her sister's grave sparkled in the light. She looked around, her mind returning to the hours spent with Alaric here, reading to him, reading to her sister.

She moved slowly, reverently, until she stood before Hana's grave, listening to the soft trickle of water. The rose quartz chips decorating the marble blocks refracted the torchlight, casting the room in a soft pink glow.

Reema reached out and placed her hand on the cool surface. This would be the last time she saw Hana's grave. For the first time, she felt no urge to apologize to her sister. She understood now that the burden of Hana's death was not hers to bear. She'd been helpless, a child before monsters of men. There was nothing she could have done to stop it. As for feeling the need to apologize for leaving ... she knew Hana would have wanted her to live.

She smiled, a single, fat tear rolling down her cheek and splashing against the rose quartz. She heard her sister's laughter echoing from the walls of their childhood home. She heard their mother and father calling after them, saying it was time to eat. She saw Hana standing atop the tallest dune, gazing into the sunset, watching as the stars burned through the painted sky.

"I love you, Hana."

She touched a finger to her lips, then to the stone.

"Next sunset I see will be for you."

CHAPTER
THIRTY-ONE

Reema was the first to enter the Hole again. This time, it looked different from how she remembered. The white marble walls were scored black, and the sunlight filtering down from above revealed smoke still lingering in the air. There was no mistaking it: this was where the Djinn had left the mines. Soon, she would follow him.

A whistle echoed around the space behind her as Omar and Ra'ad got a look at what happened to the space. They exchanged a nervous glance, as though they were suddenly doubtful about going after the Djinn. She expected that. It was one thing to talk about the Djinn, to dream about what he could do for them, but it was another to see proof of what he was capable of.

Alaric stepped next to her, his glowing brown eyes squinting up at the sunlight filtering through the Hole. He coughed, as if tasting the lingering smoke. Reema couldn't. She had been stuck in the mines for so long, exposed to torch fumes, that she probably couldn't tell the difference anymore.

"You think they'll come?" he asked.

"They will."

She had no doubt about that. The miners could all piss about and act as though they were fine enough to be in the mines, but dangle an opportunity to escape in front of them, and they'd come running.

A sound drew her attention to one of the side tunnels. Renfri appeared, her hips swaying back and forth as she held the pickaxe over her shoulder. Though she looked more like a haram girl than any sort of threat, Reema knew better.

More miners filtered out from behind her. There were more than she usually had in her gang. Some Reema recognized from Salman's gang, others she suspected were rogue miners who had heard about the gang lords dying left and right.

"You came," she said.

Renfri eyed her with a scrutinizing gaze. The smirk that had always seemed etched into her face was absent. "I did."

She scanned Reema's crew. "You've lost some of your boys."

Reema was stone faced as she answered, "I did."

Then Renfri's gaze caught on Alaric, noticing his glowing eyes. Her brows shot up, but anything she wanted to say was interrupted by the sudden appearance of miners filtering into the Hole, coming from every tunnel. They came from all territories, holding their weapons close and ready. They were no doubt worried about some inevitable trap. Smart, considering nothing like this had ever happened before.

When it seemed like the last of the miners had filtered in, Reema stepped into the center of the sunlight. She had never seen so many miners in one place. But she wasn't nervous as she raised her voice.

"Slaves of the mines of Salstsdir!" she called, drawing their attention to her. She gestured to the burnt marble around them. "Look around you. If you did not feel the shaking stone, if you did not hear word spread of his presence, then listen to me now."

She dropped her arms, her gaze bearing down on the men around her.

"A monster has been unleashed."

The crowd erupted into nervous chatter, fearful glances flicking from one person to the next. As insane as she sounded, they themselves had felt the air change in the mines. The Djinn had made his presence known as he passed through the mines.

"By you!" Renfri shouted.

Reema looked up to see Renfri striding through the crowd. She stepped into the sunlight, opposite Reema. She turned to the crowd, her finger pointed toward Reema.

"The Ifrit has slaughtered your gang lords. Mehdi, Zayd, Salman. Anyone who could stand in her way of releasing the Djinn, and now, she *has*. Do you know what she has wished the monster to do?" Renfri lowered her finger, stared at Reema with hate in her eyes. "She has wished *ruin* upon the world."

The crowd fell silent.

Reema lifted her chin, doing her best to keep her

anger chained. She knew Renfri would come at her with this.

"You're right. I released the Djinn. I was going to wish for the world to suffer, just as we all have suffered. But in the end, I did not."

Renfri scoffed, "You think that matters? All that matters is one thing. There will be no more food sent down to us. We will starve. And we will die."

The crowd began to murmur again, shocked by the sudden realization of their doom.

"You're right," Reema said, her voice carrying over the rising clamor. "About all of it."

The crowd's murmurs grew louder, spittle flying from their mouths as they yelled at her. Reema raised a hand in an attempt to quiet them, but they did not listen.

Then she shouted, her voice slicing across theirs.

"Silence!"

They quieted, waiting to hear what she had to say.

"We must leave the mines, but that cannot be where we stop. We must bring an end to the Djinn, or soon, you will hear the screams of every person you love from right here, in this very fucking cave."

The miners looked at one another, distrust evident in their postures and eyes. But she could see they were thinking about their loved ones, about the places they grew up, and the places they called home before they were made slaves.

Renfri laughed, her voice empty and hollow. "You think you can stop the Djinn?"

Reema stalked toward her, the shadows seemingly leaping from the walls to gather in her stride. Renfri staggered back a step, a hint of fear appearing in her eyes. She stopped a foot away from Renfri, and, though her voice was low, it echoed clearly across the cave.

"I can."

The crowd fell silent as they witnessed Renfri cowering before her. Somewhere along the way, she had made this gang lord fear her.

Then someone shouted from the crowd, "Why should we trust you? You brought this upon us!"

Her eyes scanned the crowd, seeing the doubt and fear etched into every face.

She glanced to Alaric, and to Asif, Omar, and Ra'ad. This hadn't been part of the plan, but she knew that she had to earn the crowd's trust. She drew a deep breath, drew her shiv, and held it toward Renfri, making eye contact with the confused gang lord.

"You will trust me, because if I fail you, then my enemy—my new second—will deliver you justice."

Renfri blinked, her gaze flicking from the marble shiv to Reema and back. Reema did not tear her eyes away, because she knew that if she did, the moment would break, and she would lose Renfri.

"What about it, Renfri?" she asked in a soft voice. "Will you serve the Ifrit? Will you hold me accountable?"

Renfri hesitated, the weight of every eye in the cave pressing down on her. The tension made it difficult to breathe, a silent standoff that seemed to stretch for an eternity. Finally, with a resigned sigh, she took the shiv from Reema's outstretched hand, her fingers brushing against Reema's in a brief, tentative exchange.

"I will," Renfri said.

A murmur rippled through the crowd, and slowly, a sense of acceptance began to spread. Faces that had been marked with fear and skepticism now looked on with cautious hope. They had witnessed a formal agreement between gang lords, something that had never happened before.

Reema turned to face the crowd, her posture commanding and resolute.

"Listen to me, all of you!" she shouted, her voice echoing off the walls, compelling their attention. "The world above has forgotten us, but we do not need them to remember. We will rise from these mines not as slaves, but as the ones to save them. And once the Djinn is brought to his knees, you will be free. I promise you that."

The miners, a sea of faces cast in shadow and light, began to nod, their initial reluctance giving way to a growing resolve.

"Asif!" she called.

Asif stepped forward through the parting crowd, glowering at the sudden loss of his position. She sent him an apologetic glance. She hadn't planned to replace him with Renfri, but there had been no other way.

"Work with Renfri and get these miners started. I long to see the sunset."

Cheers broke out among the crowd, the energy shifting to something that made her blood rush. Together, Asif and Renfri gave the miners orders, and before long, the steel of their pickaxes was smashing through marble.

As Reema stood under the Hole, light washed over

her with warmth that reached far beyond her skin. She lifted her face, soaking in the sun in a way she hadn't since she'd been a child, standing on that dune next to her sister. Behind her, the clamor of pickaxes and cheers from the miners filled the air.

But her attention was drawn elsewhere. Her gaze found Alaric standing apart from the others, his attention fixed on her with an intensity that seemed to pull at her very soul. Time seemed to slow, the surrounding noises fading to a distant hum, leaving only the two of them in the cavern.

Alaric moved toward her, each step deliberate, cutting through the crowd that parted for him. His presence was a calm force, and as he joined her in the stream of sunlight, a feeling of completeness enveloped Reema. The warmth of the sun paled in comparison to what it felt like to be next to him.

After all, this was the man whose soul had been made in measure for hers. And now, she had a chance at life with him by her side.

ALSO BY Z.R. ABADDI

The Desert of Wishes Series

Thieves of Zareen Duet

A Wish So Lost

A Wish So Wanted

Slaves of Sandspire Duet

A Wish So Dark

A Wish So Free

Champion of Morswen Trilogy

Rage to Ruin

Curse of Midnight

Whisper of Deceit

About the Author

Z.R. Abaddi is a team of husband and wife, who write in romantic fantasy and fairy tales.

They thrive in creating vast worlds full of characters who'll make you laugh and cry.

He is Jordanian American, and she is British Pakistani, and together reside in the United Kingdom where they spend time chasing down the best bubble tea.

To get in touch, visit our website at zrabaddi.com and leave a word.